The
Lighthouse Keeper

ALAN K. BAKER

snowbooks

Proudly Published by Snowbooks in 2012

Cover illustration by Daniel Acacio

Snowbooks Ltd.
Tel: 0207 837 6482
email: info@snowbooks.com
www.snowbooks.com

British Library Cataloguing in Publication Data
A catalogue record for this book is available from the
British Library.

ISBN 978-1-907777-62-2

One might almost say that the air, the invisible air, is full of unknowable Powers whose mysterious presence we have to endure.

– Guy de Maupassant

We live on a placid island of ignorance in the midst of black seas of infinity, and it was not meant that we should voyage far.

– H. P. Lovecraft

TELEGRAM FROM CAPTAIN HARVIE, MASTER OF THE LIGHTHOUSE TENDER *HESPERUS*, TO THE SECRETARY OF THE NORTHERN LIGHTHOUSE BOARD

26 DECEMBER 1900
(NORTHERN LIGHTHOUSE BOARD ARCHIVES)

A dreadful accident has happened at Flannans. The three keepers, Ducat, Marshall and the Occasional, have disappeared from the Island. Fired a rocket but, as no response was made, managed to land Moore, who went up to the Station but found no keepers there. The clocks were stopped and other signs indicated that the accident must have happened about a week ago. Poor fellows, they must have been blown over the cliffs or drowned trying to secure a crane or something like that. Night coming on, we could not wait to make further investigation but will go off again tomorrow morning to try and learn something as to their fate. I have left Moore, Macdonald, Buoymaster, and two seamen on the island to keep the light burning until you make other arrangements. Will not return to Oban until I hear from you. I have repeated this wire to Muirhead in case you are not at home. I will remain at the telegraph office tonight until it closes, if you wish to write me.

ONE

They had been on the island for a couple of hours and had finished setting up their tents and equipment. Rebecca Garratt stood on the cold, lichen-mottled concrete of the crane platform perched seventy feet above the rocks at the island's base, and she wondered why they had to camp here instead of staying in the lighthouse. The crane platform had once been used to haul supplies onto Eilean Mòr from the visiting lighthouse tenders, but it hadn't been in operation for decades. Nick had told her it was because the lighthouse was automated and they didn't have permission from the Northern Lighthouse Board, but it wasn't as if anyone were watching them out here in the middle of nowhere.

A sudden storm and rough seas had delayed their departure from Lewis, but the storm hadn't lasted, and now the sea rolled softly, the cloudless sky was a deep, luxuriant blue, and the deliciously fresh air was filled with the cries of hundreds of seabirds. Away in the distance, the six other Flannan Islands and their outlying skerries rose from the water, and for a few moments Rebecca imagined that they, too, were listening to the birds' raucous opera.

It was a pity that the beauty of the scene was marred by Eilean Mòr itself: it was quite possibly the ugliest place Rebecca had ever seen. Ancient and brooding, it rose like a clenched, misshapen fist from the ocean that stirred around its cliffs and ragged inlets: nature's violence sculpted in black and grey stone.

Nick had told her that its name meant 'Big Island' in Gaelic, but although it was the largest of the Flannans, it was still little more than a knobbly outcropping of grass-mottled rock, hunched and menacing – a place that wanted to be left alone.

A loud curse drew Rebecca's attention to the equipment tent near the edge of the platform. She stubbed out the cigarette she had been smoking and dropped the butt into her packet. She had always hated littering, and the idea of dropping the butt onto the platform or tossing it into the sea was unthinkable. She walked over to the large orange tent and poked her head through the flaps. The interior was filled with monitors and laptops and other bits and pieces of gear that were unfamiliar to her.

'What's up?' she asked.

'We've got a problem here,' said Max Kaminsky.

Rebecca squeezed into the tent. 'How so?'

'We're just running a test on the hydrophone array, but the returns don't make any sense.'

Max was from the University of South Florida and was doing postgrad work on pilot whale distribution in the North Atlantic. He had been working for the Joint Nature Conservation Committee for the last three months.

'Have you checked the wireless connection?' asked Nick Bowman, who was crouched down beside him.

'It's fine, but the readings are all out of whack.'

Donald Webb smiled. 'Would you care to define "out of whack" for us, Max?' Donald was the nominal leader of their group, and he and Max enjoyed some good-natured sparring over their cultural and colloquial differences.

'I wish I could, Don.'

Rebecca smiled as she noticed the older man wincing at the contraction of his name.

'But I've never seen anything quite like this. Come take a look, see what you think.'

Donald worked his tall, thin frame through the miniature maze of electronic equipment and joined Max and Nick at the hydrophone monitor screen. Rebecca tried in vain to interpret the images as Donald adjusted controls and tapped out commands on the computer keyboard.

'You're right,' he said. 'This is very curious.'

'What is?' Rebecca asked.

Nick turned to her. 'Looks like the hydrophone array isn't working properly. We've got returns that shouldn't be there.'

The underwater array was used to determine the location of sound-producing animals, such as whales. Three hydrophones had been installed in this region by the JNCC: one near Eilean Mòr, and the others near two other Flannan Islands. They were designed to detect the vocalisations made by means of the swim bladder sonic muscle mechanisms in many types of fish, which allowed the instruments to track the animals' movements and migration patterns.

Nick pointed to the dark shape in the lower portion of the screen. 'See, Becks, this is the northern edge of the island. But this…' His finger moved up the screen and encircled another shape with ill-defined edges. To Rebecca, it looked like someone had dropped something wet and sticky onto the surface of the monitor. 'This is wrong,' he sighed.

'All three hydrophones are working properly,' said Max.

'Could it be an animal?' Rebecca asked.

Max shook his head. 'Too big.'

'But it's making a sound, otherwise the hydrophones wouldn't be able to detect it… right?' said Rebecca.

'That's right,' said Max.

Jennifer Leigh came over and crouched down beside them. Like Donald, she was in her fifties – although she looked at least ten years younger. Her skin was smooth and lightly tanned, and the only clue to her age was her greying hair, which she kept tied back in a rather severe-looking bun. 'Then it's clear that there's something wrong with the system,' she said. 'Good lord! This is all we need.'

Donald regarded the monitor in silence for a few moments, stroking his neatly-trimmed goatee. He took off his glasses, wiped them quickly with his handkerchief and replaced them. 'All right. Let's try and correlate this. The transducer is online; I'll set the frequency to two hundred kilohertz. That should give us a clear picture of whatever it is – if it's anything at all.'

He moved over to another piece of equipment and began adjusting controls. Like the hydrophone array, the transducer was located underwater, but unlike the hydrophones, which passively listened to the environment, the transducer sent and received signals of various frequencies, which were reflected back from objects in the ocean.

They sat in front of the transducer display for several moments, waiting for the device to return an image of the ocean to the north of Eilean Mòr.

When the image appeared, it was virtually identical to the one on the hydrophone monitor.

'Wow,' said Max.

'Does that mean…?' Rebecca began.

Max cut her off. 'It means that either we've got two separate pieces of equipment malfunctioning in exactly the same way…'

'Or they're both giving accurate readings,' said Jennifer, 'and there really is something unusual out there.'

Max glanced at her. 'Unusual isn't the word for it. *Crazy* is what I'd say.'

'I have to agree with Max,' said Donald. He looked around the group. 'Has anyone ever seen anything like this before?'

'Not me, buddy,' said Max.

Nick and Jennifer shook their heads.

'Could it be a layer of plankton?' wondered Jennifer.

Max shook his head. 'It's too dense. The biomass of plankton would give a different reading. No... this looks like a solid object.'

'How big is it?' asked Rebecca.

'I'd estimate maybe two hundred square metres,' said Nick.

Donald nodded. 'Yes, I'd say that's a pretty fair estimate.'

'Whoa!' cried Max suddenly, pointing at the hydrophone monitor. 'It's gone!'

Jennifer checked the transducer display. 'From here, too,' she said.

Max whistled. '*Definitely* not plankton.'

'What on earth is going on here?' said Donald, shaking his head. 'What was it?'

'Well,' said Max, 'whatever it was, it goes like shit from a shovel.'

'That's one way of putting it,' Donald sighed. 'Jennifer, would you please make a note in the log about what we've just seen?'

Jennifer nodded.

'So, what do we do now?' asked Rebecca.

'We continue with our assignment,' Donald replied. 'Let's get the rest of the equipment up and running...' He glanced back at the monitors. 'Very interesting... yes, very interesting.'

Rebecca looked at Nick. He was still sitting cross-legged in front of the hydrophone monitor, with his chin cupped in one hand. She could see that he wasn't just intrigued by what had happened. There was a worried look in his eyes.

TWO

Rebecca wasn't a scientist. She was in the first year of her MA in History at Aberdeen University, and she didn't have to be on Eilean Mòr; in fact, she could have been with her parents at their summer house in Avignon, instead of on this ugly lump of rock in the Outer Hebrides.

But Nick was here, and as far as Rebecca was concerned, that gave the Flannan Isles the edge over anywhere else in the world.

They had met at a house party thrown by one of Nick's friends. Straight away, Rebecca had been captivated by his passion for conservation – particularly of the wildlife around the British Isles – and his work for the Joint Nature Conservation Committee. While the other young men at the party gradually drank themselves into varying degrees of stupidity, Nick seemed to become more eloquent and intense with every sip of rum and Coke, and by the end of the evening, Rebecca had decided that she wanted very much to see him again.

The problem was, he seemed to be so wrapped up in his work that she wondered if he had either the time or the inclination for a relationship. They'd bumped into each other a couple of times since that night, and while Rebecca had the impression that he was attracted to her, she couldn't shake the feeling that he considered it little more than a pleasant distraction from the really important things in his life.

She always hated it when people appeared too eager – it was such a turn-off – so when Nick told her he had signed up for this week-long expedition to the remote island of Eilean Mòr to update the JNCC database with observations of the distribution and movements of seabirds and marine mammals, and diffidently asked her if she wanted to come along, Rebecca had done her best to hide her delight. She had simply smiled, shrugged and said, 'Sure. Why not?'

She still remembered the seemingly endless list of wildlife to be found in the Atlantic Frontier to the north and west of Scotland, which Nick had reeled off that night in the cosy little pub which the postgrads and postdocs frequented. She'd had no idea there were so many different species of seabirds, cetaceans and seals (Nick called them 'pinnipeds') out here in a region she'd always thought of as wild and barren. She wanted to see them. More importantly, she wanted to see them with Nick.

Of the four people in the JNCC group, Rebecca had met only Max before, since he was a good friend of Nick's, but Jennifer and Donald were friendly and made her feel part of the group straight away.

The others were still trying to get their equipment to work properly, so Rebecca decided to do a little exploring. She had already asked Nick if it was okay to climb up to the top of the island. He had said sure but had warned her not to get too close to the edges, where the ground wasn't so safe.

The fact was, in a place this size there wasn't a whole lot of exploring to be done, but Rebecca wanted to look at the lighthouse at the island's summit, and also at the tiny drystone chapel that stood nearby. She had done a lot of background reading on the history of the Flannan Isles after accepting Nick's invitation, and she wanted to get a good look at the ancient dwelling. Centuries ago, Christian hermits had made their homes in such places, more alone than she could possibly imagine... or maybe not alone at all, at least in their own minds: in the company of their Creator, maybe they were the least isolated people in the world.

Taking her cigarettes and a bottle of water, Rebecca began to climb the rock-hewn stairs that ascended from the crane platform, winding up around the island's shoulder like a primitive necklace. The cries of the seagulls and petrels rang in her ears above the soft hiss of the ocean, and she imagined herself a Columban hermit making his way towards his new home in this strange, wild place. Of course, he wouldn't have had the benefit of the stairway; she guessed he would have had to clamber up the rocks unaided, carrying nothing with him but faith and determination.

On either side of her, the rocks sloped upwards at a steep angle, dark and damp with spindrift, and Rebecca suddenly felt herself oppressed by their ugliness and ancientness. She looked back briefly at the crane platform below and the three brightly-coloured tents perched there. She couldn't see the others, who were still inside the equipment tent, and for a moment Rebecca felt more alone than she had ever felt in her life.

How could you survive here? she wondered, thinking again of the hermit. *How could anyone survive here?*

She continued her climb towards the head of the stairway, a ragged line separating the time-worn land from the deep blue of the sky. As she approached, she caught a brief flash of whiteness flitting past the uppermost steps. She couldn't make out what it was. Maybe a bird that had alighted on the island's edge.

The climb had tired her out, and she made a mental note to do a bit more exercise when she got back to Aberdeen. She stopped briefly to take a swig from her water bottle and then continued up the remaining steps.

Made it, she thought, as she reached the edge of the sparse grass that covered the top of the island like a threadbare carpet. The first thing she saw was the lighthouse standing at the island's summit. Its whitewashed tower shone in the golden light of early evening, and although it was more than a hundred years old, it looked clean and new. It was surrounded by a low stone wall, which from Rebecca's vantage point obscured the living quarters at the base of the tower. She had Googled some pictures of Eilean Mòr back in Aberdeen and knew that the compound also contained two small outbuildings, which had once been used to store equipment and supplies for the keepers who had manned the lighthouse decades ago.

What a lonely life it must have been for them, stuck here for a month at a time in this godforsaken place!

She spotted the ancient chapel, which stood a few metres from the wall of the lighthouse compound, and made her way up the slope towards it. To call it a chapel was an overstatement: it was hardly more than a jumbled mound of drystone bricks, three metres long and a couple wide, whose corbelled roof had long since partially collapsed. In fact, the primitive building reminded her more of a fossilised turtle shell than a place of worship.

As she approached, Rebecca marvelled at the contrast between this heap of stones and the pristine tower of the lighthouse, and the long span of centuries that separated them. Their purposes were very different, but they had been equally important to the men who had lived there.

Suddenly, she caught a flicker of movement in the corner of her eye: a flash of white against the dark, mottled green. Something was moving across the grass, something smooth and elegant.

15

Jesus, Rebecca thought. *Is that a fox?*

It certainly looked like one, but its fur was pure white. *An arctic fox? Here?*

The animal was moving away from her, so that all she could see was its thick bushy tail, its haunches and the twin points of its ears. It was walking towards the tiny chapel, as if out for a stroll in the early evening. But out from where? Rebecca was pretty sure there weren't supposed to be any foxes here, and certainly not *arctic* foxes. Could it have hitched a ride on one of the ships which periodically brought maintenance crews to the island?

Still facing away from her, the animal raised its head for a few moments, as if scenting the air, perhaps looking for prey. Then it continued walking towards the chapel and disappeared into the entrance.

Probably using it as a den, Rebecca thought. *Wonder if there are any cubs in there.*

She loved animals, and spending so much of her time in the city, she rarely had the chance to observe them in the wild… and if there *were* fox cubs inside, she wanted just a glimpse. She wouldn't stay, since that would undoubtedly distress the parent… but just a quick glimpse…

Slowly and carefully, so as not to startle the fox, Rebecca bent down towards the entrance, which was hardly more than a ragged hole at one end of the building, and peered inside. The bright sunlight reached only a little way inside; the majority of the interior was dark, although she could discern the dim shapes of the stones forming the walls.

There was no sign of the fox. The chapel was empty.

What the hell?

She had definitely seen it enter the building, but there was nothing here now except darkness and a damp earth floor. Was there a small hole at the far end, through which the fox had exited? Rebecca strained to see into the gloom, wishing

16

she had a flashlight. An animal with a dark pelt would have been able to hide from her gaze, but the fox was pure, almost luminous white. If it were in there, she should have been able to see it.

Weird. There *must* have been a hole somewhere in the walls of the chapel, just big enough for the animal to squeeze through.

Rebecca was about to stand up and go looking for the fox on the other side of the building, when something caught her eye… something on the floor – or rather, just *beneath* the floor, half buried under a small mound of earth. She couldn't imagine why anyone would bury something here. For one thing, hardly anyone ever came here: the lighthouse had been automated back in 1971, and since then the only people who came to Eilean Mòr were the maintenance crews and naturalists like Nick and his colleagues. Maybe it was some relic from ages ago, perhaps centuries. Maybe, Rebecca told herself, it had been left by the hermit who once lived here. Unlikely, but an intriguing thought.

She edged a little further into the chapel, mindful of the dilapidated state of the roof: the last thing she needed was to get KO'd by a lump of stone. She looked up at the ceiling. It seemed sturdy enough, so she crawled the rest of the way inside and began to push aside the mound of earth. It was cold and clammy, and Rebecca grimaced in distaste. She never figured herself for an archaeologist, but if there were something interesting here… well, at least she'd have a souvenir to take back to the mainland. She might even give it to Nick as a present.

After a minute of pushing and digging in the darkness, Rebecca managed to free two objects from the earth's damp embrace, and she carried them out into the daylight. Looking at the results of her labours, she was a little disappointed. A weirdly-shaped lump of stone and a small package wrapped in a thick, heavy material – that was it. She hefted the lump of stone in her hands. Strange. It looked like it had been carved into that shape, but it certainly wasn't representative of anything – in fact, it was like nothing she'd ever seen before. Its surface appeared to be pitted with tool marks, like someone had chiselled it, carefully working the stone... someone with serious mental problems, by the look of it.

She put the stone on the ground and turned her attention to the cloth-covered package, which was tied together with a thong of rotted leather that fell to pieces as soon as she tried to untie it. *Must have been buried for years and years*, she thought.

Carefully, she began to unwrap the package, pulling aside the dark, stained fabric.

'Becks,' said a voice behind her, making her jump.

'Shit! Nick...'

He laughed. 'Sorry. Didn't mean to scare you.'

She smiled at him. 'It's okay.'

'What you got there?'

'Oh, it's... well, actually, I don't know. I found them in there.' She indicated the chapel with a nod.

Nick frowned. 'Rebecca, you shouldn't have gone in there. It's centuries old. If it had collapsed on you...'

'I would have been up the creek without a paddle, I know.'

'And I'd never have forgiven myself.'

She sighed and shrugged. 'I'm sorry.'

His smile returned. 'Well, no harm done. Just be careful. It can be dangerous out here, and we're a long way from help.'

'I'll be careful, I promise.' *Shit*, she thought. *The last thing I want is for him to start worrying about me. He'll end up thinking it was a mistake to invite me.* 'How's the equipment? Is it still playing up?'

'I'm afraid so. Donald and Jennifer are working on it. We just thought we'd come up and see how you're doing.'

'We?'

'Get a room, you two!' said Max as he drew up alongside them. 'Or should I say tent?'

Nick gave an embarrassed laugh, and Rebecca noticed a blush creeping into his cheeks. 'Shut up, Max,' she said with a smile.

'Becks found something in the chapel,' said Nick.

'Oh yeah? Let's see.'

Rebecca picked up the lump of stone and handed it to the big Floridian, who examined it. 'Jesus. What the hell is this?'

'That's what I was wondering,' Rebecca replied.

'It's definitely been carved,' Max added, turning the stone over and over in his hands.

'Yeah, but into what?'

'Beats me. What else you got?'

Rebecca unwrapped the package.

Nick and Max leaned in close. 'A book?' said Max.

'Looks like it.' Rebecca handed the wrapping to Nick, who examined it briefly.

'Oilskin. Pretty old... and this looks like an old logbook.'

Slowly, taking care not to damage the book, Rebecca opened it to the first page and read aloud the title.

THE TESTAMENT OF ALEC DALEMORE, OCCASIONAL KEEPER

'What's an "occasional keeper"?' asked Max.

'A lighthouse keeper,' Nick replied, 'but not a professional, fulltime one. Occasional keepers filled in on lighthouse duty when there was a shortage of staff for any reason.'

'My God,' said Rebecca suddenly. 'Dalemore... Alec Dalemore.'

Nick gave her a curious look. 'What's up?'

Rebecca looked from Nick to Max. 'He was one of the relief keepers who came to Eilean Mòr after the disappearances.'

'What are you talking about?' said Max. 'What disappearances?'

'It happened a long time ago,' Rebecca explained. 'Back in 1900.' She nodded behind them, back up towards the squat tower of the lighthouse at the island's summit. 'The light was brand new – it had been built less than a year before. It was manned by three people when the disaster happened.'

'So what's the story?' said Max.

'The three lighthouse keepers vanished from the island,' Rebecca replied.

'Vanished?'

'When their tour of duty was up and the replacement crew arrived, they found the place deserted. No sign of them. They were never seen again.'

'And this Dalemore fella was part of the relief crew?' said Max.

Rebecca nodded.

'How come you know about all this?'

'I decided to read up on the history of the place when Nick invited me out here.'

He raised his eyebrows. 'Really?'

'In case you'd forgotten, Max, I *am* a bloody historian!'

He chuckled. 'Okay, point taken. Anyway, sounds spooky, like a Scotch version of the Bermuda Triangle.'

'Scottish,' Nick corrected him. 'Scotch is a drink, dickhead.'

'Whatever.'

'You know,' said Rebecca, 'this could be a really significant find. There's never been any record of what happened when Dalemore and the other relief keepers came to the island after the disappearances. None of them ever spoke about it. And as far as anyone knew, none of them left behind any personal logs.'

Nick took the book from her and leafed through it. He frowned. 'This isn't a log, personal or otherwise.'

'What do you mean?' asked Rebecca.

Nick held the book open for her to see. 'Look. There are no day-by-day entries; it's a continuous text, kind of an autobiography, I guess…'

'A testament,' said Rebecca, 'just like the title says. Jesus…'

Nick glanced back towards the ruined chapel. 'How come it was in there? I mean… who buried it there, and why?'

'Maybe Dalemore did,' suggested Max.

Nick gave him a dubious look.

'Well, *I* don't know. Maybe you'll find the answer in there.' He indicated the book, then gave Nick a playful punch on the shoulder. 'In the meantime, buddy, we've got a bit more work to do before chow.'

'Can I help?' asked Rebecca absently, still looking at the book.

Nick regarded her for a moment, then smiled. 'That's okay. Why don't you get stuck into your own research?'

They held each other's gaze, until Max rolled his eyes and said: 'I'll be on the crane platform.' He sauntered off towards the edge of the island, whistling a Jimmy Buffet tune.

'Sorry about that,' said Nick.

'About what?'

'What old Max said about… you know, getting a tent.'

'Oh!' Rebecca laughed. 'That's okay, don't worry about it.' She found his embarrassment very attractive. She was about to say something more, but then she remembered how she had found the book and the stone. 'Nick,' she said, 'is there much wildlife on the island?'

'On Eilean Mòr?'

'Yeah, I mean, actually *on* the island.'

'Not much, apart from a few wild rabbits and the seabirds which nest here.'

'That's what I thought,' she said quietly.

'Why? What's up?'

'I saw a fox earlier on…'

'Really?'

'A white one. It looked like an arctic fox.'

Nick regarded her in silence for a few moments. 'You're kidding. There aren't any arctic foxes here, Becks. Are you sure it wasn't a rabbit?'

The comment was so ridiculous it made her laugh out loud. 'Of *course* I'm sure it wasn't a rabbit! I was thinking maybe it stowed away on one of the maintenance ships that come out here.'

'Well, I suppose it's possible. But… an *arctic* fox…?' He considered for a moment. 'It could have been an albino, I suppose… if it *was* a fox.'

She sighed theatrically and smiled.

He glanced at her, and then laughed. 'Okay, okay, it was a fox. Come on, let's get back to the platform.'

As they descended from the island's summit, Nick shook his head. 'An albino fox… wow. I'd love to see that.'

'Maybe we can look for it later.'

'Yeah, maybe we can…'

While the rest of the group continued to struggle with their equipment, Rebecca went into the tent she was sharing with Nick and Max. She dropped the carved stone onto her sleeping bag, sat down and opened the book. She leafed through it, noting that the pages appeared to have been well preserved in their oilskin wrapping. The script was small and very neat, almost a copperplate, in fact. Very few words had been crossed out, implying that Dalemore had thought very carefully about what he was writing.

Jesus, what a find! She could hardly believe she had stumbled upon it – and all because she had followed the white fox into the chapel. Okay, it wasn't exactly the Rosetta Stone, but it was still of great importance to the maritime history of this region, and might well offer some clue as to the fate of the three lighthouse keepers who had vanished so tragically and mysteriously all those years ago.

Although she had already embarked on her MA, she couldn't help thinking that this would have made a hell of a subject for a dissertation. All the same, this discovery would be a fine start to her career as a historian. She imagined being interviewed by the local press, maybe even by the local news on TV. And then, when she had completed her MA, she might even be able to use it as the basis for a PhD proposal.

Hold on, Becks. You're getting a bit ahead of yourself, aren't you?

She guessed that was true… but who knew where this might lead?

She thought about Alec Dalemore. *I'm the first person to read his journal. But why did he bury it in the chapel – if he* was *the one who buried it?* Had he written it while he was on Eilean Mòr, or had he written it later, and then returned to the island?

This was the reason for her love of history: the thrill of discovery, the piecing together of evidence that led to a new understanding of the past; the slow, steady adding to the sum of human knowledge of itself and the world. She had the feeling that she was standing at a small frontier, that she was about to learn something that no one in the world knew. She looked out through the open flaps of the tent across the slow-moving ocean and smiled. The great mystery of the sea, and the mystery of Eilean Mòr: a puzzle each for her and Nick.

She flicked carefully through the book, unable to resist the temptation to read snippets here and there. But as she scanned the text, a frown crept slowly across her brow. She stopped reading and started to look for the beginning of each chapter. She read the titles. They started off prosaically enough, but as she worked her way through the book, they became stranger. One chapter was called 'The Living Sky'; the next was called 'From the Ocean'; later on, there were chapters called 'This Night Wounds Time' and 'Another Order of Being'.

And then she found a chapter entitled 'The White Fox'. 'Shit!' she whispered. *The White Fox?*

She suddenly wanted a cigarette very badly, but Nick and Max were non-smokers, and she didn't want to mess up the air in the tent, so she grabbed her pack and her lighter and took the book out onto the crane platform. She could still hear perplexed voices coming from the equipment tent. Jennifer was outside, though. She had set up the camping stove and was heating soup and preparing smoked haddock for their evening meal.

Rebecca sat with her back against the mass of rock rising from the inner edge of the platform, lit a cigarette and read the chapter entitled 'The White Fox'.

When she had finished, she closed the book and sat very still for a while. Presently, she said quietly to herself: 'Jesus Christ.'

Jennifer glanced at her. 'Are you all right, Rebecca?'

She looked at the older woman as if she had never seen her before. 'I'm sorry?'

Jennifer regarded her in puzzlement. 'Are you all right? You look like you've seen a ghost.'

'I... I'm fine, thanks.'

'Well, our tea's ready. Donald! Nick! Max! Come and have something to eat before the soup gets cold!'

They discussed the problems with their equipment while they ate, but their words made little impression on Rebecca, who was still thinking of the chapter she had read. Nick noticed how quiet she was.

'You okay, Becks?'

'Yeah,' she nodded. 'I'm fine.'

She wanted to tell him what was in the chapter, but she knew she'd sound stupid or crazy if she even tried to describe it. So she just smiled and nodded and said yeah, she was fine.

When they had finished, Max helped Jennifer wash the dishes, and when they returned to the camp, he said: 'Hey, Becks. How about reading the book to us?'

'Book?' said Donald.

'She found it in the old chapel up there.'

Donald looked at Rebecca in surprise. 'What an astonishing find! I'd love to hear it, if you don't mind.'

'No... no, I don't mind at all,' she replied.

'Cool,' said Max. 'This is exactly what we need: a good campfire story!'

Donald lit his pipe and puffed at it contentedly as Rebecca picked up the book, which she had placed beside her while she ate, opened it and began to read.

THE TESTAMENT OF ALEC DALEMORE, OCCASIONAL KEEPER

1
HOW I LEARNED OF THE MYSTERY OF EILEAN MÒR

The Flannan Isles are wild and untamed, and when the storms of winter seize these latitudes, the seas rise like the foothills of invisible mountains, drawing the eye towards the far north and the further lands beyond, which lie at the unseen pinnacle of the world. Here at the far extremities of the British Isles, where the North Atlantic pounds with eternal insistence upon the jagged edges of the land, and the sky groans with the rage of distant thunder, it is easy to surrender to fevered imagination: to allow oneself to believe that the mundane world of the senses is but the most fleeting echo of another world – vaster, stranger and more magnificent than even dreams may tell.

Many of the older people who live in these regions, whose hearts and minds have not been swayed by the onrush of this modern age, would say that it is not merely imagination that hints at the existence of the other world. It is a reality, they say; perhaps more real than our own world, with its noisy, soulless machines and mad rushings here and there. In spite of this, the strange beliefs that once shaped the lives of all have declined over the decades, so that now they are no more than curious tales told quietly to each other by the elders around the bright, crackling hearth, while the younger folk fix their eyes and their hearts upon the concerns of the new century.

Once, I would have counted myself proudly amongst the latter group, with little time for the quaintness of folklore in far-away places. But the ages of man are but the ages of the world writ small, and just as the land is gradually transformed by the wind and the rain, the warmth of the summer and the cold of winter's chiselling frosts, by the breathing seasons of the world, so are we constantly altered and shaped by the experiences of our lives, which can mould us gently like the skilful hands of a potter, or beat our minds into new forms like white-hot metal upon a blacksmith's anvil.

Such has been my experience, and this is my testament, my account of all that happened to me when I went to Eilean Mòr to search for a man to whom I owed my life.

The man's name was James Ducat, and before I set down my later experiences, I must tell of the great service he did me, for he plucked me from the ocean's maw when my ship dashed itself against rocks near Gallan Head on the west coast of Lewis in the winter of 1899. I and my crew had thought ourselves at an end as we clung like barnacles to those unforgiving stone sentinels, and for hours we prayed for either rescue or a quick and painless death in the sea's roiling embrace. In the end, just when it seemed that God had forsaken us, a ship appeared from out of the mist and sea spray and gathered us to safety on the brooding land. A lighthouse tender it was, on its way to some far-flung splinter of rock, carrying men who would relieve those who kept the lamps lit through the long, dark northern nights.

James Ducat threw a rope to me from the heaving deck of the tender, and I snatched it with half-frozen fingers and was hauled by him to safety. How shall I describe the feelings that seized me when I took the hand of a fellow man who had risked his own life to draw me out of the shadow of death? Such experiences are not easily rendered into words. The sight of his rain-streaked face, wild and grizzled as the tumultuous sea, filled me with a gratitude and relief that were forged at once into love in my racing heart, and I wept without shame as he held me to his breast before heaving me belowdecks, along with my companions.

As I sat huddled in a blanket, with one of my fellows on one side and a cold hard bulkhead on the other, I trembled in time with the panting of the steamer's engine, which to my exhausted mind seemed like words breathed by God Himself to soothe away my terror. And as the lighthouse tender cleaved the hungry waves with its prow, heading away from the black, sea-defying splinters that had so nearly become my grave, I vowed to be a lifelong friend to James Ducat, to render him whatever service he should ask of me for the rest of my days. For how many days remained to me on this earth I knew not, save that I owed them to him.

*

My story begins in earnest on the 5th of January 1901, when I returned to my home in Stornoway after spending Christmas and the New Year with friends in the north of England. Amongst the few items of post that were waiting for me, there was a letter. I saw from the return address that it was from the Ducat family.

At first, I felt a warm surge of pleasure, expecting good wishes for the New Year. As I read the letter, however, my mood became darkened by shadows of consternation and sorrow. It was from James Ducat's wife, Mary, and the news it brought was completely unexpected and unutterably dreadful. I have the letter here beside me as I write. This is what Mary Ducat wrote:

Dear Mr Dalemore,
It is with great sadness that I write to you, to tell you that my husband and your friend, James Ducat, has met with a horrible accident while on duty at the light on Eilean Mòr. I

do not know how to describe what has happened, for in truth no one yet knows, save to say that he is gone, along with his fellow Keepers.

The Board does not know either. I received a visit from Mr William Murdoch, the Secretary of the Board, a short while ago. He is a very kind man, and I could see that it pained him greatly to tell me what he knew, which, as I say, is not so very much.

It seems that the light went out a few days ago. Mr Murdoch told me that it was noticed by the captain of a steamer bound for Leith, who reported it by wireless to his headquarters – I believe the ship was of the Cosmopolitan Line. For some reason, this was not reported to the Board, and it was only when the relief Keepers arrived on the 26th of December that they realised something was amiss.

When they went ashore, they found no sign of life. My James, along with his two companions, had vanished as if plucked from the face of the earth!

I hope you will forgive me for writing to you like this, but in truth I do not know who else to turn to, and I am well aware of the high regard you hold for my husband. The Board believes, so they say, that all three of those good men were swept away by a sudden surge of the sea. But I am not so sure. You have tended lights yourself, and you know that this cannot be true.

Forgive me again, Mr Dalemore, but I have a feeling, which I don't know how to put into words, that something else has happened to my James and the others. Something horrible that cannot be understood by those who love and fear the Almighty. I do not know what can be done, except that something must be done, to try to bring them back from wherever they have been taken.

I still recall with pleasure the visit you paid to our home last year, and the kind and wonderful words you said to my husband, how you owed him your life and would be honoured to call yourself his friend until death should finally take you. I recall the look on his face when he heard these words, and how he struggled to hold back his tears – for he is a good man who feels things very deeply.

It is with an uncertain heart that I come to the real reason for this letter. I beg you to find him, or at least to discover what really happened to him. I know you are an honourable man, who will not feel anger or exasperation towards me for making this request, impossible as it may be. I cannot bear the thought of him lost out there, desperate for the aid of his fellow man, where none may come.

To me, he is alive still, though you may shake your head in sadness at such foolishness. I cannot explain why, but I feel it to be so.

Will you please help, in whatever way you may think best?

With warmest wishes and in fervent hope,
Mary Ducat

I sat there at my kitchen table, my breakfast untouched, and re-read the letter several times while the wind whispered from its cold domain beyond the window. James Ducat, the man who had reached down from the world of light and life into the black maw of death to save me, had been taken from the world by the selfsame ocean which had sought to devour me. How unjust it was! How cruel of God to provide such a darkly ironic reward for selfless bravery.

It was then that my eye fell again on a certain sentence: *You have tended lights yourself, and you know that this cannot be true.* When I first read those words, they had seemed merely to be the understandable expression of a forlorn hope, born more of wishful thinking than pragmatism. Suddenly I understood what Mrs Ducat meant by them, and I found myself tempted to agree with her. It was a cardinal rule that no lighthouse should ever be left unmanned, and thus it was almost inconceivable that all three Keepers would be outside at the same time, unless the last man was called to attend some dire emergency.

And yet, even if such an emergency had indeed occurred, how could the last man have been summoned to it? I knew the island of Eilean Mòr (I know all that group of islands known as the Seven Hunters, to which it belongs); both landings, to the west and the east, were out of sight and too far away for any signal to be seen or cry heard from the lighthouse.

What had happened to those men?

As I rose from the table and put water on to boil for a fresh pot of tea, strange thoughts began to chase each other through the cheerless twilight of my mind, inspired by the tone of Mary Ducat's letter. She obviously believed that her husband and his companions had met a fate far stranger than merely being lost at sea. I am not a doctor, and I know little of the intricacies of the human mind, but it seemed to me that the weirdness of the letter's latter portion pointed to some kind of conflation in the poor woman's mind: a mixing of grief at the loss of her husband, together with an entirely understandable hope that, since his body had apparently not been found, he might yet be alive, clinging desperately to some fractured tooth of rock somewhere out in the ocean. I have known people who have lost loved ones at sea, and it is a reaction I have witnessed more than once: the absence of a body equates to the possibility, however remote, that the person still lives. How can it be otherwise, since hope's embers must glow in even the most despondent of human hearts?

And yet, it was clear that Mary Ducat was also entertaining other thoughts – thoughts of an altogether more extraordinary nature. She believed that something other than the sea had taken the men, something ungodly and awful. This thought was not quite as outlandish as it seemed, for superstition clung to the Flannan Isles with as much tenacity as the ocean that smashed upon their jagged shores. It was a custom among Lighthouse Keepers to say a prayer as soon as they set foot on them, whether for Saint Flann, after whom they had been named, or for their own souls it mattered little – save that the prayer was said. It was also said that the Seven Hunters were home to a wild spirit, which was ancient even before Christianity first came to this region of the world, and that the spirit resented the presence of the lighthouse and the men who tended it. This spirit was known as the Phantom of the Seven Hunters, and no one could tell of its true nature, save that it wished nothing but ill towards the living.

The extremely lucky and the extremely unfortunate often have the privilege of being able to point to the precise moment when the course of their lives changed irrevocably, leading them along a path either to happiness or perdition. For me, that moment came when I read the letter a final time (noting the shallow puckering of the paper that could only have been the result of tears falling upon it), and decided that I would do as my friend's wife had asked.

There and then, I resolved to go to Eilean Mòr and do whatever I could to discover the fate of James Ducat. And if the sea should take me in the attempt, so be it. And if something other than the sea should descend upon me and carry me towards God knew what fate, then likewise I would not flinch nor flee. Then again, if I should be forced to return with my hands and heart empty of any knowledge that could put Mary Ducat's mind at rest, then at least I would know that I had made the effort.

I had a debt to repay, and I intended, by any means necessary, to repay it.

2
THE STOLEN DREAM

I knew that the Northern Lighthouse Board would be looking for three men to replace the lost Lighthouse Keepers. Even now, there would be men stationed on Eilean Mòr, but they would almost certainly be tending the light in a temporary capacity only, until a new crew could be assigned. Realising that I had little time to lose, I packed some belongings into my battered old valise and left my house, bound for the Flannan Isles Shore Station in Breasclete.

The thirteen-mile journey took me almost directly west across the wild country of the Isle of Lewis, which is not really an island at all, but rather the northern two thirds of the largest of the Western Isles, and is joined by a mountainous tract of land with Harris to the south. As the horse and cart made their way across the green and ochre patchwork of crofts and untamed country, I turned over the contents of Mary Ducat's letter again and again in my mind. The more I thought about it, the more foolhardy it seemed for me to try to discover the fate of her husband. The Northern Lighthouse Board would conduct its own investigation into the tragedy, probably with Robert Muirhead at the helm, and it seemed impossible that I would be able to contribute anything of use to his work.

And yet, I was bound by an oath of loyalty which was impossible to deny or ignore. Would Muirhead and the Lighthouse Board think me a fool? Should I even tell them of the real reason I intended to place myself at their disposal? Perhaps there would be no need, for this disaster must surely have left them short of qualified men to tend the Eilean Mòr light.

I was not a professional Lightkeeper; I was what is known as an Occasional, my main occupation being that of carpenter. But we Occasionals are not badly regarded by the fraternity of fulltime Lightkeepers, and we are more than glad to offer our services whenever we are needed to help with the tending of the lighthouses scattered across these latitudes.

The countryside passed by as I alternately gazed and dozed, lulled into a state of semi-awareness by the cart's gentle rocking motion upon the uneven road. Hills rose in the distance on each side, dulled into shades of grey beneath a sky the colour of old milk. The wind moved invisibly among the hills as I passed Callanish, with its ancient standing stones that watched eternally over the land; it sighed and moaned, as if it were not wind at all but the unquiet souls of the dead. Perhaps it did carry their voices, along with those of stranger inhabitants of this timeless place.

Finally, I arrived at Breasclete, and from there it was a short if chilly walk through the smattering of village dwellings to the Flannan Isles Shore Station, which stood upon a low mound overlooking Loch Roag, the sea loch which offers sheltered mooring to the lighthouse tenders. Rising in the distance from its sullen waters, the island of Great Bernera appeared like the humped back of some immense, stranded whale.

The Shore Station was large and solidly built, a comforting sight, and as I walked up the footpath I could see lights in the windows. I knocked on the front door and waited.

Presently it was opened a crack, and the pale, unsmiling face of a child peered out at me. I recognised her immediately; she was Annabella, one of James Ducat's children. I believe she was eight years old. 'Hello, Annabella,' I said, in as warm and friendly a manner as I was able. 'Do you remember me?'

'Of course I do,' she replied. 'You're Mr Dalemore. You're a friend of… of my father.'

A child's grief is an awful thing to behold, and in Annabella's wide, dark eyes I saw the desolation of her little world.

'That's right,' I smiled. 'I am a friend of your father's. Do you think I might come inside for a while?'

She looked at me as if I had just said something in a strange foreign language. Just then, another voice drifted out from the hallway behind her: a woman's voice which I also recognised instantly. 'Who is it, Anna? Who's there?'

The door opened wider, and Mary Ducat stood there. 'Mr Dalemore,' she whispered, and tears started to flow down her cheeks.

'I read your letter this morning, Mrs Ducat, and I came immediately. I only wish that I could have come sooner, but...'

'Come inside, Mr Dalemore,' she interrupted in a voice that was surprisingly steady. It was the voice of one who has become used to weeping and speaking at the same time.

I stepped gratefully from the cold into the warm hallway. Now I was here, I couldn't think of anything to say beyond the commonplace things that are always said at times such as this. 'Mrs Ducat, I... I am so sorry...'

'Take off your coat, do,' she said, reaching up with trembling hands to help me. 'Mr Muirhead is here.' She carefully hung my coat on a peg by the door and then turned and gazed at me in silence for some moments, before whispering, 'Thank you for coming, Mr Dalemore.'

She led me into the large, comfortable living room, one hand draped protectively on her daughter's shoulder, before whispering something in Annabella's ear about helping her sister in the kitchen. The child wandered off along the dark corridor like a little ghost.

A fire burned brightly in the hearth, partially obscured by a tall, tweed-clothed man who stood facing it with his back to the room, his broad shoulders hunched, his head bowed as if in deep contemplation.

'Mr Muirhead,' said Mary Ducat quietly. 'Mr Dalemore is here...'

He turned from the fire and regarded me in silence for some moments, as if trying to recollect who I was, a slightly quizzical expression on his face.

Not knowing what else to do, I walked quickly across the room and held out my hand to him. After a slight hesitation, shook it. 'Good of you to come, Mr Dalemore,' he said in a voice deep and resonant with the sadness that had descended upon that house.

'I was away for the festive season. I only got back to Stornoway this morning. I found a letter from Mrs Ducat waiting for me, telling of what has happened. I... I have come to offer my services as a relief Keeper.'

Muirhead nodded, regarding me with hooded eyes, and for a moment I wondered if he were trying to decide whether to believe me or not. Presently, he replied, 'And you are most welcome, Mr Dalemore... Alec, isn't it?'

I nodded, pleased that he had remembered my Christian name – but then Robert Muirhead was well respected by all the Lightkeepers and Occasionals for his devotion to his duty, and to the men in his care. For the first time I realised how utterly devastated he must be to lose three such men in one terrible instant.

'Won't you sit down, Mr Dalemore?' said Mary Ducat, still standing by the door.

'Yes,' said Muirhead, 'have a seat, laddie.'

Annabella came in with a large tray bearing a steaming teapot and cups, and she laid it on a table by one of the chairs. Her mother reached out and stroked her hair; the child gave her a weak, trembling smile before leaving the room again.

Muirhead made to pour the tea, but Mary hurried to the table, filling cups and handing them to us.

The Superintendent returned to his post by the fire and regarded me with furrowed brows. 'Yes, you are most welcome, Alec,' he repeated. 'I hope Mary will forgive me if I set the facts before you. This horrible disaster has left the Board with a serious problem regarding manning. When the *Hesperus* discovered the... the situation on Eilean Mòr, Captain Harvie left Joseph Moore there, with three others.'

'I know Joseph,' I said. 'He's a good man, a sensitive sort.'

'Aye,' nodded Muirhead, 'that he is. He was the relief Keeper; the tender was taking him to the island to replace Donald McArthur – an Occasional like yourself – who was doing duty for William Ross, who is on sick leave.' Muirhead glanced at Mary, and I had the impression that he wished she would leave the room, so that she might be spared hearing this again. But Mary Ducat was strong, as are all the wives of Lightkeepers. She sat down by the fire and offered him a level gaze, her hands folded in her lap, a picture of dignity even in the depths of her grief.

Muirhead gave a barely audible sigh and continued. 'When they found the Flannan light deserted, Moore knew that he must stay to maintain the place until a full relief crew could be assembled, but Captain Harvie knew that he couldn't do it alone, so he asked three of his crew to keep the lad company and take their turns seeing to the equipment. They were seamen Archie Lamont and Archie Campbell, and the Buoymaster, Allan McDonald. They're good men, but they're not Lightkeepers like Moore; we need qualified men there as soon as possible. But now...' He hesitated.

'Now there is a shortage.'

He nodded. 'Aye, there's a shortage, which is why you've come not a moment too soon. We've one other Keeper on his way. We're expecting him on the *Hesperus* shortly. He's John Milne, Principal Keeper at Tiumpan Head; young Joseph will return to his position as Assistant as soon as Milne arrives on Eilean Mòr. But a third Keeper is needed, and Daniel McBride, who was to have gone, has met with an accident and broken his leg.'

Muirhead paused and regarded me with a desperate expression, which at first I couldn't interpret. I wondered whether he was tacitly offering me a final opportunity to back out, to say that I couldn't go to Eilean Mòr. I glanced at Mary, and in her face I saw the impossibility of turning away, even had I wished to.

I stood up and again offered Robert Muirhead my hand. 'You need a third Keeper, sir. I offer you my services.'

The Superintendent took my hand in his and clasped my arm in a strong grip with the other. 'Thank you, laddie. Thank you.'

*

The *Hesperus* was still an hour or so away, and I wanted to speak with Mary again before I left. Donald MacArthur's wife, Anne, had returned to the Shore Station from a long walk. Mary looked at her with great affection and sympathy, for Anne was not from here; she was a native of Gravesend, in the far south of England, and had met her husband shortly after his discharge from the Royal Engineers. Donald had brought her back to his homeland, and although she was highly regarded and well liked by the people hereabouts (she had even begun to master the Gaelic language), she sometimes found it difficult to fit in with this way of life, which was so different to what she had been used to.

After I had offered Anne MacArthur my condolences, Mary asked if she and I might take a walk outside, to which I agreed. Although the sky remained overcast and the wind snatched at the shore, the rain had eased, so that now the air was dampened only by occasional sea spray and pierced with the cries of hovering gulls.

As we walked slowly down the path leading from the Shore Station to the edge of the ocean, Mary looked at me, her face furrowed against the wind, and said, 'Thank you again for coming, Mr Dalemore.'

'Please call me Alec.' It seemed to me that formality was lost in this situation. I had wanted to ask her about the things she had said in her letter, but now that the moment was upon me, I found it unaccountably difficult to broach the subject. Fortunately, Mary took the job from my hands.

'I think I should apologise for writing the things I did. They must have seemed like the ravings of a madwoman...'

'Not at all,' I said. 'There is a mystery here; that much is plain. I can't understand why all three of the Lightkeepers would have gone outside at once.'

'Nor can I. Nor can Mr Muirhead.'

'You mentioned something else in your letter. Something I confess I didn't understand.'

'Yes. I am sorry for that. I wrote it while I was thinking of the dream I had.'

'A dream? What did you dream about?'

'The strange thing is, I can't remember. I think I dreamed of James and the other keepers, but something seemed to reach into me, something strange and terrible, and snatched the dream away.' Her voice had grown halting, punctuated with stifled sobs. I placed a hand on her arm, trying in vain to comfort her. Without thinking about where we were heading, we had arrived at the pier where the lighthouse tenders were moored. The sides of Loch Roag, weather-worn and misty, rose away on each side.

'It's so difficult, Alec,' she continued. 'I dreamed I was on Eilean Mòr, looking up at the lighthouse. James and Thomas and Donald were there, on the balcony, looking out to sea. It was night, and mists were covering the island, and every half-minute the light flashed out, turning them into dark silhouettes. I called out to them – to James – but they couldn't hear me above the roar of the ocean. They seemed to be looking at something in the sky, but I couldn't see what it was. They were grabbing each other and pointing; two were wearing their oilskins, but the third wasn't... perhaps they were outside at first and rushed in to tell him that something was happening, and together they climbed in the greatest haste to the top of the tower.'

Like everyone else, I was aware of the so-called 'forerunners', phantoms of those lost – or about to be lost – at sea, who appeared to their loved ones as if to prepare them for the tragic news they would soon receive. They were said to appear sometimes in dreams, sometimes in the waking world.

'What do you think they saw?' I asked quietly.

'I don't know,' Mary replied. 'I looked up into the sky, but all I could see was the rain and mist and the spray of the ocean. And the light... the light swinging round every half-minute to turn them into black phantoms!'

She buried her head in her hands. I wanted to put my arms around her and hold her close, but felt that such a gesture, however innocently intended, would be presumptuous. And so instead, I placed a hand on her shoulder. After a few moments, she recovered a little and drew apart from me, her gaze fixed on the ground between us.

Something occurred to me then; a question which I wondered whether I should ask her. It might sound as though I were being dismissive, and yet I could not stand to see her so consumed with horror, and I knew that I had to seize any opportunity to bring her back to the world of sane thoughts – even if those thoughts were also unbearable.

'You say that your dream was stolen from you. If that's the case, how can you remember it?'

Her reply surprised me. 'I've wondered that myself.

Perhaps dreams are *things*… things that drift through the mind, of which the mind is aware. And when they go, they leave behind memories of what they were, and if something *takes* them, you remember that, too.'

I did not know how to respond to this. I believed that Mary Ducat's mind was so filled with horror and grief that it was in danger of becoming unhinged. I was afraid for her, and for her children. I said nothing, as the wind flew in from the mouth of the loch and snatched at us as if trying to carry us out into the heaving waters beyond.

THE TESTAMENT OF JOSEPH MOORE

The lighthouse tender *Hesperus* ploughed through the cold northern ocean, bound for the Flannan Isles, the Seven Hunters; bound for the heart of the terrible mystery that had descended like a carrion bird to cast a shadow of despair over us all.

John Milne, the Principal Keeper, had introduced himself to me soon after we got under way. He seemed an affable, capable man, a man of steady nerves who was untroubled by the lonely life of a Lightkeeper. Not every man is suitable for this profession, which requires him to spend long periods in isolated and dangerous places.

Lightkeepers are divided into three grades: Principals, Assistants and Occasionals. During the daytime, our duties include cleaning the Station and painting if necessary. We must maintain the equipment, making sure that the light is in proper working order, the oil fountains and canteens filled, the lenses polished and the wicks properly trimmed. At night the Keepers are required to keep watch in the lightroom to make sure that the light is working properly and flashing correctly to character, and also to keep a constant fog watch, and be ready to operate the fog signal in the event of poor visibility. The Lightkeepers must be men of many talents and abilities, with a good working knowledge of engines, and also a healthy respect for the capricious and destructive power of the sea. They must be good handymen and decent cooks, as well as genial and pleasant companions – a more important requirement than one might think, since they are required to man Rock Stations for four weeks at a time.

John Milne was such a man, and I felt confident at the prospect of spending a month in his and Joseph Moore's company. I must say, however, that this feeling did not seem to be reciprocated; for although Milne seemed affable enough, I had the impression that this was only a pretence born more of good manners than something genuinely felt. Whenever I looked at him, he averted his gaze, and his smile seemed distracted, artificial. I didn't know why this was, and I did not feel confident enough to ask him outright. In the end, I put it down to the sadness we all were feeling.

For the remainder of the voyage out to the Flannans, he avoided me, and even the tender's crew refused to look me in the eye. The only man who treated me differently was Superintendent Muirhead, who had come with us to look over the island and talk to Joseph Moore. Nevertheless, several times I even caught Muirhead looking at me with that same expression of sadness and trepidation.

*

It was late in the afternoon when the *Hesperus* made its approach to the Flannan Isles. The turbulence of the Atlantic was mirrored in the sky, where the clouds boiled ceaselessly. Cold, hard rain lashed the decks, and the sea raised white-flecked claws against the vessel, thrashing and pounding it this way and that, so that the engine wheezed and panted its hunger for more coal. As we approached Eilean Mòr, I went out onto the deck and seized the rail to steady myself, so that I might have an unobstructed view of our destination.

The world is full of beautiful things; some bring delight to the heart, and others possess a terrible beauty that inspires fear and wonder. The calm waters of a loch, shimmering like quicksilver in the summer sun, can lift the soul and make one grateful to be alive. And yet on other days in those parts, the soul can tremble at the sight of rocky crags reaching naked and primal into a stormy sky, and one feels the need to hide one's eyes from the limitless power of nature.

But Eilean Mòr inspired neither delight at nature's beauty nor fear at its perilous splendour. The sheer ugliness of the place gave rise to a terrible kind of awe: if a shape can be said to be violent, then its shape was that. It seemed an expression of all that is dangerous and inimical in nature: its rocky crags and sheer cliffs, the deep gouges of its inlets, as if something huge and malign had reached up from the depths of the ocean to claw mindlessly at it, sent a flood of sickness through me – a sickness that had nothing to do with the rolling of the ship as we made our approach.

Muirhead came up beside me and grabbed the rail, planting his legs far apart on the heaving deck, his hair plastered across his forehead by the sea spray. 'Cap'n Harvie's going to try for the West Landing,' he shouted.

I nodded and turned back to the approaching bulk of the island. Harvie had already sounded the tender's horn, and a lone figure had emerged from the lighthouse and waved to us. From this distance I couldn't tell who it was, and he and the lighthouse were quickly obscured from view by the misshapen rock of the island's flanks, which rose precipitously into the furious sky.

The swell heaved us closer to the West Landing, with its semi-submerged steps clinging to an ascending outcrop of rock, constantly washed by the boiling sea. I was unashamed of the fear that seized me as jagged forms reared up on either side of the tender, threatening to smash us to smithereens at any moment. Fear and respect kept men alive in places like this, and at any rate, James Harvie was an experienced captain who well knew what he was doing. Twice he guided the *Hesperus* towards the landing, and twice the tender was coughed back out into the open sea. But on the third attempt, the island accepted us. William McCormack, the second mate, hurled a rope over the railing. The loop found the capstan, and the tender's crew secured her at the landing.

And then something happened that made the steamer's crew glance at each other uneasily. The sea that had been thrashing in the inlet containing the West Landing suddenly calmed, as if defeated by our successful mooring. The deck on which we stood ceased its heaving and began to bob gently up and down. It was as if the elements, exhausted by their attempts to deny the island to us, had finally admitted defeat and let us be.

I breathed a great sigh of relief and turned from the railing. As I did so, I caught sight of John Milne standing at the steamer's prow, looking at me, his face devoid of expression.

*

Five of us went onto the island: myself, Captain Harvie, William McCormack the Second Mate, John Milne and Superintendent Muirhead. We laded ourselves with backpacks filled with supplies and made our way carefully up the slippery steps which curved upward around the island's flank. The going was painstaking, for although the sea had unaccountably calmed, the wind still lashed at us, and the cold rain felt like a million tiny teeth gnawing incessantly at our faces. We took full advantage of the iron safety railing bolted onto the rock, clinging to it and hauling ourselves up the steps.

Presently we reached the wide concrete platform, about seventy feet above sea level, containing the crane used to transfer heavier supplies and equipment onto the island, and the terminus of the miniature tramway which was used to haul them up to the lighthouse. The first crane had been washed away during a violent storm the previous winter. Its replacement was in good order, the jib was lowered and secured to the rocks, and the canvas covering and the wire rope on the barrel were firmly lashed.

Everything seemed normal at first, with no clue to hint at the disaster that had overwhelmed James Ducat and the other Keepers. But as we made ready to leave the platform and climb the final flight of steps that would take us to the top of the island, we saw that part of the safety railing had been ripped from its stanchions, and what remained was horribly twisted out of shape. A large block of stone that must have weighed upwards of twenty hundredweight had been dislodged from its position higher up and carried down and left on the concrete path leading from the terminus of the tramway to the steps.

Milne paused at the remains of the safety railing, and slowly and tentatively reached out to touch the twisted iron, as if it were a length of electrical cable that might still be live. William McCormack came up and stood beside him. 'Dear God, what could have done that? The sea?'

'The sea has carried off more than this from the island, Mac,' the Keeper replied. 'It took the first crane with no trouble.'

'And yonder stone,' added Captain Harvie, pointing ahead at the fallen block.

McCormack shook his head. 'All the same, Cap'n, a crane and a big lump of stone, they give the water something to hold onto... but the railing here... I've never seen the sea do that.'

Captain Harvie glanced at me and then clapped his Second Mate on the back. 'Come along now, Mac; let's get this gear up to the light. I'm sure the lads up there will have some hot tea waiting for us – and perhaps something a wee bit stronger.'

'Aye, my nerves could do with it,' muttered McCormack as he followed the captain onto the final flight of steps.

We found the man who had waved to us waiting at the top of the steps, and I saw that it was Joseph Moore, who had been first onto the island on the 26th of December. He greeted us all with a shake of the hand, although he didn't smile; in fact, there was a great fear in his eyes and a pallor to his face.

46

Moore led the way up the sloping top of the island towards the lighthouse. Superintendent Muirhead walked with him, turning his head and saying things periodically, but the wind snatched his words away before they could reach me.

The lighthouse tower was squat and sturdy, rising some sixty feet into the air. At its base stood a large whitewashed house and a couple of stone outbuildings, where the equipment and supplies were kept. Gratefully we passed through the entrance gate in the low wall surrounding the small enclosure and entered the house through the kitchen door.

Inside, we found a fire burning brightly in the grate, and the table was laid for afternoon tea. Archie Lamont was pouring hot water from the kettle into a large teapot and called a friendly 'hello' over his shoulder as we relieved ourselves of our heavy backpacks and slumped into chairs around the table.

As I gratefully received a steaming mug of tea, I noticed that Joseph Moore was standing beside the kitchen door, as if reluctant to stay here. Lamont noticed it, too; he walked up to the lad and placed a comforting arm around his shoulder. 'Come on, Joe, sit down and have some tea.'

'How are you, Joseph?' asked Captain Harvie.

Moore ran a hand through his thick, sodden dark hair and offered a weak smile. 'Oh, I'm all right.' He sighed. 'Yes… I'm all right.'

'Joe's a good lad,' said Lamont. 'It wasn't easy for him, being the first to find… well…' He broke off and brought a large plate of oatcakes and apple scones to the table.

'I understand,' said Muirhead. 'This is a terrible business, but I promise you we'll get to the bottom of it. Where is Mr McDonald?'

'Up in the lightroom.' Lamont turned to Moore again. 'Joe, will you ask Allan to come down? I daresay Captain Harvie'll be wanting his shipmate back, eh Cap'n?'

Harvie nodded; the Buoymaster Allan McDonald would be leaving on the *Hesperus* when it departed. I glanced at Moore again and saw a yearning in his eyes that told more eloquently than words ever could how dearly he wanted to be away on the lighthouse tender when it left Eilean Mòr behind. Without a word, he retreated from the kitchen.

Lamont took a bottle of whisky and some glasses from a shelf and placed them on the table. 'Now, who will take a wee dram?'

We all mumbled our agreement, and as Lamont poured, he said, 'I don't mind telling you that young Joseph has had an awful time this week. The shock of what he found – or rather what he *didn't* find – has been almost too much for him to bear. He's a sensitive lad, and that's all to the good, but his nerves have been frayed ragged, having to stay here.' It was clear that this was addressed more to Muirhead than to any of us others.

The Superintendent nodded. 'Believe me, Archie, I understand what you're saying. But the fact is I need him here for a while longer. I'll certainly consider a transfer in due course, if that's what he wants, but for the moment…'

'Aye, Mr Muirhead, I know.' Lamont sighed and sipped his whisky.

An uneasy silence followed, which Lamont broke by turning to me. 'I don't believe we've met, laddie.'

'Alec Dalemore,' I said, shaking his hand. 'Occasional, standing in for Daniel McBride, who's on sick leave.'

Archie Lamont exchanged the same uneasy glance with the others around the table that I had noticed onboard the *Hesperus*. 'Aye,' he said at length. 'Well… good, laddie. Good!' He raised his glass. 'Let's drink to the health of the relief Keepers – Mr Dalemore and Mr Milne!'

We all raised our glasses as Joseph Moore returned with Allan McDonald, who was clearly overjoyed at seeing his shipmates again.

While McDonald took a glass of whisky, Superintendent Muirhead beckoned to Moore to have a seat at the table. 'Now Joseph,' he began, but Moore cut him off.

'I know, Mr Muirhead. I know what you're going to ask me, and I'm ready to tell what happened on that day, although to tell you the truth, I've been dreading it this past week.'

Muirhead poured a little more whisky into his own glass and slid it across the table to the young Lightkeeper. 'Take your time, laddie....'

'Well,' Moore began. 'As you are aware, the *Hesperus* came to anchorage on the 26th of last month, and we did not see the Lighthouse Flag flying, so we thought that the Keepers didn't see us coming. Captain Harvie' (he glanced furtively at the tender's Master) 'sounded the horn several times, but there was no reply, and no one came out to greet us. So the Captain ordered the rocket to be fired – still nothing. It was too rough to make the West Landing, so we tried for the East Landing instead and succeeded in lowering a rowboat and mooring there.'

Moore took a swallow of whisky, grimaced, and continued. 'I was on the boat, along with Mr Lamont and Mr McCormack, although I was the first to go ashore. I went up, and on coming to the entrance gate, I found it closed. I made for the door leading here to the kitchen and found it also closed. I came into the kitchen and looked at the fireplace, and I saw that there was nothing but cold ashes in the grate. It looked like the fire had not been lit for some days. The kitchen was clean, the dishes had been washed and were on the draining board. Everything seemed normal, except that the clocks had stopped, and one of the chairs was turned over and lying on the floor.'

I looked across at Muirhead. The Superintendent was watching Moore intently, paying close attention to every word.

'I called out to the men, but there was no answer. I thought they must all have fallen sick and taken to their beds. Yes...' he paused, remembering, 'that's what I thought. I called again and went to each bedroom, but there was no one there, and the beds were neatly made. The whole place... there was no sound but the howling of the wind and the battering of the rain on the windows. I didn't search anymore, since I knew then that something serious had happened. I ran from the house, back to the East Landing where Archie and Mac were waiting for me.

'I shouted to them that the place was deserted, and Mac came ashore, and together we returned here. I suppose I should have checked the tower and lightroom first, but...' He faltered and fell silent.

'I understand, Joseph,' said Muirhead quietly. 'You wanted to report back to your shipmates as quickly as possible...'

For the first time since our arrival on the island, Joseph Moore smiled, but it was a small, sad smile. 'No sir, that's not the reason. I... I just didn't want to be here alone. We searched the house again and then went up to the lightroom. There was no one there, although everything was in order: the lamp was cleaned, and the oil fountains were full. So we returned to the *Hesperus* and reported to Captain Harvie, who told me that someone had to stay on the island to light the lamp and make sure it kept working. The task fell to me, since I was the only Lightkeeper on the boat, but Mr Campbell and Mr Lamont came with me, and also Mr McDonald, the Buoymaster.

'We came ashore again and went straight to the lightroom and lit the lamp that night and every night since.

The following day, we searched the island from end to end, but we found no sign of the men and no clue to convince us how or why they disappeared. We even checked the bothie out there.' He jerked his head towards the kitchen window. He was referring to the tiny dry-stone chapel that stood in ruins a few yards from the lighthouse: a relic of the time when Christian monks first came to these islands centuries ago.

'We went to the East Landing, but nothing appeared touched to show that they were taken from there. The ropes were in all their proper places in the shelter, just as they were left after the relief of the 7th. On the West Landing, it was different. There was an old box halfway up the tramline, for holding the mooring ropes and tackle, and we saw that it had gone. Some of the ropes had got washed out of it: they lay strewn on the rocks near the crane. And the handrail...'

'Aye, lad,' said Muirhead. 'We saw.'

Moore shook his head. 'We couldn't believe that. It was as if some great hand had reached up from the sea and wrenched it away.'

Up from the sea, or out of the sky, I thought, remembering Mary Ducat's dream.

'Even so,' Moore continued, 'there was nothing at the West Landing to give us an indication that the men lost their lives there.'

'What about the log?' asked Muirhead.

'The last entry was on the 15th. It was written on the slate but hadn't been transferred to the logbook.'

I glanced at the slate on the kitchen wall. It was used to record meteorological conditions such as wind direction, barometer and thermometer readings, which were marked in chalk before being copied into the logbook at the end of each day.

'And the last entry in the logbook?'

'That was on the 13th.'

Muirhead nodded. 'The steamer *Archtor* from Philadelphia passed the Flannans on the 15th, and reported no light visible. So it would seem that whatever happened, it happened on the 14th.'

'Don't forget the chair,' said Moore suddenly.

'The chair?'

'The chair was upturned, on the floor.' Moore indicated the chair in which Archie Lamont was sitting. Lamont shifted uncomfortably.

'Ah, yes,' nodded Muirhead. 'As if someone got up in a hurry. The West Landing can't be seen from here, is that right?'

'Yes, sir, not even from the top of the tower.'

'And you found one of the oilskins still on its peg.'

'That's right. The other two were gone.'

'And you made a complete search of the island, you say.'

Moore nodded. 'We searched the cliffs and crags and the hollows in them – everywhere we could. We called out to them until we were hoarse. But they were nowhere to be seen.' Moore closed his eyes, swallowed and lowered his head. 'They're not on the island, Mr Muirhead.'

'That's right,' said Archie Lamont. 'We searched from one end to the other, and more than once: young Joseph here insisted on it.' He offered Moore a sad smile. 'If they were still here, trapped somewhere on the island's edge, we'd have found them...' Lamont broke off, as if at a loss for further words, and he too bowed his head.

'I see.' Muirhead nodded again, absently, clearly lost in thoughts of his own. Presently, he began to speculate aloud, his eyes unfocussed, gazing out through the rain-streaked kitchen window. 'We know there was a powerful storm that night. James Ducat must have been worried about the landing ropes. Six months ago, the tackle at the West Landing was carried off in a storm and had to be replaced. Ducat would have known that if it happened again, it would make relief all the more difficult. Nobody goes out of a lighthouse in bad weather if they can help it, but Ducat had to be sure that the ropes and tackle were safe.

'Later in the afternoon, the wind starts to drop, so Ducat and one other man put on their sea boots and coats and make their way to the west side of the island. The third man is left in the lighthouse, according to the rules. Ducat and his companion come to the safety path, which runs at right angles to the stairway, and continue towards the crane where the box for stowing the landing ropes is situated.

'Suddenly, a wave much bigger than the other ones comes in and sweeps one of them into the sea...'

'From the crane platform?' interrupted Lamont in disbelief. 'Such a wave would have to be a hundred and fifty feet high, at the least! How could that be, if the weather had calmed enough for them to go outside in the first place?'

Superintendent Muirhead knew these islands better than most, and a much greater area besides: after all, it was his job. He fixed Lamont with an intense, grim stare, which he then gave to each of us in turn. 'A high roller,' he said.

He was met with blank stares from all of us, except for John Milne, who was the most experienced Lightkeeper there. 'I know what you're speaking of, Mr Muirhead: the chasm in the rocks near the West Landing. It's like a blow hole; when the sea rears up in a storm, a wave pattern is set up – a freakish thing – the water floods in through the inlet and is cast up onto the land, a sudden torrent, tearing up the cliff-face to crash against the platform. Aye... maybe that's what did it.'

Lamont nodded. 'It has the ring of truth to it,' he said quietly, his eyes lingering on Joseph Moore. I wondered what the young man had been thinking and saying to the others during the long nights of the past week.

Muirhead continued with his speculations – speculations that seemed sound for all that. 'So, a sudden torrent floods in through the inlet, carrying one man into the sea. The other man – there's no way of knowing who it was – makes his way as quick as he can back up the island's shoulder to the lighthouse, shouting through the doorway what has happened. Perhaps the cook has just finished washing the plates and has sat down at the table; he springs to his feet, knocking the chair from under him, and rushes out, without taking his coat.

'Grabbing a heaving line, the two men make their way back down to the west side, hoping to throw the line to their comrade. But it is all in vain, for another torrent comes pounding in through the inlet, and carries them both to their deaths.'

'How can you be so sure that that's what happened?' asked Moore.

'I'm not, Joe,' Muirhead replied. 'But it seems the most plausible explanation to me. Whatever happened, it happened fast: that's why you found the chair turned over, why one oilskin was left on its peg. Its owner went out of the lighthouse in his shirtsleeves: no one would do that unless he was in a great hurry. I need to go back down to the West Landing to examine the place properly. Will you come with me, Joe?'

Moore nodded. 'Aye, Mr Muirhead, if you think it'll help.'

'I think it will.'

John Milne gave me a long look before saying, 'If you've no objection, Mr Muirhead, I'll come too – at least as far as the top of the cliffs, so I can keep an eye on the both of you while you're down there.'

'Thank you, John.'

The three men put on their oilskins and went out through the kitchen door, leaving me alone with Captain Harvie, Archie Lamont and Allan McDonald, all of whom looked at me in silence.

THE CHAPEL AND THE SONG

The silence continued for several moments, so that I grew increasingly uncomfortable. It was clear that these men entertained the same misgivings about me as John Milne, and I was at a loss to explain what they were. Was it just unfamiliarity, combined with the natural taciturnity of seamen? Or was it something else – perhaps the fact that, as an Occasional, I was not a fully-fledged member of the fraternity of Lightkeepers?

Presently, though, their inherent good nature came to the fore, and they tried to strike up a conversation with me. They asked about my family and my profession of carpenter. I answered their questions readily, and with all the friendliness I could muster, but after some time the conversation stalled, and to save them any further embarrassment I excused myself, saying that I felt like taking a short walk in the open.

'There isn't a great deal to see, Alec,' said Archie Lamont with a brief smile.

'True enough,' I agreed, 'but I might have a look at that bothie nearby.' In fact, I just wanted to be out of the house for a while.

'Stay away from the cliffs, Alec,' said Captain Harvie. 'The weather's easing a little, but the sea is still high.'

'Aye, I will,' I said and went out through the kitchen door.

The air was heavy with spindrift, and my hair was soon damp again upon my brow. I gathered the collar of my waterproof tight around my neck and walked the short way to the chapel.

To call the poor mound of stone a chapel was to do it a kindness it no longer deserved – if indeed it ever had. And yet, as I stood gazing at its low, corbelled roof with the wind shouting in my ears and the clouds boiling through the sky, I became aware of a strangeness rising in my heart, and with it a fear I had never known existed, so that I could neither name nor understand it.

Suddenly, I no longer wished to look upon that mean little heap, which seemed to contain an emptiness that was more profound and frightening than the mere absence of objects or human inhabitants, but neither did I want to return to the lighthouse just then, and so I walked slowly around the chapel, trying to imagine what life must have been like here, so lonely and hard with nothing but the sea and the sky for company. I imagined some long-forgotten Columban hermit sitting alone in the chapel, whispering to God, his words of devotion carried away by the wind's mournful groan and the sea's mocking whisper.

The clouds were etched with the dancing forms of puffins and petrels that swooped and glided through the air, searching for fish upon the surface of the sea. Their cries stirred a wretchedness in my breast, and again the strange fear arose, as if it were a living, breathing lonely thing that had arrived from outside, settling upon me and growing comfortable in my presence.

I shook my head and pulled my coat collar tighter about my throat, reluctantly preparing to return to the lighthouse and my companions.

It was then that I became aware of another sound beyond the groan of the wind and the whisper of the sea, a sound that seemed to come from all directions at once and none at all, as if made by the very air itself. Beautiful and mournful it was, rising and falling against the background of groan and whisper, like a pipe played by a lonely player, like a song from the limitless past telling of things long forgotten.

I stood rooted to the spot beside the ancient chapel, listening to the phantom pipe-song that seemed to come at once from the sea and the sky, and it is a measure of my frame of mind that it took so many moments for me to realise its source. *A whale*, I thought. *Yes, a whale, a minke or a pilot, in the ocean somewhere nearby*. I relaxed somewhat at the realisation that the sound came from an inhabitant of this world – albeit a part of the world that was mysterious and fathomless to human understanding, and I wondered what the whale was saying: was it calling to its mate, or singing of its loneliness, or perhaps giving voice to thoughts forever incomprehensible to the mind of man?

I let out the breath I had been holding, wiped the sea-spray from my face and gave a quiet laugh. 'Yes... a whale,' I said in a low voice that was caught and discarded by the wind.

But then, as I was about to turn back towards the lighthouse, another sound came across the sea, and I stopped and listened, again holding my breath in my lungs like a precious possession.

I strove in vain to recognise the sound. If I describe it as a metallic shimmering, a hard and distant trembling of the air that seemed both to approach and recede at the same time, of something moving through the atmosphere that was not meant to do so, then perhaps I may present the most fleeting impression of what it was like.

For many moments I stood there, transfixed and unable to move as the sound washed over me, making me tremble from more than mere cold, making the very air tremble with its presence. And riding upon the sound, as rain rides upon a storm's chaotic winds, a whisper came to my ears, as of voices that issued not from the throats of men, but from something that was nevertheless capable of speech.

I still do not know whether they really were voices, or whether my imagination, thrown into uncontrolled and fevered speculation, sought to influence my senses, to build some recognisable framework with which to apprehend what I was hearing.

And as I stood, grimacing with cold and concentration, one hand clutched upon the collar of my waterproof while the spindrift stung my eyes to blindness, I strained to hear what the 'voices' were saying. And presently, I did begin to pick out whispered words flung upon the wind from God knows where. And the voices, it seemed to me, were saying, over and over again:

'Let us be gone. Let... us... be... gone.'

My eyes darted across the horizon, my gaze like a stone skipping upon the water, as I tried to ascertain from which direction the whispering voices came, but it was useless, for they seemed to come from every direction at once, and from none at all. It was as if the world itself were speaking, making a desperate, unfathomable entreaty.

I shuddered again and tried to banish the repeated words from my awareness, to convince myself that they were an illusion born of the strange environment in which I found myself, this wild part of the world where men did not belong. But it was no use, for once within my mind, the words could not be unthought, and I could no longer believe that they were merely part of the moaning wind and the ocean's hiss.

Looking away from the rolling horizon, my gaze fell upon the entrance to the ruined chapel, an irregular patch of blackness framed by the crazily-piled, ash-grey stones.

'Let us be gone.'

My breath came quick and shallow, as the voices sighed upon that shimmering metal sound and the wind rose and fell like the waves that besieged the island. I stared at the chapel's doorway, at the impenetrable darkness within, darker than the sky at midnight, unable to tear my gaze away.

I strained to hear the song of the whale, for in that moment I felt a strange kinship with the creature, felt a desperate need to hear its voice, for it was something known and knowable out there in the wide ocean that surrounded me and which contained so much that was unfathomable.

But the whale had fallen silent.

'God preserve us,' I whispered, the words springing unbidden to my lips.

'Let us be gone.'

THREE

MONDAY 20 JULY
6.45 AM

Rebecca awoke to clattering sounds outside the tent. Groggily, she realised that someone must be making breakfast. As she got dressed, she could hear someone fumbling around on the other side of the partition, in the half of the tent that Nick and Max were sharing. She poked her head through the flaps and saw Nick outside, hunched over the portable gas stove. She hurried herself, glancing over her shoulder at the partition; it sounded like Max was getting dressed as well. Maybe, if Donald and Jennifer were still in their tent, she could grab a few moments alone with Nick outside, maybe give him a hand with breakfast.

She ran a brush quickly through her hair, bemoaning the fact that she would spend the next week without access to a shower, and tied it back in a ponytail before leaving the tent. The air was cool and fresh, with a light north-easterly breeze, and the sky was clear and blue once again. She stood and stretched and smiled at Nick, who still had his back to her. The sea breathed with a loud but soothing hiss all around them.

Rebecca continued to watch him for a few more moments. He was stirring the pot with the intense, deliberate concentration of a complete novice. *No great shakes in the kitchen department, eh?* she thought. *What about the bedroom...?*

Any further speculation along such pleasant lines was interrupted when he said: 'Morning, Becks.' He hadn't turned, and Rebecca smiled, flattered that somehow he had known it was she rather than Max.

'Good morning. What's for breakfast?'

'Porridge with honey and dried apples. And coffee.'

'Mmm... sounds good.'

Nick crumbled some dried apples into small pieces and sprinkled them into the bubbling porridge.

'That's a hell of a story you've got there,' he said.

'Yeah... it is.'

She thought of the first four chapters of Alec Dalemore's testament, which she had read aloud last night before tiredness finally overcame them and they agreed to stop and turn in. 'What do you think about it?' she asked, sitting down cross-legged on the concrete next to him.

'I think it's interesting.'

'More than interesting,' she said. 'Damned weird.'

He chuckled.

'You don't think so?'

'Well, yeah... I guess, in places.'

'Mary Ducat thought that something supernatural had happened to the missing lighthouse keepers.'

'Yeah, but she was a grieving widow. Bereavement does bad things to a person's mind, Becks. Everyone knows that. Dalemore says as much himself, doesn't he?'

'Yeah, I suppose.' Rebecca shrugged. She was still thinking of the white fox she had seen yesterday, and how Dalemore and the other relief keepers had seen something like it during their stay on the island.

She could have told Nick about it right there and then, of course. But she was still reluctant: he had enough on his mind already. He and the others had come to Eilean Mòr to do a job – a job which had nothing to do with what three men might have seen or not seen a century ago. And the unforeseen complications with the hydrophones and transducer made her even less willing to start bothering him with the half-formed speculations that had started to grow in her mind.

Better to just read the chapter to them and see how they reacted – or more specifically, how Nick reacted.

But those speculations continued to grow and develop, having taken root in her awareness as she lay awake in their tent last night. She had a strange sense of some connection being made, as if something were reaching out to them across a hundred years, something that had been awoken by her discovery of the stone and the manuscript.

The thought of it made her shudder. Nick noticed and glanced at her. She smiled at him and said: 'I believe you mentioned coffee.'

'Oh, yeah.' He poured some into a large aluminium camping mug and handed it to her.

She murmured in pleasure as she inhaled the aroma. Funny how such simple things seemed so luxurious when one was away from civilisation. She realised it was a feeling she could get used to – as long as she didn't have to get used to it here.

She took a sip, then said: 'What do you think that was yesterday?'

'Hm?'

'That thing the equipment picked up... what do you think it was?'

'Dunno, Becks. Probably nothing.'

'Nothing?'

'No piece of equipment's completely infallible. Sometimes we get weird returns, stuff that doesn't make any sense. It's rare, but it happens. The Yanks call it "ratty data".'

'Do you think that's what it was?'

Nick spooned porridge into two bowls and handed one to her. 'I'm not sure what else it could be.' He regarded her for a moment and then broke into a broad grin. 'Do you think it was a sea monster?'

She laughed. 'Of course not!'

He regarded her through narrowed eyes. 'Are you sure?'

She sighed. 'Yes, I'm quite sure, piss-taker. But I was just thinking…' She hesitated. 'Are *you* sure there's something wrong with the equipment? I mean, Max said it was pretty unlikely that the hydrophones *and* the transducer would be returning the same false image…'

'Well, that's true – but I honestly don't know what else it could be.'

As he turned to her, his eyes caught something, and he stood up from the stove and waved. Rebecca turned away from the sea to face the wall of rock rising from the crane platform. High above them, a figure was standing at the edge of the island.

'Who's that?'

'Max. Up bright and early, and probably ready for breakfast.'

'Max?'

'Yeah. What's up?'

'Max is… he's in the tent.'

Nick laughed. 'What are you talking about, Becks? Look, here he comes.'

Rebecca watched as Max carefully descended the winding rock-hewn staircase towards the platform, and suddenly she felt something cold and heavy in her stomach, as if she'd seen something she shouldn't have, or been told something she didn't want to hear.

'But I heard him moving around in the tent while I was getting dressed,' she said in a small, quiet voice.

Nick shook his head, chuckling. 'I suspect that what you heard was the breeze rippling the fabric. Haven't done much camping, have you?'

Rebecca was about to say something else. She was about to say that there *was* someone on the other side of the partition, that she heard and felt another person there. She'd heard movement, heard *breathing*…

But she said nothing, because suddenly the sea was too vast and the sky was too cold, and she was aware of how very far from home they all were. Instead, she went back into their tent, took a deep breath and unzipped the partition.

Max's and Nick's belongings and some spare clothes were there, but apart from that, the other side of the tent was empty. Rebecca sat down in her half and forced herself to breathe deeply, to calm down.

Stupid, she thought. *Don't be stupid. Nick's right. It was just the wind rippling the fabric. Max wasn't in here… he wasn't in here. It was just the wind.*

Then she got up and hurried out of the tent. Even though she knew that Nick must be right, she didn't want to be in there alone.

*

For the rest of that morning, Rebecca said nothing more about the sounds she'd heard from the other side of the tent's partition. Her silence was for Nick's sake: she didn't want him worrying about her when he and the others had so much work to do. But it continued to play on her mind, resisting all her attempts to shrug it off, in spite of the logic of Nick's explanation.

And yet, maybe Nick *was* right: maybe it was just the sound of the tent's fabric rippling in the wind. After all, Rebecca had never really been one for the outdoor life – had never even camped out in her back garden when she was a child, and she'd certainly never been to such a wild and remote place as this. She wanted very much to believe that that was the explanation, and by lunchtime she had almost convinced herself.

Nick came out of the equipment tent as she was heating soup on the little stove. He looked worried.

'Everything okay?' she asked.

'Not really,' he said. 'We've just spent the morning running diagnostics on the equipment, recalibrating it – you name it…'

'And?'

'And there's nothing wrong with it.' He hesitated and took a deep breath. 'But now we've got another problem.'

Rebecca stopped stirring the pot and looked at him. 'What is it?'

Nick offered her a bewildered look. 'There's nothing there.'

'What do you mean?'

'The area that gave the anomalous return yesterday… it's empty of marine life. No fish, no seals, no plankton. There's no life in that section of ocean to the north of the island.'

Nick turned away from her, shaking his head.

Rebecca stood up and walked slowly across the crane platform to him. 'What does that mean?'

'I don't know. It's as if something just scooped up every living thing within that area.'

Max came out of the tent. He looked just as worried as Nick. 'Still nothing,' he said. 'Hydrophones and transducer are working, but they're not picking up anything. This is really weird, man. I mean, this is freakin' *weird*. Even if some large predator had cleaned out the area during the night – not that I'm saying that's even possible – but even if it had, then the area should have been repopulated with life from the surrounding ocean. It's almost as if…'

'As if the other life is staying away,' said Rebecca.

Max gave a short, humourless laugh. 'It's not a very scientific hypothesis, but yeah, that's what it looks like.'

'Do you think it could be a giant squid?' asked Nick.

Max shook his head. 'Doubtful. Their profile doesn't match what we saw yesterday. And anyway, not even a giant squid could do... *that*.'

'A giant squid?' said Rebecca, glancing from Max to Nick. 'You mean they really exist?'

'Oh yeah, they exist,' said Max. 'The largest one ever recovered was about thirty feet long. And we think there are even bigger ones out there. You can see their sucker marks on whales sometimes...'

'They attack *whales?*'

'And whales attack them,' said Nick.

Rebecca glanced towards the ocean. 'Jesus Christ.'

Nick put a hand on her shoulder. 'Don't worry, Becks. Max is right: it wasn't a giant squid.'

'No, from what you're saying, it was something even bigger and weirder!'

Nick gave a brief half-smile, lowered his eyes and took his hand from her shoulder. She suddenly found herself wanting him to put it back.

Max shrugged. 'Well... yeah, I guess that's what we're saying. Man, I can't figure this shit out...'

'None of us can,' said Donald, who had just emerged from the equipment tent. They all turned to him. 'At least, not yet. But I'm sure we'll be able to, if we just put some thought into it – some thought and some further observation – instead of wild theorising about giant squid and other monsters of the deep.' He gave Nick and Max a stern look.

Max sighed. 'Okay, Don, I guess you're right. But I gotta tell you, I've been thinking about this, and I'm wondering whether it might be something like the Slow Down or the Bloop.'

Donald looked at him in silence.

'The Slow Down?' said Rebecca. 'The Bloop? What are they?'

'Sounds,' Max replied, 'recorded in the deep oceans. No one knows what made them. The Slow Down was recorded in 1997 on a hydrophone array in the Pacific Ocean. During the Cold War, the US Navy established a huge network of underwater listening devices to keep tabs on Soviet nuclear submarines. The array was composed of hydrophones placed at 3,000 km intervals in a deep layer of ocean called the "deep sound channel", where the combination of low temperature and high pressure allows sound waves to propagate across great distances. When the Cold War ended, the US Navy allowed the array to be used for scientific research. The Slow Down was detected by three hydrophones at a distance of 2,000km, and slowly descended in frequency over a period of about seven minutes, hence its name. The sensors were able to triangulate its location at approximately 15° S, 115° W. This type of signal had never been detected before and hasn't been detected since. Its origin is completely unknown.'

Rebecca nodded, taking all this in. 'And what about the Bloop?'

Nick answered: 'A few months after the Slow Down, the same array detected another mysterious ultra-low frequency sound on several occasions at about 50° S, 100° W. The sound rose rapidly in frequency over a period of about one minute, and was apparently generated 3,000km from the nearest sensor. The researchers had no idea what it was, what to call it, so they called the "Bloop". The strange thing is, the characteristics of the Bloop match those of a living creature, although the fact that the sound was detected from such a great distance means that such an animal would have to be truly colossal – much larger than the blue whale, the largest known animal on Earth.'

'And you think that whatever caused the Slow Down and the Bloop is here, now,' said Donald. He sounded a little incredulous, but Rebecca thought she detected something else in his voice… something like uncertainty.

'I'm just saying that something strange is goin' down here,' Max replied. 'Something we don't understand.' He caught the look in Donald's eye and added: 'And I'll tell you something else right now: I don't feel happy about camping here. It's too exposed, too near the sea.'

'We're on a small island,' said Donald reasonably. 'Everywhere here is near the sea. And besides, the crane platform does offer protection from the wind.'

'Yeah, well, it's not the wind I'm worried about,' said Max, and he went back into the equipment tent.

'I think he may be right, Donald,' said Nick.

Donald gave him a disbelieving look. 'Oh, come on!'

'Wait, hear me out. We detected something on our instruments yesterday, and today an area of approximately a square kilometre is barren of marine life. I'm sure you'll agree that's a pretty unusual event. I don't think we should stay here: it *is* too exposed.'

'Are you worried that something's going to come up out of the sea and carry us off?'

'No, of course not. It's more than likely there's nothing out there that's a threat to us. I'm just saying that we shouldn't take chances with our safety if we don't have to.'

'Are you suggesting we radio the mainland and request an evacuation? Because I can tell you that the JNCC aren't going to be too impressed with our reason.'

'No, not at all. I want to get to the bottom of this; I want to find out what happened. Something important is clearly going on here, and it's our job to investigate it.'

Donald folded his arms and regarded Nick. 'Then what do you suggest we do?'

Nick indicated the cliff face rising from the crane platform. 'We can move our camp up there, to the lighthouse. We can pitch the tents against the wall around the tower and the outbuildings.'

'And our equipment?'

'We'll leave the equipment tent here. We can still do our work during the day, and at night we'll go up to the top of the island.'

Donald considered this for a moment, and then he sighed in resignation. 'All right, Nick. If it'll make you feel better, we'll move our camp after lunch. Then perhaps we'll be able to get on with the job in hand, eh?'

With a sigh and an irritated shake of his head, Donald went back into the equipment tent.

'Did you do that for my benefit?' asked Rebecca, softly.

'Not really, Becks – or rather, for your benefit and everyone else's.'

She regarded him in silence for a moment. 'You're serious, aren't you? I mean… you're really spooked by this.'

Nick hesitated, then replied: 'Not spooked. Just careful. Respectful.'

'Respectful?'

'Yes. Respectful of the sea. You know, my dad spent years in the merchant navy. I've been around the sea all my life, and people who *know* the sea. I grew up listening to tales of all the things that can happen to ships and their crews.' He laughed softly. 'Oh sure, some of them are taller than a ship's mast. But some…' His voice drifted off, like the call of a departing seabird.

'Go on,' said Rebecca. '*Some* of them…'

'Some of them make you wonder… about what's really out there, in the deep places where no one's ever gone, or maybe will ever go. That's what fascinates me about the sea, Becks. We know more about the surface of the Moon than we do about the deepest seabeds, the great ocean trenches. We have no idea what's down there. It's a mystery as profound as space, but it's right here in the world, within our grasp.'

Rebecca stood in silence for a while, looking out at the vast sapphire sweep of the ocean. 'What do you think happened yesterday, Nick?'

He paused before replying: 'I honestly have no idea.'

*

It took them a couple of hours to move the two accommodation tents and their contents from the crane platform to the enclosure containing the lighthouse and its outbuildings. They might have got the job done a lot quicker if Donald hadn't suggested that Rebecca and Nick do the moving, while he, Max and Jennifer continued with their observations. Nick had glared at him, while Max simply shrugged and gave him a wry smirk, as if to say: 'Sorry, buddy, he's the boss.'

Although Nick was mightily pissed off at Donald for demonstrating his scepticism in this way, Rebecca silently thanked him, since it would give her some extra time alone with Nick. But that wasn't the only reason she felt a sense of gratitude towards the group's leader: she had been unnerved by the sudden, unexplained absence of marine life in the sea to the north of the island, and Donald's obvious exasperation with the idea that it might be necessary to move their camp reassured her. She sympathised with Nick and appreciated his unwillingness to take unnecessary risks with their safety, but she was also glad that Donald so obviously didn't believe that they had anything to be afraid of.

While they were transferring the contents of the tents, Rebecca glanced at Nick from time to time. She was curious as to how he behaved when he was in a bad mood. It was something she always watched out for, ever since the first year of her BA back in York, when she had got into an argument with Steve, her then-boyfriend, and he had settled the matter by punching her repeatedly in the face. Her flatmate, who had witnessed the attack, ran from the room and called the police. Steve was charged with assault, given a suspended prison sentence and sent down from the university. Rebecca never saw him again after the trial. For a while, she wondered whether he might try to get back at her somehow, but she supposed that if any such thought had crossed his mind, it was banished by the look of cold hatred her father had given him during every session in court (in fact, she honestly believed that her dad would have beaten Steve to within an inch of his life if she and her mother hadn't begged him to stay calm and let the law take its course).

Deep down, Rebecca knew that Nick wasn't remotely like Steve, but she kept glancing at him all the same, as he muttered under his breath while lugging backpacks and cooking utensils up the winding stone staircase that led from the crane platform to the shoulder of the island. Once, when they were approaching the lighthouse, he glanced at her and saw that she was looking at him. His angry frown quickly vanished, and he gave her a smile.

'You think I'm being childish, don't you?' he said.

Rebecca shrugged. 'A bit.'

'Nah.' He shook his head. 'A *lot*. I guess I just don't like it when people feel they have to make little points like that.'

'Maybe you need to look at it from his side. You've got lots of work to do, you've had problems with your equipment… he just sees this as a waste of time. But if it makes any difference, I'm glad we're moving the camp up here, and I know Max is too.'

Nick sighed. 'You're right, Becks. Yeah… you're absolutely right. And in any case, it certainly isn't worth getting bent out of shape over.'

Rebecca giggled.

'What?'

'Bent out of shape?'

Nick chuckled. 'I think I've been hanging around with Max too long.'

'Well,' she said, 'I hope I make a nice change.'

He looked at her for a long moment. 'You make a *very* nice change.'

They had come to the low wall around the enclosure. Rebecca put down the backpack she was carrying and moved closer to him. '*How* nice?'

He put down his own pack and put his arms around her waist. They looked at each other for a few more seconds, enjoying the game of delaying the kiss. Then, just as his lips were about to meet hers, Nick froze.

Rebecca pulled back a little. 'What's wrong?'

His eyes were open and gazing into the distance behind her. 'Becks,' he whispered, 'you were right. There it is!'

'What?'

'The fox. I think it *is* an albino!'

Oh God.

She drew further back, taking his arms from around her, and turned to look in the direction he was looking.

It was there, near the edge of the island. It was quite far away, and she couldn't make it out in detail, but it was clearly the same animal she had seen yesterday.

'Amazing!' Nick breathed, shaking his head. 'I wouldn't have believed it. I'm sorry I doubted you, Becks.'

'It's all right,' she replied in a quiet voice. *It's really all right… it isn't the same one… not the same one as in the book.*

The sleek white form glided across the grass, apparently unmindful of their presence. Nick narrowed his eyes, peering intently at the distant shape. 'What's that on its face?'

Rebecca didn't answer.

'See, Becks? There's something on its face…'

'I can't see anything,' she said.

'Look… there, d'you see? Can't make it out… too far away. Shit, my binoculars are in the camp. And my camera! Come on, let's try and get closer.'

Christ, it couldn't be the same one!

Reluctantly, she followed as Nick began to walk towards the fox.

'Shouldn't we finish moving the camp?' she said.

'We're nearly done. I just want to get a closer look.'

No, you don't.

'Nick,' she said, taking hold of his hand. 'I don't want to.'

'Why not?'

'Because I know what's wrong with its face.'

He stopped and turned to her. 'What do you mean?'

'I've seen it before.'

'Up close? When?'

She shook her head, and gave a desperate sigh. 'I don't mean I've seen it up close myself. I mean… I've seen it in the pages of Dalemore's manuscript.'

'I don't understand.'

'They saw it – Dalemore, Milne and Moore.'

'Becks, you're not making much sense.' He was about to say something else, but the expression on Rebecca's face stopped him. Her eyes had filled up with fear as she gazed at the fox's retreating form.

'They saw it!'

How can it still be here? How the fuck *can it still be here?*

'Rebecca, foxes don't live for a hundred years. If they *did* see one, this isn't it.'

'Yes it is,' she said, her voice lowered in sudden resignation. 'It's the same one.'

'How do you know?'

'Because it isn't a fox.'

'Then what is it?'

She glared at him. 'You think I'm crazy, don't you?'

He shook his head. 'Of course not. But I don't understand what you're talking about.'

'You will. Listen, Nick, the others will want me to read some more from the book tonight, after dinner. But I want you to read, okay?'

He shrugged. 'Okay, I'll read tonight. But I still don't get what all this is about.' He glanced back over his shoulder, but the fox was now nowhere to be seen. 'Gone,' he said. 'Maybe its den is over there somewhere.'

'It'll be back,' said Rebecca.

*

They ate dinner in their new camp at the foot of the lighthouse. Donald, perhaps feeling a little guilty, made a point of thanking Nick and Rebecca for their work. Nick smiled and nodded, and the atmosphere in the group thawed a little.

'In fact,' said Nick, 'I want to thank *you*: if you hadn't given us the job, we wouldn't have seen the fox.'

'Huh?' said Max around a mouthful of bread and cheese. 'Foksh?'

'Yeah, and get this: it's an albino.'

'Are you sure?' said Jennifer, putting her plate down and leaning forward in interest.

'That's what I said to Becks when she saw it yesterday. But yes, I'm sure.'

'How extraordinary!' said Jennifer. 'I wonder how it got onto the island.'

'Becks suggested that it somehow found its way onto a ship.'

'That's the only explanation,' agreed Donald.

'Jeez,' said Max. 'I'd love to get a look at that little critter!'

Nick glanced at Rebecca, who was eating in silence without looking at any of them, before adding: 'I couldn't be sure, but I think it has some kind of deformity.'

'Oh yeah?' said Max.

'There's something not quite right about its face. It was too far away when we saw it to know for sure. But... just something.'

Rebecca felt his eyes on her and returned his gaze without saying anything.

Max noticed the strange, wordless exchange, coughed and said: 'Well, I guess it's time for another instalment, huh, Becks?'

Nick went into their tent and brought out the book. 'If no one minds,' he said, 'I'll read tonight.'

With a final glance at Rebecca, he opened the book to the fifth chapter and began to read aloud.

THE DEPARTURE OF THE HESPERUS

Late on the afternoon of the 5th of January 1901, the lighthouse tender *Hesperus* made ready to cast off and leave Eilean Mòr. She would be carrying the men who had accompanied Joseph Moore while he waited for relief to arrive from the mainland. We all said our goodbyes with a lightheartedness that was forced and artificial, but which was no less essential to our state of mind for all that.

As he was about to leave the house, Robert Muirhead stopped at the threshold and, turning to me, said, 'Alec, will you walk a little way with me?'

'Of course, Mr Muirhead,' I replied.

As Archie Lamont, Archie Campbell and Allan McDonald moved on ahead, Muirhead hung back, walking more slowly, so that I was forced to lessen my own pace. We walked in silence for some moments.

'The wind has fallen,' Muirhead presently observed, without looking at me.

'Yes, and the sea's a little calmer; you shouldn't have too much trouble getting under way.'

'When Joseph and I came up from the West Landing, I saw you outside...' He glanced at me, but I did not reply. 'You heard it too, didn't you, Alec?'

Surprised by his forthrightness, I lessened my pace still further and looked at the Superintendent.

Muirhead met my gaze, a faint smile which I could not interpret trembling upon his lips. 'That sound... and the voices... you heard them, didn't you, just as Joseph and I heard them?'

I nodded and continued on towards the stairway. The others had already disappeared from view.

'What did they say?' he asked, and I guessed that he was seeking confirmation of what he had heard, or thought he heard.

I saw no point in prevaricating, and truth to tell, I was glad that I had not been alone in hearing the shimmering metal sound and the voices that whispered upon it. 'I think that they said, "Let us be gone."'

Muirhead let out a breath. 'Yes... yes, that's what we heard.'

And then, suddenly and without warning, he seized my arm. 'Alec, listen. You must look after Joseph. I wish to God I hadn't asked him to go with me to the landing; I wish he hadn't heard what I did while we were there. I wish...'

'You wish you could take him back with you on the *Hesperus*, back to the mainland, away from here,' I completed.

Muirhead sighed and nodded. 'If you could have seen the look on his face when we heard that sound, and the voices...'

'A trick of the wind,' I said suddenly, with a force and conviction that made the Superintendent glance at me again. 'That's all it was. The same kind of trick that deceives us into seeing faces in clouds in the sky and flames in the hearth.'

Again, that vague tremble of a smile. 'Yes, I suppose you're right, Alec. At any rate, I have no choice but to leave Joseph here with you, until other arrangements can be made by the Board. But do please look after him, you and John: as I said to you before, he's a sensitive young man, and this terrible business does not sit easily with him.'

'Nor with any of us, but I'll do as you ask, Mr Muirhead, on my word I will.'

'Thank you, Alec.'

We had reached the top of the stairway. Far below, the *Hesperus* waited, rising and falling gently upon the quicksilver sea.

Muirhead regarded the lighthouse tender in silence for a few moments, then said, 'May I ask you one more question?'

'Of course.'

'What did Mary say to you in her letter?'

I was taken aback by this and hesitated. Muirhead apologised, said that it was of course a personal matter, and that he shouldn't have asked.

'No, no, it's all right, Mr Muirhead. She... she told me what happened, of course, since I'm a friend of the family, and that the Board would be short-staffed. She suggested that I offer to stand watch here with the other replacement Keepers...'

I stumbled into silence, quite certain that the Superintendent knew I was not telling the whole truth. But at that moment, I did not want to describe the true contents of Mary Ducat's letter and the strange fears she had expressed, both in the letter and in person when she and I had taken that walk by the Shore Station at Breasclete. I did not want to describe them, nor even to think of them.

Muirhead stood in silence then, lost in thoughts of his own. Presently, he reached for my hand and shook it with warmth and vigour. 'Well, I'll be on my way. You can be assured that I will not rest until I find out exactly what happened to those men. I believe my theory is sound enough, but even so, it will require proof...'

'I believe your theory is sound, Mr Muirhead.'

The frown that had clouded his brow lifted a little, and he offered me a broad, if strained, smile. 'Good luck, Alec, and thanks again.'

With that, he turned and began to make his way down the winding stairway, towards the waiting ship. I did not want to watch the vessel's departure, and so I turned around and began to make my way back up the island's shoulder, towards the lighthouse.

My limbs felt tired and heavy as I walked with a dismal heart, up the slope, past the ruined chapel (from which I averted my eyes), towards the tiny, fragile outpost of humanity that was the Flannan Isles light. The sky was thick with grey clouds that had stopped their racing as the wind died down, as if they too were exhausted and were pausing to gather their strength.

For the next four weeks, I mused, I would be alone, with only the other Keepers, the wind and the sea for company. Almost immediately, I upbraided myself. The thought was inappropriate; it was the wrong attitude to take: it was we three Keepers, *together*, who would be alone, here on this ugly, brooding island, with its cold, damp harshness, its frightening ancientness, and the mystery that hung upon it like an unclean fume.

Four weeks to brood upon the reason for the disappearance of Ducat and the others, trapped in the place from which they had disappeared.

*

I found John Milne in the kitchen when I entered. He had washed and put away the tea things, and on the stove a saucepan of leek and potato soup was bubbling away. I breathed in the hearty aroma gratefully as I took off my waterproof and hung it upon the peg with the others.

'Where's Joseph?' I asked.

'Up in the lightroom,' he replied, without looking at me.

Since Milne seemed disinclined to talk, I thought it might be best to go up and speak with Joseph, perhaps to offer a few words of comfort and encouragement, to repeat what I had said to Muirhead about the voices, that they were surely nothing but the deception of the wind. The fact that I myself found it difficult to believe mattered little, it seemed, at that moment.

I was about to leave the kitchen, when Milne turned away from the sink. 'Alec.'

'Yes, John?'

He hesitated, and behind his back, through the kitchen window, I saw raindrops begin to fly against the glass. He inclined his head, evidently distracted by the sound they made, like tiny fingernails tapping insistently upon the pane.

'A storm's gathering,' he said quietly. 'I think we're in for a rough night.'

I moved away from the door. 'Are you all right, John?'

Milne said nothing but walked to the kitchen table and sat down. I supposed that he wanted me to join him, and so I sat down opposite him and waited for him to speak.

Presently, he said, 'I was talking to Joseph, while you were seeing Mr Muirhead off...'

Of course, I knew what he was about to say, and I let him describe his conversation with Joseph Moore: how the lad had told him of the shimmering metal sound and the voices that drifted upon it, which he and Muirhead had heard while they were at the West Landing earlier.

'You were outside, then, Alec,' he concluded. 'Did you hear it?'

I replied that I had and gave Milne the same assurance I was about to give to Joseph.

Milne shook his head, and his gaze dropped to his big, gnarled hands which lay clasped together on the rough wood of the kitchen table. I noticed that the skin of his hands was the same colour as the table, his protruding knuckles like knots of wood from the same tree. I thought that this was a strange comparison to make and briefly wondered why it had come to me.

'I'd like to believe that,' he said. 'I'd dearly like to believe that's all they were... just a trick of the wind and the sea...'

'But you don't.'

He shook his head.

'John, I'm only an Occasional, and I wouldn't presume to tell you your job, or how to behave, or what to think. But we cannot be ruled by our imaginations, not here, and not now. The imagination is what separates us from the animals, but sometimes... well, sometimes it is not our friend. Sometimes it betrays us and leads us towards superstition and senseless fear...'

'Are you a religious man, Alec?' he asked suddenly.

'As much as anyone,' I replied carefully, unsure as to why he had asked the question.

'My father was a minister in Aberfoyle,' he said. 'A wise and gentle man, he was, well-read in the history of the church. He taught me a good deal about the early days of Christianity and the first Christian historians. Have you heard of Josephus?'

I had to admit that I had not.

'Well, Josephus was a first-century Jewish historian, who described how the Romans destroyed the Temple in Jerusalem in the year 70. He wrote that, just before the Temple was torn down, the priests heard a sound, a great and terrible sound, as if a great multitude were crying, "Let us remove hence."'

'"Let us remove hence,"' I echoed in spite of myself. '"Let us be gone."'

'My father said that some saw this as a warning, the sound of the divine presence departing...'

Our eyes met and held each other across the table that was the same colour as John Milne's hands.

Presently, I managed to say, 'What do you think this means?'

'The sound you heard, and the voices, the words that they said...' He sighed deeply, a thin, ragged counterpoint to the raindrops tapping against the windowpane. 'I wonder if it means that God has forsaken us. I wonder if it means that God has no power here.'

I said nothing, but I thought of the ruined chapel outside, of its half-collapsed entrance, and of the impenetrable darkness within. 'God has power everywhere,' I replied at length. 'For otherwise, it surely is not God.'

'Perhaps,' said John Milne.

'There is no "perhaps", for we must believe it. I hold with Mr Muirhead's theory, that poor Ducat, Marshall and MacArthur were taken to their deaths by a high roller...'

'And the voices? And what they said?'

'There were no voices, John,' I whispered, my breath coming in quick bursts, as it had outside. *There were no voices!* And the sound like shimmering metal was just the wind and the sea: it was nature playing a cruel jest on the ears of mournful, frightened men.'

'I pray you're right, Alec,' said Milne.

I stood up from the table. 'I believe I am,' I replied, my words carrying a conviction I did not feel.

'Well, at any rate, supper will be ready soon.' Milne went back to the stove and stirred the bubbling pot of soup. 'Yes,' he said, apparently talking more to himself than to me. 'Supper will be ready soon. We'll all feel better with some food inside us. I'll set the table.'

As he stirred the soup, he looked out through the kitchen window, at the wind-driven raindrops that wrote incomprehensible words upon the glass.

'Are you a decent cook, Alec?'

I smiled, relieved that he had turned his attention to more prosaic matters. 'Aye, decent enough. I live alone and can ill afford a housekeeper to keep me fed.'

'You're not married?'

'No.'

He smiled. 'Strange that we know so little about each other, the three of us being here, alone.'

'Well, we have four weeks to get acquainted. I'm looking forward to becoming your friend, Mr Milne.'

He nodded, still looking out through the window at the rising storm beyond. 'Aye…'

I offered him a smile which he could not see and turned to go through the door, into the hallway containing the spiral staircase that led up to the lightroom. It had been my intention to go up and see Joseph, to try to lessen the nervousness Muirhead had told me he was experiencing. But there was no need to go up to the lightroom, for I found Joseph Moore sitting at the foot of the staircase, hands clasped in front of him, head bowed, eyes closed, as if in prayer.

The Logbook and the Light

John Milne had been right about the storm. That night, it descended upon the island with a fury that was terrible to behold. The sky became a maelstrom of black, churning clouds, and the gale-force winds came from every direction, as if stirred by the flapping of vast, unseen wings. The rain seethed and thrashed against the island and the lighthouse, so that our ears were doubly assaulted by the wind's enraged wailing and the terrible clattering of a million icy drops of water.

Within the lighthouse, however, all was in order. The storm lamps cast a warm, steady glow throughout, and the shadows they threw upon walls and floor were comforting in their familiarity and stillness, in their soft counterpoint to the raging chaos outside. On a calm night, I supposed, there would have been a certain homeliness to the place, for it was clean and cosy, and the furnishings, while basic, were comfortable. But that night, it was easy to believe that humanity was gone from the earth and that we three were the last of a race and a civilisation that was no more, cast to oblivion by a storm that covered the entire world with destruction.

Milne was up in the lightroom, keeping watch over the great 100,000-candle-power kerosene lamps that flashed twice every thirty seconds, flinging their handfuls of illumination into the seething night. Visibility in the region was very low, and so periodically he sounded the foghorn, which, in addition to the light, would let passing ships know of their dangerous proximity to the Flannans.

I was in the sitting room with Joseph, who had just made a pot of tea. His hand quivered slightly as he poured the steaming brew into three mugs. He handed one to me, which I accepted gratefully, and without a word took another for Milne and disappeared through the door. He had not mentioned the sounds we had heard earlier that day, and although it had been my intention to try to put his mind at rest, I now felt oddly disinclined to broach the subject with him. Perhaps, I felt, it was better not to bring it up again: perhaps he was trying to forget and would not thank me for reminding him of it.

Presently, Joseph returned from the lightroom and walked across to one of the whitewashed walls and a shelf lined with a large number of books. Reading is a great pastime amongst Lightkeepers, including those who had never thought to do so before taking the job, and during the long, lonely days and nights of lighthouse duty, most take great comfort from losing themselves in the worlds to be found within the pages of a book.

But it was not just any book that Joseph plucked from the shelf: it was the lighthouse logbook, which Milne had recently updated with the meteorological information that had been chalked upon the slate on the kitchen wall.

'I heard what you said to Mr Milne, Alec,' Joseph said as he leafed through the logbook, his voice almost lost to the howling and clattering of the storm.

'I thought as much. And so, what do you think, Joseph?' I asked as he found the page he was looking for and handed the book to me.

He didn't answer directly. Instead, he said, 'You haven't read what Marshall wrote in the log, before...' His voice trailed off into silence as he sat down across from me, his unblinking gaze making me suddenly profoundly uncomfortable.

I looked down at the pages, and read the last entries made by Thomas Marshall.

December 12: Gale, north by northwest. Sea lashed to fury. Stormbound. 9 p.m. Never seen such a storm. Waves very high. Tearing at lighthouse. Everything shipshape. Ducat irritable.

I glanced at Joseph, who nodded at my confused expression. 'That's right, Alec. Lewis is only twenty miles away, and yet no storm was reported there on the 12th of December.'

'That is strange,' I conceded, 'as is the reference to Ducat's temper. I wouldn't have thought he was the kind of man to be easily angered.'

'Especially since he was an experienced Lightkeeper,' Joseph added. 'But read on.'

The next entry was just before midnight on the same day.

Storm still raging. Wind steady. Stormbound. Cannot go out. Ship passing sounding foghorn. Could see lights of cabins. Ducat quiet. MacArthur crying.

Again I looked at Joseph. 'Crying? Why would MacArthur be crying?'

Joseph's gaze had fallen away from me. He was now looking at the floor, his eyes glassy and unfocused, as if lost in a mournful contemplation of things that passed his understanding. 'He was a man of the sea; he knew it well. And he was a hard man, too, Alec. I've seen him in more than one brawl on land, and he always came out best, believe me.' Joseph's eyes found mine again. 'What could have happened to make such a man weep?'

I read the entry for the next day.

December 13: Storm continued through night. Wind shifted west by north. Ducat quiet. MacArthur praying.

'On the 12th, MacArthur was crying,' I whispered. 'On the 13th, he was praying.'

Joseph's voice had also dropped to a whisper. 'Read on,' he repeated.

12 Noon. Grey daylight. Me, Ducat and MacArthur prayed.

'They all prayed together,' I said. 'Perhaps they were giving thanks for coming safely through the storm?'

Joseph caught the hint of desperation in my voice and offered me a slight, grim smile. 'I knew these men well, Alec. They prayed in church, of course, but I've never seen them pray outside. They were all experienced men, with long service to the Lighthouse Board. They lived through many storms.' He shook his head. 'Fear of a storm wouldn't have made such men fall to prayer, either during or after, I'm sure of it.'

I said nothing, but read the last of Thomas Marshall's entries in the logbook.

December 15: 1 p.m. Storm ended. Sea calm. God is over all.

I read the last sentence aloud. 'God is over all. What does that mean?'

Joseph said nothing, and I glanced again at the log entries, aware of another mystery. 'And why did Marshall write such things at all? Such observations have no place in a logbook. This is for noting facts: dates, times, weather conditions.' I shook my head, perplexed. 'Why would

Marshall make note of his personal feelings and the moods and actions of the others? No Lightkeeper would do that...'

Joseph was about to reply but was interrupted by the cacophonous blast of the foghorn. He waited patiently for the numbing sound to die away, then opened his mouth to speak. But the horn sounded again, immediately, before the echoes of the previous sounding had had time to die away.

Our eyes flew to the ceiling.

Joseph jumped to his feet and rushed from the sitting room. 'There must be a ship nearby, coming too close!' he called over his shoulder.

I followed him out into the hall and up the spiral staircase leading to the lightroom at the top of the tower. We found Milne with his back to us, facing the all-but-invisible ocean to the west of the island, his hands pressed against the lattice of triangular window panes. Behind him, at the centre of the cramped room, the large lens assembly rotated around the lamps, its clockwork mechanism muttering with the click of mechanical escapement.

'What is it, John?' asked Joseph as we joined him at the windows. 'A ship?'

Beyond the triangular panes, all was darkness, a brutal void of gale-driven rain that battered the tower with unutterable violence and fury. The odour of kerosene hung strangely upon the air, as if the great lamps were living, breathing things exhaling in watchful silence.

'Yes, I believe it's a ship. Look.' Milne pointed out into the darkness, through the wildly flying rain that flashed to quicksilver stars in the lamps' bright illumination.

Off in the distance, a light hung and flickered in the feral maelstrom.

'How close is it?' I asked, my mind clouded with horrible visions of sailors dashed to pieces upon the storm-thrashed islands.

'Hard to say,' Milne replied. 'Perhaps half a mile.'

'That puts them close to Roaireim,' said Joseph. 'Good God, the sea is high! Look at it!'

'I'm looking, Joseph,' said Milne quietly. 'Too high… too high.'

I understood what he meant, for as I peered into the storm, I could see how high the light from the ship was hanging… and it *was* too high. 'If you're right, John, and it is half a mile or so away…'

'It shouldn't be in that position,' Milne completed. 'Aye… it shouldn't be.'

'Could it be further out?' I asked, glancing from one Keeper to the other.

Milne shook his head, and I saw that he was frowning in confusion. 'It doesn't look that way. I would swear that it's…'

'For God's sake, John,' Joseph cried suddenly. 'Why don't you say what you're thinking? It isn't *on* the sea… it's *above* it!'

Milne cast him a furious glanc, and sounded the foghorn again. 'I'll not listen to talk like that, Joseph,' he said. 'It's a ship, out on the ocean – nothing more, nothing less, and if the storm is playing tricks on our eyes, then that's no more than we've seen before in these parts. Am I not telling the truth, laddie?'

Joseph lowered his eyes, unwilling to meet Milne's fierce stare. 'Aye, John, you're right. I'm sorry.'

'Do you think they can see us in this?' I asked. I knew it was a stupid question, but it was born of the fear and helplessness I felt at that moment, and Milne did me the service of offering a reasonable answer.

'Aye, they can see us, Alec, have no doubt of that. And hear us too. But it may be too late to do them any good.'

I moved closer to the window panes, as if an extra couple of feet could afford me a clearer view. At that moment, I felt like what I was: an Occasional, not a true Lightkeeper. I felt small and useless in the face of the immensity outside. I thought again of the night James Ducat had saved my life, drawing me out of the sea, defying its rage and hunger to carry me back to the world of men. And as I gazed helplessly into the churning darkness beyond the windows, I thought of the poor sailors on that ship who would have no such salvation, and no witnesses to their fate, save three powerless men watching from afar.

'What can we do?' asked Joseph Moore, his voice small and drowned in sadness. 'What can we do?'

I glanced at John Milne and saw an expression of bewilderment on his face; his frowning eyes were unblinking, and he shook his head, slowly, from side to side.

He whispered something I couldn't catch.

'What? What are you saying, John?'

He spoke a little louder, and his voice trembled in a way I did not like. 'Why is it so still?'

I looked back through the windows and saw that he was right. In the mournful extremity of the last moments, I had not realised, had not registered the truth that was now so plain to see.

The light was not moving.

I stepped back from the windows.

'A ship,' said Milne, 'out on that ocean… shouldn't be so still.'

I glanced from Milne to Joseph Moore and saw something in his face that made me turn quickly away. In desperation I searched for an answer; even one that made no sense would do for me, then. 'The light from a house, on another island west of here. That's what it is. It isn't a ship. It isn't in the sea.'

Milne shook his head. 'There are no inhabited islands out here, Alec. No houses, no people. It can only be a ship.'

'A ship on the stormy sea,' said Joseph. 'But a ship that *doesn't move.*'

Again I pressed close to the windows, my face reflected in the glass, an ugly apparition peering back at me from out of the storm. For many moments I gazed out into the tumult, at the light that hung perfectly still while the black sea rose and fell and beat and thrashed.

'I think Joseph is right,' I said at last. 'I'm sorry, John, but I think he is right. It isn't on the ocean, it can't be. It *is* above it – though how in God's name it can be…'

'Yes,' said Milne, and there was resignation in his voice. 'Yes, it's above the ocean.'

For how long we three looked out at that impossible light, I don't know. But presently, without warning, it went out, leaving only the darkness and the frenzy of the storm.

Milne walked unsteadily to a chair and sat down. He put his head in his hands but said nothing. I looked at Joseph, who was still standing at the windows, his face suddenly blank and impassive.

'God is over all,' he said, more to himself, I thought, than to us. 'God is over all… but which God?'

'That's enough, Joseph,' said Milne. He stood up and went to the windows.

'John…' I said.

'It's late,' he said, interrupting me. 'You'll be wanting your beds.'

Without another word, Joseph shuffled towards the staircase that led down into the house. Just as I turned to leave, I caught sight of Milne's reflection in the windows. His eyes were fixed on me, and I waited a moment to see if he wanted to say anything more. He didn't, but he instead turned and looked at me, and his face held an expression I could not at first interpret. I thought again of his behaviour on the *Hesperus*, that strange, artificial smile he had given me, when he could bring himself to look at me at all. In his eyes I now saw something that might have been fear or mistrust, and suddenly I had the overwhelming feeling that the fear and mistrust were of me.

An Unwelcome Truth; a Strange Speculation

The sun rose upon Eilean Mòr, but we did not see it, for the sky was covered with thick clouds that transformed its golden light into a dull grey pall. I have always been early to rise, ready to greet each new day with a hopeful heart, but that morning was different, and I confess that I felt a strange, dreary lassitude creep over me as I looked out across the slow steady heave of the grey ocean stretching to the horizon.

John Milne had manned the light for the remainder of the night, and I supposed that he was now in his room, trying to get some sleep. But if my own night offered any indication, he would find it difficult to rest.

I shaved, dressed and went along the corridor to the kitchen. As I approached the door, which was standing a little ajar, I heard voices: it seemed that Milne had not yet taken to his bed. I was about to enter when Milne said something that made me stop and listen.

'He's a good man, Joseph, I can tell. I won't believe that of him.'

'I've no doubt that he's a good man,' Joseph's voice replied. 'But I can't get the thought from my mind.'

'Superstition, laddie… nothing but silly superstition.'

'You know why MacArthur was here with Ducat and Marshall.'

'Aye.'

'He was an Occasional, doing duty for William Ross, who is on sick leave…'

'I said I know why MacArthur was here!'

'Shh! Please keep your voice down, John, otherwise he'll hear. MacArthur was an Occasional, doing duty for a man on sick leave. *Dalemore* is an Occasional… doing duty for Daniel McBride, who has broken his leg and is on sick leave!'

'Superstition,' Milne repeated.

'This is tempting Providence, John. Ducat, Marshall, and MacArthur the Occasional. Milne, Moore, and Dalemore the Occasional. MacArthur and Dalemore covering the duty of a sick man. I tell you, it's not a good sign.'

Neither of them spoke for several moments, and then John Milne said, 'No... it's not a good sign.'

I left the kitchen door and walked quietly back along the corridor to my room, where I sat on the edge of the bed and looked out through the window.

So that was it: the reason for the strange looks I had received from the crew of the *Hesperus*, and even from Superintendent Muirhead himself. My presence on the island was a bad omen; I was a potential bringer of ill fortune, perhaps even of another catastrophe. It was nonsense, of course, for how could any such similarities as Joseph had described have any bearing on what was to happen over the next month? Did he and Milne seriously think that my presence could influence the elements and bring the sea crashing upon us, washing us away to oblivion?

I wanted to go to the kitchen and say this to them, to put their minds at rest, but I knew that it wouldn't do any good. I was already an outsider, and in their eyes *worse* than an outsider. Any protestations I made would simply have marked me as one who does not known the ways of the sea, and men of the sea, and Lightkeepers.

And, perhaps, all the more dangerous for that.

What was I to do, then? The answer was obvious and came to me immediately: I was to do the job I had come here to do, to the best of my ability, and not be found wanting in any of my tasks. *Thus* would I reassure my companions that they had nothing to fear from my presence!

I heard the sound of footsteps in the corridor as Milne went to his room. They seemed to pause briefly outside my door before continuing on. I stood up, left my room and went back to the kitchen.

Joseph had set the table for breakfast and was boiling water for tea. 'Good morning, Alec,' he said quietly.

'Good morning, Joseph.'

He looked out through the window. 'The weather hasn't turned yet. It's calm now, but it'll be raining auld wives and pike staves by this afternoon.'

'Aye, I wouldn't be surprised.'

'I wonder if it will come back tonight,' he said quietly, and I was struck by the casual way he said it, in the same tone he might have used had he been wondering what was for supper this evening.

'I don't know,' I replied. Then I asked if Milne had mentioned any further disturbances after we left the lightroom last night. Joseph shook his head. 'What do you think it was?' I asked.

'I can't say… but didn't you have the feeling it was watching us, Alec? Be truthful with me, now.'

I gave a chuckle as I took the kettle and poured boiling water into the teapot.

'No, Alec! Don't treat it lightly,' Joseph said suddenly and with great vehemence. 'It's a bad thing to do, to laugh at it!'

I turned to him. 'And what would you have me do, Joseph? Cower under my bed like a wee trembling mouse, waiting for the cat to pass by? We saw something strange last night, I won't deny that; something that shouldn't have been there, but there's an explanation for it, Joseph, even if we don't know what it is – an explanation that makes sense. And we're still here and unharmed, and we have a job to do.'

'Why didn't it move, Alec?' he demanded suddenly. 'What can cause a light to appear above the sea, to make it hang there without moving in a sky full of gales?'

'A star,' I said. 'A star in the sky does not move, at least not fast enough to be seen.'

Now Joseph laughed, but it was a humourless sound, bitter and desolate as the sea. 'It wasn't a star, Alec; you know that as well as I do. No stars shine in a sky full of thick clouds.'

'Well then, a break in the clouds,' I countered in desperation. 'A sudden break in the clouds, allowing a single star to shine through.'

Joseph shook his head. 'The clouds were as deep as the ocean last night. There were no stars in that sky. And the light was too *big* to be a star – you saw it with your own eyes.'

'Then I'll ask you again,' I said, trying to keep the irritation from my voice, for poor Joseph had begun to grate on my nerves, and I felt his fear and superstition passing to me like an infection. 'What do *you* think it was?'

He said nothing for some moments. Turning from the window, he walked slowly to the table and sat down heavily, as if he had just spent many hours at some back-breaking toil.

'Well?' I prompted.

'I've heard old folk speak of such things, now and then,' he said. 'My parents and grandparents have spoken of them on many occasions. Things that live in the wild places, where people have no business; things that guard their places jealously, ever mindful of the world of human beings.'

'You're speaking of the fairy-faith,' I said, and he nodded.

'I was raised with a hundred tales of such things, Alec, as perhaps you were yourself.'

'I never set much store by them,' I confessed.

'I know what you mean. Many people consider them no more than stories to pass away a long winter evening by the fire, or to frighten bairns into doing what their mothers and fathers tell them. But I've always wondered whether there's some truth in them.'

'If there is,' I ventured, pouring tea for us both, 'then the spirit that haunts the Flannans is not to be trifled with.'

'Did you know that it was once the custom to say a prayer the moment you set foot on the Flannans, Alec? They used to say that the Seven Hunters are home to a wild spirit, which was ancient even before Christianity came here, and that this spirit doesn't like men to come here. It's known as the Phantom of the Seven Hunters, and no one can tell of its true nature, save that it wishes nothing but ill towards the living.'

He shook his head. 'No, none of these things are to be trifled with. Not the Phantom of the Seven Hunters... nor the great black birds that live in the lochs of Argyllshire... nor the Brown Man of the Muirs, nor the Brollachan...'

'The Brollachan?'

'A Gaelic word. The Brollachan is a creature of the night, a thing that has no shape. And then there are the kelpies...'

'Aye, I've heard of them.'

'Most people have. They are the water horses that can change their shape to that of a man. They haunt the rivers all across the land, and leap out to cause mischief with the unwary traveller. These lands of ours are home to as many spirits as people. There are more than I can name, and I can name many.'

'So you think that the light we saw last night was a fairy spirit,' I said. 'Something from beyond the world of men.'

Joseph regarded me in silence for a moment, then gave a small, embarrassed laugh. 'I'm sure you think me a fool.'

I shook my head. 'No, Joseph, I do not.'

He took a contemplative sip of his tea, and continued,

'There are so many legends, Alec, so many stories... hundreds, thousands, and many that are forgotten, and some that will soon be forgotten for the lack of telling. Are they all no more than fantasy? Can simple folk have invented them all, every last one? Can they really be explained away so easily? Or is there a seed of truth at their heart?'

I didn't answer – how could I? I had all but forgotten the tales told to me in my own boyhood, nor did I have the education and learning of a scientist who might have found a rational explanation for what we had seen the previous night. I felt as if I were trapped between two worlds: that of misty legend and that of the scientific intellect of modern man. I felt lost in a limbo between the spirit and the machine, besieged by both, and truly understanding neither.

I sipped my tea and nibbled at an oatcake, since I didn't have much of an appetite, and while I did so, I stole the occasional glance at Joseph. He was a strange one: not ten minutes ago, he had been voicing his fears regarding my presence to Milne, and now he was confiding in me, telling me of the superstitions that clung fog-like to the Flannan Isles, and with which he clearly had more than a passing sympathy.

I didn't know what to make of him. It was as though his experience of finding the lighthouse empty eleven days ago had slightly unhinged him, drawing his mind towards a strange world in which I refused to believe. His natural sensitivity was like a raw nerve that had been touched by something hard and unyielding, and I pitied him.

I pitied all of us.

8
THE WHITE FOX

The light did not come back that night, nor the next, though each of us who manned the lightroom in the days that followed watched uneasily for its return. In fact, we never saw it again, and I have often wondered, since returning to the mainland, what its true nature was. There is still a part of my mind that refuses to believe that it was anything other than a star, whose light had somehow managed to filter down through the clouds, and whose apparent size had grown by some trick of the atmosphere.

Yes, in spite of everything that happened to us subsequently on Eilean Mòr, I still cling uselessly and forlornly to that naive hope. Such thoughts seem to depend on my mood, by which I mean that when I am feeling well, and my mind is clear of the memories of the island (an infrequent occurrence, I have to say), I can almost convince myself that that is indeed what it was, and the other things that happened were no more than the fantasies of minds besieged by solitude and the elements.

But for the most part, I cannot help but return to that night in my memory, to dwell morbidly upon it, and to wonder whether the light was actually a harbinger of what was to come… or perhaps even the *means* by which subsequent events occurred – although by what mechanism such a thing could happen I cannot say, save that I am troubled by such thoughts most often when the north winds press upon my window, and the thought that those winds have also touched the lighthouse on Eilean Mòr makes me cringe.

I confess that I do not like to go out when the wind blows from the north.

*

The light, then, let us alone, and for the next few days we performed our duties normally. We took our turns manning the lightroom, keeping the oil fountains full, the wicks trimmed and the clockwork lens assembly properly wound. We performed routine maintenance on the buildings during the day, and in the evenings played a game or two of cards, or tried to lose ourselves in books. I like to think that I acquitted myself well in the kitchen; certainly I had no complaints from my companions, and more than one nod of appreciation.

By common, tacit consent, we did not speak of the light, and we fell to our allotted tasks with all the more enthusiasm for the distraction they offered from our private thoughts. During those first few days, both John Milne and I kept a careful eye on Joseph Moore. Milne appeared to be very fond of the lad, and I felt my own affection for him growing with each passing day. He was hardworking and diligent in the performance of his duties, and his gentleness – a poet's gentleness, one might say – made him a good companion.

That very gentleness and sensitivity, however, had caused the disappearance of Ducat, Marshall and MacArthur to weigh most heavily upon him. It was obvious enough that his nerves had been frayed badly by his discovery that the three Lightkeepers had gone from the island; his human qualities had been doubly assaulted by the loss of his friends and colleagues, and the horrible mystery of the circumstances surrounding it. This, I supposed, had forced him to give vent to his fear when the light had appeared and also to speak to Milne of his fears regarding my presence, and there were occasions when I sensed a great unease in the lad's bearing and demeanour.

John Milne was a different matter. He was older and more experienced than either Moore or I, and he possessed a quiet strength and dependability born of his many years in wild and lonely places. I knew that he harboured the same misgivings about me as Joseph, at least during those early days on the island, but he never voiced them or allowed them to influence his conduct towards me. It may sound foolish to say so, but during the time we spent on Eilean Mòr, I came to regard Milne as a kind of lighthouse himself: a beacon of calm, offering quiet reassurance in the incomprehensible darkness that grew to surround us.

*

In looking back over these words that I have just written, I realise that they form a kind of preamble to the first of the events that truly defy all reason and logic – events that made the strange, still light seem as commonplace as a sprig of heather. And in writing them, I have expressed a just defence of my friends, of their character and the high regard in which I still hold them. It feels correct to do so, and so I will let the words stand, for what they are worth.

It happened on the 9th of January, towards the end of our first week of duty. The day was bright, the weather mercifully calm; the storm had spent itself, and the elements were quietly gathering their strength for their next bout of rage. Milne, Moore and I took advantage of the day's clemency to perform some maintenance on the lighthouse, replacing some roof slates and sweeping out the tiny yard that surrounded the tower, the house and the outbuildings. A couple of petrels lay dead in the yard; having been attracted to the light, they had dashed themselves against the wall of the tower. I gathered their bodies and cast them into the ocean.

It was a pleasure to feel the sun on my face after so many days of cloud and rain, and more than once I took a few moments to pause and look out across the calm ocean at the other islands and skerries of the Flannans, their forms rising serenely in the distance, mottled with shades of grey, green and brown. The sky was clear and good; the bruises of the storm had healed, leaving a vault of deep, jewel-like blue that was filled from horizon to horizon with the flitting shapes of puffins, fulmars, storm-petrels and a dozen other types of seabirds, and I listened to their raucous calls with a glad heart. Out on the ocean, seals and minkes broke the water's surface like capering children, and for some moments I stood watching them, envying their apparent freedom from care.

I went into the kitchen to find Milne preparing smoked haddock and potatoes for the midday meal. The room was bright and fresh with its recent airing, and the first of the day's meteorological notes had been written on the blackboard on one wall, ready for transfer later to the lighthouse logbook. Milne offered me a smile and a nod as he dropped the peeled potatoes into a pot of boiling water, and for the first time since receiving Mary Ducat's letter in distant Stornoway, I began to feel a certain ease of mind.

'Where's Joseph?' I asked.

'On the West Landing, checking the ropes and tackle. He should be back shortly.'

'Shall I brew a pot of tea?'

'Aye, I'll take a cup, and I'm sure Joseph will too,' he said, and for a brief moment I felt as if this were a normal tour of duty, as if no disaster had recently occurred on the island, as if no men were missing and probably dead and we were merely tending the light as many had done over the past year, and as many would do in the years to come. I am quite sure that Milne felt the same at that moment, but it was only a moment, for presently the smile faded from his lips, and without a word he returned to his cooking.

While I spooned tea into the pot, I glanced out of the window. A lone figure was approaching up the slope of the island's shoulder. 'Here's Joseph now,' I said, and I hesitated before adding, 'Do you think he'll be all right?'

'I believe he will,' Milne replied. 'I believe we all will.'

There was a quiet determination in his voice which I found comforting. 'We have a job to do, and we'll do it well,' I said.

'Yes,' Milne replied, and the determination was still present as he added, 'Whatever happens, we'll keep the light burning.'

I hesitated and turned to him. 'Do you think something else will happen?'

He shrugged. 'How can I say?' And then he smiled a small, sad smile. 'I'm sorry, Alec. I shouldn't have said that – it was a bad choice of words.'

I recalled my earlier conversation with Joseph. 'John… that night, when we saw… well, you manned the light until morning.'

'Aye.'

'You didn't see anything else, did you?'

'I told you I didn't.'

'If you had, you'd have told us… and even if you didn't want Joseph to know, you'd still have told me, wouldn't you?'

'You sound as if you *wanted* me to see something,' he replied, and I caught the sudden irritation in his voice.

'No, I'm not saying that…'

'Look, Alec,' he said, turning to me, 'if I had seen something else, I would have told you both, and for a good reason: there's only the three of us here, and if anything happens that might put us in danger, we *all* have to know about it.'

I looked into his eyes and saw no hint of deception there, and I believed unequivocally that John Milne was being honest with me as he said, 'I saw nothing else that night. Nothing.'

I nodded and returned my attention to the window. Joseph had come to a halt and was standing a few yards from the low stone wall that surrounded the lighthouse and its buildings, and a few yards from the ancient chapel. He was looking at the entrance to the chapel, which was hidden from our vantage point, and even from there in the kitchen I could see the expression on his face.

Instinctively, I clutched Milne's shoulder and pointed through the window. He looked and suddenly became very still and watchful, as if waiting for some event to unfold, the outcome of which was utterly unknown.

Outside, Joseph too had become as still as a statue – except, that is, for his face, which was contorted by an expression of terror and confusion the likes of which I had never seen. His mouth opened and closed as if he were talking to himself, and presently he began to shake his head vigorously from side to side, and took several faltering steps backwards away from the chapel.

'What's he seen?' whispered Milne.

Without answering, I rushed across the kitchen, threw open the door and ran out into the yard. I had barely reached the gate when Joseph ran frantically up and vaulted it in a single bound, colliding with me and knocking me to the ground. Badly winded, I tried to call out to him, but already he had disappeared inside the house. I heard Milne shouting his name, his voice at once confused, angry and fearful. Evidently, Joseph paid no heed, for Milne's voice, still shouting, faded further into the house.

Painfully, I got to my feet, nursing a bruised shoulder, and went back into the kitchen. A few moments later, Milne came back in.

'What happened?' I asked.

He shook his head. 'I don't know. He's shut himself in his bedroom. I tried the door, but he's jammed it closed with something.'

I looked out through the kitchen window again, out at the island sloping away to the cliffs and the tranquil blue sea beyond, out at the sky and the distant flapping forms of the seabirds, out at the peace of the world, and I could not guess at what Joseph had seen to make him flee in such panic.

And then my gaze fell upon the ruined chapel standing there, its shivered stones still and silent with the weight of abandoned ages. Joseph had stopped in front of it, facing the ragged hole of its doorway. Had he caught sight of something inside?

My first instinct was to go out and see for myself, for there was a part of my mind that told me there could be nothing in there to cause a man such fear. The chapel had stood in empty solitude for centuries – and might stand for centuries more – containing nothing but the lost history of a man who had long since gone to meet the object of his lonely devotion. And yet, from elsewhere in my being there came a voice whispering with the greatest urgency, *Don't look. Don't go out there.*

'What did he see?' asked Milne, and as he spoke he edged hesitantly towards the door leading to the yard.

'Leave it, John,' I said. He glanced sharply at me. 'There's nothing out there. The lad's nerves must be frayed worse than we thought.'

'But you saw his face,' said Milne.

'There's nothing out there,' I repeated. 'We'd spend our time better if we tried to calm him down.' I walked towards the door leading to the sitting room, and when Milne still hesitated before the outer door, I called his name sharply. 'Come on, now. If we can settle his nerves, perhaps he'll tell us himself what happened.'

After a pause, Milne nodded. 'Aye, perhaps you're right.'

*

It took us nearly half an hour of coaxing to get Joseph to remove whatever barricade he had placed against the door to his room. When finally he allowed us inside, I saw that he had used a stout rocking chair, for it stood out of place in the centre of the room, rocking slowly back and forth, back and forth.

We asked him to come back to the kitchen with us, to have a cup of tea and take a bite to eat, but he refused with a vehement shake of his head and sat himself on his bed with silent determination.

Milne turned the rocking chair to face him and sat down, while I stood with arms folded by the window. From my vantage point I could see into the small courtyard and beyond to the chapel. The raucous cries of the seabirds were muted but still audible through the windowpane.

'Now then, Joseph,' said Milne with a gentle, friendly smile. 'What's got you into such a bother?'

Joseph regarded him in silence for some moments, then gave a loud, ragged sigh. 'It was in the chapel,' he said in barely more than a whisper.

'What was?' asked Milne.

'The fox.'

There was a pause, and then I said, 'The fox?'

'Aye... the white fox.'

Milne shook his head. 'Laddie, there are no foxes on Eilean Mòr. There's a few wild rabbits... but no foxes.'

'I saw it in the chapel,' said Joseph, his voice rising a little, his breathing growing faster. 'I saw it through the door... it was sitting there in the dark, watching me.'

'Could it have been a rabbit?' I asked. 'You said yourself that it's dark in there.'

Joseph gave a short, hysterical laugh. 'For God's sake, Alec! Do you think I can't tell the difference between a fox and a rabbit?'

I sighed. 'Sorry, Joseph. I just thought…'

'And it was watching me… and I saw its face… and…' His voice trailed off as he closed his eyes tight.

'What about its face?' asked Milne, but Joseph merely shook his head and would not answer.

Milne looked at me helplessly. I could only shrug and say, 'I'll go and have a look.'

'That might help,' said Milne, but Joseph leaped to his feet and took me by the shoulders, and I winced as his fingers bit into the bruise I had taken when I fell down outside.

'Don't, Alec! It might still be there. Oh, God save us, *it might still be there.*'

I had heard enough. Roughly I shook Joseph's hands from my shoulders. 'I'll not take fright at the sight of a wee fox, whether it belongs here or not! And what about its face? Why won't you tell us that?' Joseph remained silent, and so I repeated the question in a shout that brought Milne to his feet.

'Easy now, Alec; don't be hard on the lad.'

'Are we men or bairns, John?' I shot back. 'Will you listen to us! What are we doing?' I lapsed into a confused silence, for the memory of Joseph's face as he looked into the chapel sprang unbidden before my mind's eye. Presently, I turned to Joseph. 'I'm sorry, but if you won't tell us what frightened you so, then I'll go and see for myself.'

Joseph turned away from me towards the window, and at that moment he let out a moan of such despair that I felt my heart falter in my chest. 'There,' he said. 'There it is, Alec, John… there it is!'

He backed away from the window, and Milne and I huddled together and peered through the glass. The fox was walking away from the chapel, and it was perfectly white, from its nose to the foaming fur of its tail. It was large, and it walked slowly, pausing periodically to take the scent of the rough grass that covered the island. Its ears twitched as it raised its head, as if surveying the limitless ocean beyond.

And then it turned and looked at us.

John Milne and I gasped in unison as we instinctively recoiled from the window. We both looked at Joseph Moore, who had sat upon the edge of the bed and buried his head in his hands.

The white fox turned and looked at us, and we saw its face so clearly that there was no room for doubt, for the blessed possibility that we might be mistaken in what we saw.

There was no mistake.

The white fox had five eyes.

FOUR

Nick stopped reading and looked at Rebecca. She returned his gaze without a word.

'Five eyes?' said Max. 'Jesus Christ.'

Donald glanced sharply at him.

'It's the same one we saw,' said Rebecca, looking at each of her companions in turn. 'It's still here.'

'That's impossible,' said Donald. 'Foxes don't live for a hundred years.'

'I *know* that, but I'm telling you it's the same one.'

'How do you know, Rebecca?' asked Jennifer.

Rebecca looked at Nick. 'There's something wrong with its face – you said so yourself.'

'Yeah, but…' He hesitated, clearly trying to recall the animal, to picture it in his mind. 'It was quite far away… I'm not sure that's what it was.'

Rebecca regarded him in silence for a moment, then said: 'Yes, you're sure.'

Everyone looked at Nick, waiting for him to respond, but he lowered his eyes and said nothing.

'What the hell happened here?' said Max, looking up at the lighthouse. The automated light swung around every fifteen seconds. The sun was gone, leaving a blue-black wash

110

of sky in which the stars began to gather their strength. 'And what about that light they saw, during the storm?'

'Dalemore was right,' replied Donald. 'A bright star, seen through a break in the clouds... or do you think it was a flying saucer?' he added with a smirk.

Max gave him a dirty look but said nothing.

'What do *you* think, Rebecca?' asked Jennifer.

'Me? I...' She sighed. 'I'm not sure. I know it sounds crazy, but I just know that Nick and I saw the same thing the lighthouse keepers saw. And that light above the ocean wasn't a star. But I don't know what it all means.'

Jennifer smiled and nodded. 'Natural versus supernatural. It's an interesting dilemma, isn't it?'

'It's no dilemma at all,' said Donald decisively. 'There's a rational, logical explanation for everything. The light they saw *was* a star.'

'And the fox?' said Jennifer.

Donald shrugged. 'A deformity, a genetic aberration, or perhaps a set of facial markings that only made it *look* like it had five eyes. And as for the animal Nick and Rebecca saw... well, I think it most likely that there's a colony of foxes on Eilean Mòr – whether they're arctic foxes or albinos makes no difference – and the one they saw is simply a descendant of the one the lighthouse keepers saw, with the same genetic traits.'

'I doubt it,' said Jennifer.

Rebecca glanced at her. 'Why?'

'It would have to be a fairly large colony to survive for a century or more. I doubt there's enough food here to support such a group, and even if there were... then where are the rest of them? Why haven't we seen foxes all over the island?'

'Perhaps they're hiding from the flying saucers,' said Donald.

Jennifer gave him a look which struck Rebecca as being full of sweetness and understanding. 'You're the one who's hiding, Donald,' she said.

He made a dismissive sound. 'Hiding from what? Fairy stories?'

'No, not fairy stories. From mysteries which can't be theorised away at the drop of a hat. Strange, for a man of faith.'

'I have faith in science.'

'And God.'

'Yes, in God too.'

Rebecca looked at him in surprise. She wouldn't have figured him for a religious man. She'd never been able to understand how scientists could believe in God – surely the two world views were mutually exclusive? Science was all about proving that things were true or false, whereas a belief in God could only ever be supported by faith in the absence of any real evidence.

'And yet you want to separate the natural world from its First Cause, the supernatural agency which created it.'

Donald sighed. 'We've been over this before, Jennifer. I believe that God created the Universe, but He designed it to follow the immutable laws that He also created. Those laws cannot be broken, but God gave humanity the faculties of reason and logic to *understand* them, and to apply that understanding in order to solve the mysteries of creation. I don't try to separate the world from its Creator, but I *do* try to separate it from woolly-headed mysticism and pseudo-science.'

'So how do you explain what we saw on your equipment?' asked Rebecca. 'That object in the ocean, the disappearance of the marine life, the fact that all the other life seems to be avoiding that area?'

Donald smiled at her. 'I can't explain it. But that doesn't mean it can't be explained. As I said before, all we have to do is put a bit of thought into it – thought and observation – and we'll solve the mystery.'

Rebecca turned to Jennifer. 'What do *you* think about this?'

Jennifer replied with a question of her own. 'How, exactly, did you find Dalemore's manuscript? If it was buried under the floor of the chapel, you couldn't have simply stumbled upon it.'

Rebecca couldn't stop herself from smiling. The answer, she felt, was yet more evidence that something truly strange was happening on Eilean Mòr. 'The white fox led me to it,' she replied.

Nick shook his head. 'Bccks…'

'It's true, Nick.'

She told them all how the fox had disappeared into the tiny, ancient building, how it wasn't there anymore when she'd looked inside, and how she had noticed the mound of earth concealing its strange treasures.

'The fox led me to it,' she repeated. 'To the manuscript… and to the stone.'

Donald puffed on his pipe in irritation. 'So you think it's intelligent, that it wanted to show you where they were buried.'

'I know it sounds insane…'

'Indeed!'

Rebecca was about to say more, but she hesitated and lapsed into silence. How could she convince him of something which she didn't understand, something which she herself doubted because it *did* sound insane?

Donald smiled condescendingly at her. 'All right, let's assume, for the sake of the argument, that it *is* intelligent, that it's something other than an ordinary animal… why is it here? And why did it want you to find these things?'

'How the hell should I know?' Rebecca snapped. 'I'm sorry,' she added quietly.

'It's all right, Rebecca,' said Donald. 'Being in strange, remote places can play tricks on the mind – and I'm not saying that to be patronising, believe me. Many people have experienced it – explorers, researchers, adventurers – and when certain unusual or puzzling events are experienced, such as our own little mystery in the ocean, the mind tends to fill in the gaps in its knowledge with speculation. It's perfectly natural – and from what I've heard so far from Mr Dalemore, it also happened to those three lighthouse keepers a century ago.'

'Which three?' asked Max, pointing to the book. 'These three, or the three who vanished for no apparent reason?'

Donald sighed and shook his head. 'May I remind everyone of the reason we're here? We are here to observe the distribution of seabirds and marine mammals, to update the JNCC database. We are *not* here to conduct paranormal investigations, using a hundred-year-old manuscript as our guide.'

'Perhaps that *is* why we're here,' said Jennifer, more to herself than to anyone else.

Rebecca was about to ask her to explain her comment, but Donald stood up and said: 'I doubt it. And I've heard quite enough for one night. I'll see you all in the morning, bright and early.' Before ducking into his tent, he turned and said with a chuckle: 'Pleasant dreams, everyone.'

The others decided that they had best turn in as well. As she helped to clear away their things, Rebecca found herself looking at Jennifer Leigh in a new way.

FIVE

During breakfast, Donald made a point of focusing the conversation on what they had to do that day. It was clear that, as far as he was concerned, the matter of the white fox was closed: he had come up with a theory that satisfied him, and now they could return their attention to the tasks at hand. No one contradicted him, which didn't surprise Rebecca, nor did she hold it against them. They *were* here to do a job, after all, and she understood that the mystery of the white fox was an unwanted distraction.

Nick, Max and Donald went up to the top of the island to make a visual survey of the seabirds in the area, while Jennifer remained in the equipment tent to continue working with the hydrophone array and the transducers.

Rebecca briefly considered reading more of Alec Dalemore's testament, but she realised that she didn't want to – at least not then. The truth was, she was frightened by what the manuscript contained and how the events of a century ago seemed to be sending strange echoes into the present. She felt the smallness of the island pressing in all around her, and the impossibility of leaving until their pickup arrived in a little under a week's time made the breath catch in her throat. It was like a weird combination of claustrophobia and agoraphobia: she couldn't decide which was more oppressive, the smallness of Eilean Mòr or the vastness of the sea and sky.

Rebecca poked her head through the flaps of the equipment tent. 'Hi,' she said.

Jennifer turned away from her displays and smiled. 'Come in, Rebecca.'

'How's it going?'

'Everything seems to be working fine now. Sit down, have some coffee.'

'Thanks.' Rebecca poured herself a cup from Jennifer's thermos and sat beside her. 'What are you doing?'

'I'm working on a way to reroute shipping from areas where whales gather in high concentrations.'

'Oh,' said Rebecca. 'Is that a serious problem for shipping?'

'Actually, it's more of a problem for the whales. Many of them are killed each year as a result of collisions with ships.'

'I didn't realise that.'

Jennifer nodded. 'I'm afraid so. We're hoping to establish a programme for deploying hydrophones along the world's main shipping lanes, which would enable mariners to detect the presence of whales in real-time and avoid the high-concentration areas. There's also an international project to install fish-finding sonar in the bows of vessels, which would allow them to detect whales that are just below the ocean's surface.'

'How would that work?' asked Rebecca, leaning forward and watching the images flickering on the displays.

'They use equipment similar to our transducer here, which sends and receives high-frequency signals, typically between twenty and two hundred thousand cycles per second. The pulses detect the air in the swim bladders of whales and fish, and the energy is reflected back to the detector. Look at these.'

Jennifer pointed to several dark-coloured arches scattered across the display, like shallow, inverted 'U's. 'These are called "fish arches". Each one represents a fish.'

'Why do they look like that?'

'The beam transmitted by the transducer is like a cone, which spreads out with distance. The mark you see here begins when the fish enters the outer edge of the cone; then, as it swims through the cone, the distance between it and the transducer decreases, and the mark curves upwards. Then, as the fish continues towards the other edge of the cone, the mark curves downwards again, and stops where the fish exits the cone. And that's how we know what's in the ocean, how big it is and how far away it is.'

'I see,' said Rebecca. 'And that thing that showed up soon after we got here, on Sunday... what do you think it was?'

'I've been thinking about it ever since. The short answer is "I don't know."'

'What's the long answer?'

Jennifer gave a short chuckle. 'There isn't one.'

'Oh.' Rebecca took another sip of her coffee. 'Do you think Max might be right – that it might be the same kind of thing that made those sounds they detected in the Pacific? The Slow Down and the Bloop?'

Jennifer considered this for a moment. 'I suppose it's possible. Oceanographers believe that there are still many undiscovered species in the deepest oceans... and some of them may be very large and very strange. Mind you, the idea that one of them could have come so close to the surface here... well, it's a little hard to accept, but it *is* possible.'

Jennifer regarded her in silence for a few moments, then turned back to the displays. 'Eilean Mòr guards its secrets well, doesn't it?'

'I certainly think it has some to guard.'

'Hm.'

'Although Donald doesn't seem to think so.'

'Donald's a very nice man… but he has no time for things which can't be weighed and measured and placed within an entirely rational world view.'

'And yet he's also a religious man.'

'And you don't understand how the two can be reconciled.'

Rebecca sighed. 'No, I suppose not.'

'Well, the fact is, neither do I.'

'But the thing you detected – that was measurable, wasn't it?'

'Yes, but apparently not repeatable, which is another rule of the scientific method. It came, and it went, and it hasn't returned – a bit like the Slow Down and the Bloop, in fact. Donald's view is that we can do nothing more than record the event, since speculation is useless in the absence of further data.'

Rebecca was silent for a few moments, trying to think of the best way to say what she wanted to say. 'Last night… when we were talking about all this, about the manuscript, about what happened back then… you seemed to see things differently from Donald – not *scientifically*, if you'll forgive me for saying so…' She hesitated.

'Go on,' said Jennifer.

'Well, it was as if you were willing to accept that something strange, something genuinely *unknown* is happening…'

'Not quite: I accept the *possibility* that something genuinely unknown is happening. The fox which you and Nick saw, for instance. I can't explain that, and I certainly don't believe that there's a colony of foxes on the island, for the reasons I mentioned last night.'

'So why does Donald think there is? Just clutching at straws, maybe?'

'Yes, that's probably it.'

'I don't understand that. Surely it's the job of a scientist to observe unusual phenomena, not to deny that they exist.'

'Yes, but where do you draw the line? Donald can only go as far as the scientific method will allow him to go. Imagine, for instance, that we all saw the fox up close. Imagine that it walks into our camp this evening, allowing us to examine it closely.' Rebecca repressed a shudder at the thought. 'Even if it does have five eyes, Donald would admit only that it suffers from some congenital or genetic abnormality. He still wouldn't accept that it's the same animal that the lighthouse keepers saw a hundred years ago. His background and training wouldn't allow him to.'

'Is that the only reason?'

'What do you mean?'

'Do you think he might consider such an idea, such a creature... blasphemous? Do you think he's afraid of what it might actually be?'

Jennifer was about to answer, but she was interrupted by shouts coming from outside. Someone was calling their names. They hurried from the tent and looked up at the wall of rock rising from the crane platform. Nick, Max and Donald stood at the top, high above them. Max was pointing to a neighbouring island a few hundred yards away, which looked like a half-submerged whale. Rebecca tried to remember its name – Nick had told her, but the Gaelic language was strange and difficult to hold in her mind. Eiean Tighe... was that it?

Jennifer placed a hand on Rebecca's shoulder, and together they looked at the island in the middle distance, and then Rebecca realised that the men were not looking at the island: Max had been pointing at the sky... all three of them were looking at the sky. Rebecca wondered what they were looking at. Maybe it was some species of seabird they hadn't expected to find here.

And then Rebecca realised that it wasn't a bird that had caught their attention. There was something in the sky – or rather, something *about* the sky that seemed to have got them in a panic. She couldn't make out just what it was, but something was happening to the sky, as if it had become fragile and insubstantial, like a vast sheet of blue tissue paper, wrinkling and undulating in a way she had never seen before. The phenomenon increased, until the sky looked more like the surface of an ocean, a rippling, swelling, multifaceted surface extending in all directions from horizon to horizon.

'What's happening?' she said. 'Jennifer, *what's happening?*'

Jennifer shook her head. 'I don't know.'

Was it some kind of weird weather phenomenon? Something like the Northern Lights? But Rebecca could hear raised voices from the men at the top of the island. They were gesticulating wildly, pointing and shaking their heads in an almost comical way. Surely they would know about something like that, but it looked as if they were as surprised as Rebecca.

In the midst of the rippling and undulating field of blue, Rebecca could discern other movement. Something was growing: a shape, a rectangle which seemed to contain within its perfectly straight borders the sky as it *should* have been: flat and blue, featureless, normal. She wasn't sure which direction it was coming from, or whether it was growing in size or approaching from a great distance, and as she watched, she had the impression that it wasn't a rectangle, but a cylinder, for it was revolving, and as it turned, its two ends became rounded, periodically transforming the thing into a circle. Although she had no idea why, she didn't want to look directly into the circle: she has the impression that there was something in there which should not be seen.

As the cylinder continued to revolve above them, a sound came to her ears, a sound which she recognised from Dalemore's description: shimmering, metallic, as if simultaneously surrounding her and coming from a great distance. Suddenly, inexplicably, an image of the colour bronze leaped into her mind, shading her thoughts with a strange, frightening lustre.

This was so far beyond the range of Rebecca's experience that she began to tremble uncontrollably. Jennifer seized her and held her close.

What is it? Christ, what is that?

Somewhere in the depths of her terror, she wondered if this was what an animal felt like when it instinctively knew that its existence was threatened. Her eyes filled with tears, and she started to weep silently.

She turned away from whatever was in the sky, buried her face in Jennifer's shoulder, and waited for what was to come.

THE OUTBUILDING

I did not want to return to the window, to see again the impossibility that was watching us from outside. The thought of those five eyes burning blackly in the fox's slender white face filled me with such confusion, shock and disbelief that I could do nothing but stand there in the centre of the room, my gaze fixed upon the floor. At once, I understood why Joseph could not bring himself to describe in full what he had seen: the words themselves would have been easy to say, but I am sure that his own terror, and the certainty that Milne and I would not have believed him, robbed him of the ability to say them.

Milne, however, was built of sterner stuff than I, for he returned to the window and looked out, all the while muttering the words 'Good God' over and over again.

'Is it still there?' asked Joseph, remaining perched on the edge of his bed.

'Aye,' replied Milne. 'It's still there, watching us.' He shook his head slowly from side to side. 'What in God's name could cause such a thing?'

'I don't know,' said Joseph, 'and I don't want to know. I would give ten years of my life to get off this island right now.'

Milne said, 'We can't do that, Joseph.'

And the lad sighed, 'I know.'

'Could it be a deformity?' I asked, and both men turned to look at me. 'I mean… I'm no farmer, but I do know that sometimes animals are born deformed.'

Milne and Moore glanced at each other, and I continued quickly, 'That could be it… and here we are, three grown men, terrified of some poor wee beastie that wasn't born as it should have been. Why, if we were any kind of men, we'd go down there right now and put the poor thing out of its misery!'

Joseph shook his head. 'I don't want to go near it.'

'Then John and I shall go. What do you say, John?'

'I don't know, Alec,' Milne replied. 'I can see there's sense in what you say… but how did it get on the island? Where did it come from? And what could *cause* such a thing?'

'It must have come from the mainland; perhaps it found its way onto a tender, looking for food, and was brought here. It might even have come with us on the *Hesperus*, who knows? And as to the cause, well, I'm no veterinarian any more than I'm a farmer; I can't say how this poor animal was born the way it was   perhaps only God Himself can say. But we shouldn't be afraid of it.' I forced myself to smile at my companions, forced myself to go back to the window and repeated, 'We shouldn't be afraid of it.'

I looked at Milne, and I could see in his eyes that he desperately wanted to believe that I was right, that the white fox was merely a victim of some cruel jest of nature, that it was harmless, and that we were fools to be fearful of it.

'If you're right,' he said, 'then perhaps we should just let it be. I'm not one to go killing things for no good reason. And after all, it doesn't look like it's suffering.'

As I regarded the fox, which was still sitting there a few yards from the ruined chapel, I found that I had to agree with Milne. The animal looked up at me with what appeared to be great serenity and stillness: it didn't look to be in any kind of pain, in spite of the horrible strangeness of its appearance.

'Perhaps you're right, John,' I said, and tried to lighten the mood by adding, 'And anyway, I wasn't relishing the prospect of chasing it around the island.'

I went across and sat on the bed beside Joseph. 'How are you feeling now?'

'A little better, I suppose,' the lad replied. 'Perhaps it was foolish of me to take fright so.'

'Ach, away with you!' I said, clapping him gently on the back. 'I'm quite sure that John and I would have done just as you did, if we'd been the ones to see it first out there.'

'Aye, you'll hear no argument from me on that score,' agreed Milne, moving away from the window.

'All the same,' Joseph added, 'I'll not rest easy in my bed, knowing it's wandering around the island.'

'I'll not sleep easy in this month of duty, with or without our wee friend out there,' replied Milne quietly, and both Joseph and I nodded our agreement.

I stood up and moved to the window again. 'At any rate,' I said over my shoulder, 'it's gone now.'

Milne joined me, and together we looked out at the chapel and the dwelling. Of the five-eyed white fox, there was no sign.

*

The rest of the day passed uneventfully. Joseph stood watch in the lightroom, having calmed down considerably since his initial fright, while John Milne and I made a circuit of the lighthouse, the living quarters and the two outbuildings. We did not say much, keeping our conversation to matters of maintenance, with the occasional remark concerning the state of the buildings. The lighthouse, of course, was only about a year old, and so everything was in good repair; however, the climate in those latitudes is as harsh as can be imagined in winter, and it soon became apparent to us that some painting would be in order during our stay. In fact, we agreed that, should the weather remain clement over the next day or two, we would do a little whitewashing of the house.

As we performed our examination, I found myself wishing to broach the subject of Milne and Moore's discussion, which I had overheard while standing outside the kitchen. It had pained me to hear them speak of me that way, as a bringer of ill fortune, a carrier of some incomprehensible curse. I wanted to say something, to reassure Milne that such thoughts were contrary to rationality and good sense, that God would watch over us and would not allow such things to occur. But it was impossible to mention it without betraying the fact that I had stood and listened to them without their knowing – that I had been eavesdropping. I believed I knew Milne at least well enough to know that he would not have taken kindly to such an admission. And so I said nothing, telling myself once again that the best way to reassure them that they had nothing to fear from my presence would be to do my job well, and to earn their trust and friendship.

The sky was still bright and blue, but the air was cold, and Milne lost no time in retiring indoors as soon as we had finished our inspection. I, on the other hand, found myself wishing to linger outside a little. I am not certain why this was; I think that perhaps I wanted to prove to myself that I *could* remain outside alone, that the wildness and remoteness of Eilean Mòr held no fear for me. The sudden and unexpected appearance of that poor deformed beast had given us all a bad shock, as if the veil of normality had fallen from the face of the world, revealing things we had no idea existed, or could possibly exist. In desperation my mind had clutched at a rational explanation for the appearance of the poor brute, and in their own terrible anxiety, my companions had gladly accepted my theory.

I saw no reason to doubt my suggestion now, and as I looked around the rounded hump of the island, I sincerely believed that I would not succumb to fear, should the white fox return. Pulling my coat tight around my neck to ward off the biting cold, I made another solitary circuit of the lighthouse, this time on the outside of the enclosure. As I walked, I looked out at the sea, extending in a disc of dark rippling blue-green out to the flat, calm horizon. In that place, it was easy to believe that this was the entire world: a flat plain of water floating in an empty blue firmament, but a place where silence would never reign, such were the unceasing cries of the seabirds and the insistent whisper of the ocean itself.

I came to a halt at the entrance to the chapel and realised that I was standing at the exact spot where Joseph had stood when he saw the white fox in the darkness enveloped by the ruined jumble of stones. For some moments I stood there, and although I tried to move on, I felt myself unaccountably held before the ragged entrance, as if by unseen hands. I bent over, placing my hands on my knees, and peered inside – although what I expected to see I had no idea. The fox was not there, nor was anything else: nothing but dense blackness and memories hidden from me by the veil of an unknown man's death.

The air suddenly breathed a frigid wind that tugged at my coat, penetrating the heavy fabric and seizing my bones, making me shiver. For a moment, I fancied that I saw the blackness inside the chapel ripple like the waters of a deep loch at midnight, although I supposed that this was caused by my eyes watering in the sudden chillness of the wind.

At any rate, I decided that I had taken enough fresh air. The sky's brightness was fading, its vivid blue now tinted violet by the approaching sunset. I straightened and turned away from the chapel and walked back to the gate in the low wall surrounding the lighthouse. After making sure that it was securely fastened, I walked across the yard, past the outbuildings, and entered through the kitchen door.

Milne was in the kitchen, preparing the evening meal. I asked him if he needed any help.

'No, that's all right, Alec. Why don't you take a wee bit of time for yourself?'

It was my turn to man the lightroom that night, so I thanked him and went into the sitting room. The lamps had been lit, and a fire crackled quietly and soothingly in the hearth. I sat in an armchair and dozed for a few minutes, but I was not tired, and my eyes opened of their own accord. Joseph was still at his post, and I did not feel like making idle conversation with Milne (or rather, I felt that the prospect of idle conversation was rather remote, and I did not wish to discuss anything more significant with him), and so I rose from my chair and looked at the books standing on a shelf to one side of the fireplace.

One book in particular caught my attention: a large, battered volume that had obviously seen a lot of use over the years. I guessed it had been left here by one of the previous keepers, perhaps even by one of those who had vanished. I took it down and looked at the title page.

A DESCRIPTION OF
THE WESTERN ISLES OF SCOTLAND
BY
Martin Martin

I had heard of this book, although I had never read it. If memory served, it had been written in the latter years of the seventeenth century and was a comprehensive account of these latitudes, their lands, people and customs. I returned to my armchair and began to flip desultorily through its faded pages.

In former times, the Flannan Isles were noted for their pasturage and were home to large numbers of sheep. I recalled from other reading that it was the custom of MacLeod of Lewis, to whom the islands had once belonged, to send his clansmen to the islands to slaughter the sheep. In Martin's pages, I read of several unusual customs observed by the men of Lewis when they came ashore here, and I marvelled at the strangeness of superstitious belief in centuries past. One custom in particular was observed even prior to landing on the islands. I read how the men of Lewis, who came here to collect seabirds and their eggs, along with quills, down and feathers, would turn their boats around and return home without daring to land here if the wind's direction should change from the east to the west.

In one passage, I read of the ancient observances associated with fowling on the Seven Hunters, of the rules which the clansmen considered it essential to follow. If one among them should be an apprentice, with no knowledge of these observances, he would be placed under the supervision of another member of the party, who would instruct him in what should and shouldn't be done. Having secured their landing place, the men would scale the cliffs by means of a wooden ladder, and would then thank God for allowing them to reach the island safely. Then they removed their upper garments and went to the ruined chapel, where they would spend some time in prayer and meditation.

I read more of these strange customs. One passage in particular intrigued me:

The biggest of these islands is called Island More; it has the ruins of a chapel, dedicated to St Flannan, from whom the island derives its name. When they are come within about twenty paces of the altar, they all strip themselves of their upper garments at once, and their upper clothes being laid upon a stone, which stands there on purpose for that use, all the crew pray three times before they begin fowling; the first day they say the first prayer, advancing towards the chapel upon their knees; the second prayer is said as they go round the chapel; the third is said hard by or at the chapel, and this is their morning service. Their vespers are performed with the like numbers of prayers. Another rule is that it is absolutely unlawful to kill a fowl with a stone, for that they reckon a great barbarity and directly contrary to ancient custom. It is also unlawful to kill a fowl before they ascend by the ladder. It is absolutely unlawful to call the island of St Kilda (which lies thirty leagues southwards) by its proper Irish name, Hirt, but only the high country. They must not so much as once name the islands in which they are fowling by the ordinary name, Flannan, but only the country. There are several other things which must not be called by their common names, e.g., Visk, which in the language of the natives signifies Water, they call Burn; a Rock, which in their language is Crag, must here be called Cruey, i.e., Hard; Shore, in their language expressed by Claddach, must here be called Vah, i.e., a Cave; Sour in their language is expressed Gort, but must here be called Gair, i.e., Sharp; Slippery, which is expressed Bog, must be called Soft, and several other things to this purpose. They count it unlawful also to kill a fowl after evening prayers. There is an ancient custom by which the crew is obliged not to carry home sheep suet, let them kill ever so many sheep in these islands. One of their principal customs is not to steal or eat anything unknown to their partner, else the transgressor (they say) will certainly vomit it up, which they reckon as a just judgement. When they have loaded their boat sufficiently with sheep, fowls, eggs, down, fish, &c., they make the best of their way home. It is observed of the sheep of these islands that they are exceedingly fat and have long horns.

How strange, I thought, that there should be such complicated and rigorous rules associated with staying on these islands. I had the impression that the men of Lewis were genuinely afraid of contravening them, and that both their customs and their fear owed more to pagan beliefs than to Christianity. It seemed that those ancient clansmen were aware of some great and incomprehensible power at work here, and that to anger it would bring dreadful misfortune upon them. For the first time, I had a sense of the Seven Hunters as being a kind of meeting point between the pagan and the Christian worlds, and that this meeting point was like the collision of opposing weather fronts, resulting in dangerous and unpredictable storms.

For what seemed like a long time, I sat in the armchair and looked out through the window, and presently I realised that I had watched the sky deepen into night.

The sudden clatter of a pot being placed upon the stove brought me out of my reverie, and for lack of anything else to do, I replaced the book on the shelf and returned to the kitchen, where I was surprised to see Milne still preparing the meal. How long had it been since I had left him? What had he been doing in that time?

'Alec,' he said over his shoulder. 'Would you please bring in a can of oil from the store-room? We'll be needing to fill up the fountains this evening.'

'Of course, John,' I replied and, lighting a storm lantern with a piece of kindling from the stove, I stepped out through the kitchen door into the yard. The night air was still and silent, and I shivered suddenly in the deep cold. At a height of some sixty feet above me, the light turned twice every thirty seconds, casting sudden, brief daylight into the depths of the bitter darkness. Overhead, the stars glistened like hoarfrost on a vast, black windowpane, and the sea whispered its secrets in the distance.

I hurried across the yard to the larger of the two outbuildings, which served as our main storage room, and threw the iron bolt that secured the door, which opened inward, but to my surprise it did not move easily. Thinking that perhaps something had fallen across the threshold and was blocking the door, I pushed harder, holding the lantern awkwardly in my left hand as I did so.

Slowly, the door began to open under the heave of my shoulder, and I wondered what could have fallen in front of it to impede it so. When I had succeeded in forcing it open eight or nine inches, I stopped and thrust the lantern through the opening, hoping to see the obstacle.

Craning my neck, I put my head around the edge of the door and peered inside, with my arm held out before me. The light from the lantern dimly illuminated the interior, but such was my position that I could not see very much. From what I could see, all of the equipment and supplies in the outbuilding were in order and in their proper place. Lowering the lantern, I looked down at the floor, but could see nothing that might have prevented the door from opening.

Perhaps there was something lying just beyond my field of view, I thought, and in growing puzzlement, I withdrew my head and arm from the opening, and prepared to heave against the door again.

At that moment, the door slammed shut in my face with a loud crack of wood against stone.

In shock, I recoiled and staggered a few paces back across the yard. 'What in God's name…?' I whispered, and felt fear and incomprehension rising in me like a rolling wave. 'There is someone in there,' I said quietly to the night, my words all but lost in the distant whisper of the sea. But how could there be? We three keepers were alone on the island. And yet the door to the outbuilding had been pushed closed with great force, from the inside. Had there been a storm, I might have believed that the wind had seized it and thrown it shut – but there was no storm, and no wind.

And then a thought occurred to me, which filled me with a mixture of great hope and a strange, unaccountable fear, and I dashed across the yard and threw open the kitchen door.

'John!' I cried.

Milne turned from the stove, saw the look on my face and said, 'Alec, what's wrong?'

Breathlessly, I told him what had just happened, and as my words rushed out, a dark frown of alarm spread across his face. 'John,' I concluded, 'I don't think we are alone on the island.'

'What are you talking about? Of course we are alone. Who else could…?

His eyes widened as realisation dawned.

'That's right,' I said. 'It could be one of the missing keepers – Ducat, or one of the others. Come on, it'll need two of us to get the door open.'

Without waiting for a reply, I rushed back across the yard, and again threw myself against the door to the outbuilding. Milne came up beside me and lent his efforts, and for several moments we pushed with all our might against the door.

'Who's in there?' Milne called out. 'Whoever's there, let us in! It's John Milne and Alec Dalemore! Ducat, Marshall, MacArthur! Let us in!'

But the door remained shut, and in another minute we had both all but exhausted ourselves and leaned breathlessly against the wall of the outbuilding.

'Why won't they let us in?' I wondered desperately, my words carried on the ghostly white vapour of my breath. 'If it's them…'

I was interrupted by a soft, quiet creak as the door moved open an inch. Milne's eyes flew to the narrow band of darkness, and he bent down to retrieve the storm lantern from the ground. Holding it above his head, he reached out slowly, gingerly, and pushed open the door, which now gave easily, and we both stepped inside.

Milne held the lantern before us, swinging it left and right, so that the whole of the interior was illuminated.

But there was no one inside, and every item of equipment was in its proper place, undisturbed.

'There's no one here,' whispered Milne, and my heart trembled at the confusion and despair in his voice. 'Oh God, Alec... there's no one here.'

SIX

TUESDAY 21 JULY

8.15 AM

They were all sitting in the larger of the two accommodation tents, the one used by Rebecca, Nick and Max, and Max was repeatedly running his hand through his hair and saying: 'What the hell was that?' over and over again. He was hunched forward and shaking his head, as though trying to rid himself of the memory of what they had seen.

Everyone was silent, except for Donald, who merely said, 'I don't know.'

'I mean, for Christ's sake! What happened to the sky?'

Max looked at them each in turn, but no one said anything.

It had been about ten minutes since the sky returned to its normal state. Rebecca had been certain she was about to die, and she still couldn't quite believe that the phenomenon hadn't killed them all. But it had passed, like a cloud or a shower of rain: the rotating cylinder, which had seemed to contain the sky as it should have been, had reached the island and then expanded, sweeping across the strange rippling and finally dissipating it. And then the sound, too – that horrible, shimmering metallic sound – had ceased, leaving only the cries of the seabirds.

Max turned to Nick. 'Have you ever seen a weather phenomenon like that?'

Nick shook his head.

'I don't believe any of us has,' added Jennifer.

'Perhaps some kind of optical illusion,' Donald suggested. 'Something like heat haze…'

'Bullshit!' Max poured himself a cup of coffee from the flask Rebecca had prepared for them. Donald looked hurt, and Max sighed. 'Sorry, Don. It's just… I'm a little rattled over this.'

'Things aren't right here,' said Rebecca quietly.

Max glanced at her. 'No kidding, babe!'

Rebecca picked up Dalemore's testament and held it close to her chest. 'That sound we heard just now… while the sky was… anyway, Dalemore heard the same thing, soon after he arrived on the island. So did Joseph Moore and Robert Muirhead; they all heard the same thing.'

'That's right,' said Jennifer, looking at the book. 'It was exactly as he describes it.'

'Ever since we arrived, things have been happening,' said Nick. 'Things we can't explain. Those anomalous readings from the hydrophones and the transducer, the absence of marine life in that area of ocean, the white fox… whatever just happened now…'

'And the sounds I heard in the tent yesterday morning,' added Rebecca.

Max looked at her. 'What sounds?'

'When I woke up, I heard someone moving in the other half of the tent, behind the partition. I thought it was you, Max, but it wasn't. You were already outside. Nick said it was just the sound of the tent's fabric rippling in the breeze, and for a while I thought… well, I wanted to believe that was the explanation.'

'Maybe I was wrong about that,' Nick conceded.

'I'll try to bear that in mind when I'm in bed tonight,' said Max glumly.

'Whatever happened to Dalemore and the others is happening again,' said Rebecca.

Donald was about to say something, but then he hesitated and shook his head.

Rebecca looked at him. 'I'm sorry, Donald, but it's true. I don't know what's happening, or why... but *it's happening*.' She opened the book to the eleventh chapter and pointed to the handwritten text. 'This chapter is called "The Living Sky".'

'*What?*' said Max. He took the book from her. His eyes flashed back and forth as he speed-read the text. 'Holy shit. They saw something... something like what happened here just now.'

'I'd like to hear some more,' said Jennifer in a voice devoid of inflection. 'We've reached the chapter which describes the white fox... now I'd like to hear some more.'

'What's the point?' asked Donald.

'The point,' said Jennifer, 'is that Dalemore and the others spent a whole month here. They may have experienced something that might give us a clue as to what's happening now – perhaps something that they wouldn't have understood, but we might.'

'We're wasting our time,' said Donald.

'Christ, Don!' said Max, so loudly that Rebecca jumped. 'Aren't you even *curious* about this?'

Donald closed his eyes. 'Max, will you *please* stop using that language?'

'*What* language?'

'You shouldn't take the Lord's name in vain.'

Max looked at him aghast, then shook his head. 'Oh man. With all this shit that's goin' down... you're worried about me swearing.'

'Max.' Jennifer placed a hand on his shoulder and shook her head.

'You're all reading too much into this,' said Donald in a quiet, measured voice. 'We've encountered some unusual natural phenomena... some unusual *natural* phenomena. I won't deny that they're strange – unprecedented, even. But there's nothing supernatural occurring here, do you understand?' His voice rose a little, as he added: '*Nothing* supernatural. Now... we have a job to do here, and we're going to do it. We only have until the end of the week, and we have a timetable to keep to. So I suggest that we put all of this nonsense to one side and get on with our work.'

There was silence for a few moments, then Nick indicated the book and said: 'Max, carry on from where we left off.'

Donald gave Nick a furious look. 'I am in charge!' he shouted.

Max laughed and said: 'This ain't boot camp, Don. Fuck you.'

Donald's face became impassive as he replied: 'Very well. Since you all seem to have lost interest in this project, I'll carry on by myself.'

Without another word, he left the tent. Jennifer gave Max a reproachful look and made to follow Donald, but Nick stopped her. 'Jennifer,' he said, 'let him be. You wanted to hear more...'

Jennifer regarded him in silence.

'You may be right,' he continued. 'There may be something here... some clue...'

Jennifer hesitated, glanced through the open flaps of the tent, then sat down again. 'All right,' she said. She looked at Max. 'Go ahead.'

10
THE CARVED STONE

John Milne and I came back into the kitchen and sat facing each other on opposite sides of the table. Neither one of us spoke for a long time. We were confused and fearful; I was thinking furiously about what had happened, and trying to understand what it meant, and I assumed Milne was silent for the same reason.

Presently, Milne said, 'We should not tell Joseph about this.'

I looked at him askance and replied, 'But you yourself said that we should keep no secrets from each other.'

'I know what I said, Alec,' he replied quietly. 'Anything that has a direct bearing on our safety, on our ability to do the job at hand, should be reported immediately. But I don't think this comes under that category, do you?'

I shook my head. 'I suppose not – although what category to place it under is beyond me.'

'And me,' he agreed.

I sighed. 'For some moments, I thought… I thought that the others were not gone, that they were still here, alive.'

'So did I. It feels as if we've lost them a second time.'

I felt an awful sadness rising in my breast, and kept my silence for fear that any words I spoke would unlock the tears in my eyes. Presently, I said in a measured tone, 'All right, John. What was it? We're not children; we're men, with the minds of men. We have lived and worked in strange and dangerous places – you especially…'

'Me?' he retorted. 'You think I have the answer, simply because I've seen more storms than you, because I've spent more days away from people, and the places and things of people?' He shook his head and lowered his voice, as if afraid that we would be overheard, although Joseph was still above in the lightroom. 'I'm sorry, Alec. I have no answer for this, nor for the light we saw that first night... nor for that infernal creature we saw today.'

I glanced at him sharply. 'Then you don't think it was just some poor deformed beast?'

He gave a grim, dismissive chuckle. 'Well, perhaps it was, and perhaps it wasn't. If it had only been that... if we hadn't seen the light, and,' he pointed at the kitchen door and the yard beyond, 'if this hadn't just happened, I might have held with your theory. But the truth is, Alec, I've never experienced anything like this before. It seems that Eilean Mòr is a place of cruel wonders indeed.'

'Perhaps so,' I replied. 'But why *this* place? Why Eilean Mòr?'

'Who knows? Perhaps these things happen more often than we might think, out here in the wild regions of the world, where men have yet to set foot with their civilisation and their sensible thoughts. Our science and our cities are manacles on the feet of Nature; we bind it to our will, and most of us have forgotten what it was like when we lay naked and defenceless in its hands.'

'Nature is one thing; this is something else entirely!'

He smiled at me. 'Are you so sure, Alec? Do you really know what Nature is? Are you really so familiar with all of the parts that make up the whole of the world? Can there be such a thing as the "supernatural"... or are such things simply parts of Nature which we don't understand?'

'I'm no philosopher,' I said.

'Nor I. But sometimes I wonder whether the lowliest beastie scampering through the forest knows more of the world than we men.'

*

I awoke on the morning of the 12th of January to the sound of mournful gales and the shouting of the sea beneath a grey-painted sky, and a single thought hung in my mind like a great, dark seabird riding motionless upon a rising wind: *Three more weeks*.

Three more weeks of duty in this humanless place, with the wind and the sea and the sky… and mystery upon terrible mystery.

I rose, washed and dressed, and went to prepare breakfast. Milne had taken over from Joseph in the lightroom, and I brought him a mug of tea before returning to the kitchen to see about some porridge. I was due to relieve him in an hour's time, at nine o'clock, and once the breakfast was made, I swept out the kitchen and made sure that everything was clean and in order for the rest of the day.

I was glad to be performing these mundane tasks, for they soothed my mind and reminded me that, first and foremost, we were Lighthouse Keepers, with responsibilities to fulfil for the sake of the men who guided their ships through these regions. When I went up to the lightroom later, I would continue to perform my duties: to trim the wicks of the lamp to make certain that its light was clear, to fill the oil fountain and polish the lens assembly, to wind up the escapement mechanism that kept the lens turning smoothly.

It was only when I recalled that a new can of oil was needed that my gladness departed, and disquiet returned to my mind like an unwelcome guest, for the oilcans were kept in the outbuilding, where three nights ago Milne and I had heaved aside the blocked door to find that nothing was blocking it.

I thought of asking Joseph to go there with me, to lend a hand, but the truth was that each oilcan could be lifted by one man, and so there was no reason – no *obvious* reason – to ask him to accompany me. It would be an act of cowardice to avoid going into the outbuilding alone, and Joseph would almost certainly suspect that something about the place was wrong. I still intended to comply with Milne's wish that Joseph not be told, although I still did not know whether I agreed with him, but he was the Principal Keeper, the one in charge of our small group, and I was experienced enough to know that, while on lighthouse duty, the Principal's instructions had to be followed.

And so I went out through the kitchen door and into the yard. Closing the door firmly behind me, I paused for some moments, looking at the outbuilding, with the wind rising in my ears like the moan of some great waking beast, and the vast grey blanket of sky looming overhead.

And it was then, just as I began to walk reluctantly across the yard towards the outbuilding, that something happened which I am at a loss to explain. While still in mid-stride upon the cobbles of the yard, I suddenly and without warning nor any intervening period of time, found myself hunched over in near-total darkness.

Instead of hard cobbles beneath my hands and knees there was cold, damp earth. I remember crying out – an ugly animal cry of uncomprehending shock, harsh, guttural and filled with terror. My senses were overwhelmed with the twin immediate sensations of darkness all around and cold dampness beneath; they filled my awareness, obliterating all rational thought, and for I don't know how long, I cowered there like an animal in its burrow, my breath coming in quick hard gasps.

Presently, my mind cleared somewhat; the behaviour of a civilised man reasserted itself to the extent that I was able to look around. There was a wall, apparently made of drystones, on three sides, while a glance behind me revealed a ragged doorway leading outside. I saw land rolling towards the grey foam of ocean in the distance, and I realised, with a sense of dizzying incomprehension that threatened to overwhelm me again, that I was crouching inside the ruined chapel that stood a few yards from the lighthouse.

A single question pulsed in my mind like a beating heart: *How did I get here?* I had been walking across the yard towards the outbuilding with the intention of fetching a can of oil for the light. And then… and then, in the instant between two neighbouring moments, I had come here…

The thought occurred to me that there was something profoundly wrong with my mind, that for several moments I had ceased to be conscious and had walked to the chapel and crawled inside for reasons utterly unknown to me now. That was the only explanation I could think of, and yet it raised another question that was no less daunting and terrible: if I had lost my awareness and, in effect, sleepwalked away from the lighthouse, might it happen again? And what if it happened while I was on duty in the lightroom? And what if next time I walked further, off the edge of the island?

'Oh, God,' I murmured. 'This place… this place.'

I realised that I would have to report this episode to Milne, to make him aware that it was entirely possible I could no longer be relied upon to perform my duties. This dismal thought made me groan aloud, for such an admission would only confirm Milne and Moore's belief that I had brought ill fortune to them, that I was possibly dangerous and not to be trusted.

I was about to crawl back out of the chapel into the light, when my hands fell upon something half buried in the damp earthen floor. At first I thought it was simply a lump of stone, and I would have ignored it were it not for something in its shape, felt half-blindly in the darkness, that stayed me and made me pull it from the earth's cold, damp embrace.

Outside, I stood up straight and held the thing before me, and it was like nothing I had ever seen before, nor even imagined. That it had been carved by the hand of man I had no doubt, such were its intricacies, its planes and folds, its rounded bulbs and deeply chiselled clefts. But as to what it was intended to represent, if anything, I had no idea. Small clods of earth clung to it, and I tried to smear them away, but they held tenaciously to its surface.

Who had carved it? I wondered. And what strange inspiration had taken hold of them to produce such an object? Although I had no evidence for such a supposition, the thought occurred to me that the stone might have been carved by the long-dead Columban hermit who had spent his lonely days on the island. But again the question rose in my mind: why carve a lump of stone into this shapeless shape? Perhaps, I thought, the terrible harshness and isolation of his existence had unhinged his mind.

Perhaps I was holding in my shivering hands the product of a man's insanity.

Slowly, as if in a dream, I walked back to the yard, retrieved the oilcan from the outbuilding and took it into the kitchen. John Milne was there, ladling porridge into a bowl.

'Good morning, Alec,' he said.

'Good morning, John.'

'What have you got there?' he asked, glancing at the carved stone.

'I'm not certain.'

'Where did you find it?'

'In the chapel.'

Milne stopped what he was doing and looked at me. 'What were you doing in there?'

'I… I don't know.'

He regarded me in silence, and for the first time the thought occurred to me that it had not been some random mental aberration that had taken me to the chapel. For some reason, I had been drawn there against my will – against even my direct knowledge… drawn there to find the carved stone.

I put the oilcan down and took the stone to the sink. I took the kettle and poured boiling water over it to clean away the lumps of earth. Milne stood beside me and watched.

'What do you mean you don't know?' he said. I did not reply immediately, and he repeated the question with urgency.

I could not bring myself to lie to him, could not even think of a convincing lie to tell. 'I was walking across the yard to fetch an oilcan for the fountain,' I said. 'And then I was inside the chapel, and I don't know how I got there, and I have no memory of getting there... but there I was, and I found this half-buried in the floor, and I don't know what it is or what it is meant to be, but I have a notion that it was made by the Christian hermit who once lived here.'

'You have *no memory* of going into the chapel? What the devil are you talking about?'

'I'm sorry, John,' I said. 'But that's the truth of it.'

Milne looked down into the sink, at the stone that now lay clean and unobscured there. 'It looks horrible,' he said. 'Why would any Christian make such a horrible, misshapen thing?'

I said nothing.

'The Flannans have been visited many times over the centuries,' Milne said. 'Clansmen used to graze their sheep here, and came to hunt seabirds for their meat and feathers.'

'I know.'

'Perhaps this was left by one of them for some reason. They had some strange customs.'

'Perhaps.'

Milne hesitated, then continued, 'It's only a stone.'

'If it's only a stone, then what happened to me? Why was I taken into the chapel, if not to find it?'

'I don't know. But I will tell you this: I'm very alarmed that you have no memory of it.'

'I don't think it will happen again.'

'How do you know? This is not the place to...'

'To what? Lose my faculties?' I shook my head. 'I don't think that will happen again, John.'

'I hope not, Alec,' he said, staring levelly at me.

I lifted the stone from the sink and turned it over in my hands, running my fingers along its folds and crests. 'Whoever made this made it for a reason... but why?'

'It's the product of a diseased mind,' said Milne with distaste. 'I don't like it, and I don't want it here. Do you understand me, Alec? I want you to put it back where you found it – or better still, throw the thing into the sea.'

'It was made for a reason,' I repeated.

'It looks like some horrible beast from the bottom of the ocean, something that should never see the light of day. I don't want it here.'

'It's nine o'clock,' I said. 'I'm going up to the lightroom.'

I picked up the oilcan and walked out of the kitchen.

But I kept the stone with me.

The Living Sky

There was a table and chair in the lightroom. I placed the stone on the table and sat and looked at it, while the wind moaned around the tower and the clouds rolled and tumbled across the sky and the grey mass of the breathing sea rose and fell. Several times I stood up and walked restlessly around the confined space, but always I would return to the chair and sit hunched forward to examine the stone, while the hours moved by in their slow, inexorable procession.

I thought again and again of Milne's words, of his reaction to the stone's appearance. 'Something that should never see the light of day,' he had said. I recalled the expression on his face: a frown of deep concern, mixed with something akin to revulsion, as if the ocean had indeed thrown up some strange form of life, an aberration of Nature, a defect in God's world.

I wondered whether he was right in suggesting that one of the clansmen of centuries past had left it here. I recalled Martin Martin's description of the customs they followed while on the island, how they would take off their shirts and pray and meditate around the chapel, and I decided to consult his book again at the first available opportunity, to see if he made mention of anything like this.

In the meantime, I could not rid myself of the conviction that the stone had been created for some reason by the unknown man who had lived here in ancient ages, and I continued to examine it, with the sounds of the wind and the sea in my ears, and as I regarded it with greater and greater intensity, I began to feel its bizarre and incomprehensible shape enter my mind, as if I were a child learning to read, attempting to make sense of strange symbols on sheets of paper. If I could only interpret the lines of the stone, the intention behind its form, the guiding principle that had inspired it, might I then gain some insight into the mystery of Eilean Mòr?

My reverie halted at that thought. Why should this be so? I wondered. What could this object possibly tell me about the island and what we had seen here? 'What a strange notion,' I whispered to myself. I recalled that outside, I had wondered if the stone were the product of madness, and yet, I reflected, it made a curious kind of sense to suppose that whoever had carved the stone had been attempting to express something, to describe something that words alone could not describe – a feeling, an event, a revelation... or perhaps an obscure epiphany.

Had Milne sensed something of this when he saw the stone? Was that the reason for his curious reaction, which had surprised me in its vehemence? He had not wanted it in the house, had wanted me to cast it into the ocean; he had seemed genuinely afraid of it. For my part, I was still deeply concerned at the unexplained means by which I had come upon the stone, but my own fear had been overwhelmed by the question of its existence, which grew in importance to me with each hour that passed.

At a quarter to one, Joseph came up to the lightroom with some food for me. He put the plate of stew on the table, glanced at the stone and left quickly, without saying a word. I assumed that Milne must have told him about it; perhaps he had also described how I had found it. If so, then it was reasonable to suppose that he considered this situation to be potentially dangerous, for I guessed that he would not have mentioned it to Joseph otherwise.

As I half-heartedly dipped the thick slice of bread into the stew, I felt a sudden wave of depression seize me: a profound sense of isolation, not only from the rest of mankind, but also from my companions here on the island. I did not like the feeling of being up here alone in the lightroom with the others downstairs, probably discussing me in worried tones.

I wondered if something like this had happened to the lost keepers, Ducat, Marshall and MacArthur. Had some strange event turned them against each other? Perhaps one of them had lost his mind and murdered the other two, and then thrown himself into the sea in remorse, or perhaps to make a desperate escape from whatever madness had seized him. It was possible, I supposed, but if that were the case, then were the lethal events now repeating themselves?

I sighed deeply and miserably and put my head in my hands, besieged by horrible, unanswerable questions. The best thing to do would be to follow Milne's wishes and cast the stone into the sea; my mind understood that well enough, but my heart refused to let go of the feeling that the stone held some secret which might, if revealed, provide an answer to the enigmas we had so far experienced.

Perhaps I should lie to the others: tell them that I had thrown the thing away, while secretly keeping it in my room and examining it in private. Yes, I could do that. Then perhaps they would believe that I could be trusted. I needed them to believe that, and I needed to believe it myself.

Feeling a little better, I finished the stew and stood at the windows, surveying the land and ocean to the south. From my vantage point I could see the twin islets of Làmh a' Sgeir Bheag and Làmh an Sgeir Mhòir, and beyond them the neighbouring island of Eilean Tighe, clustered in dull green-greyness together upon the hissing, clasping sea.

The clouds billowed like thick smoke overhead, as if Heaven itself were on fire, and somewhere far off there was a dull explosion of thunder. The wail of the wind rose yet further, and I could almost feel its pressure upon the leaded panes of glass that surrounded me. And as I looked out at the clouds filling the sky, I realised that I did not like the way they looked, for there was something about them that I had never seen before: a regularity that had no place in the chaos of an approaching storm.

Pressing my hands against the window panes, I watched in disbelief as the clouds slowly arranged themselves into vertical columns, like the pillars of some ancient Roman temple, and I listened as the wind fell away to leave an unnatural silence all about. It was as if the sky was not the sky anymore, as if it had been supplanted by something of an entirely different order.

I rushed to the top of the staircase leading down through the tower from the lightroom into the house and sounded the house-bell, shouting, 'John! Joseph! Come up here, now!'

Within moments I heard the sound of boots upon the stairs, and my companions joined me.

'What is it, Alec?' said Milne.

I pointed through the windows. 'Look.'

The others gazed in silence at the columns of cloud that now surrounded the island.

Joseph shook his head. 'God preserve us... what's wrong with the sky?'

'A trick of the wind,' said Milne a little too quickly.

'But there is no wind,' retorted Joseph.

'Not now, but there was until just a few moments ago. The wind can make strange shapes out of clouds, we all know that, Joseph.'

Milne looked at me, as if seeking my agreement. I nodded. 'John must be right,' I said, for suddenly I felt immensely weary and realised that I could not face more strangeness. I felt like a man sick to his bones with pneumonia, who is confronted with the prospect of a long walk through freezing wind and rain. I could not face it: I craved peace and normality as much as a sick man craves warmth and rest. I gladly agreed with John Milne, even while I realised that he was mistaken, that no wind could ever make clouds into the shapes we saw.

Joseph must have recognised the lie in my voice, for he said, 'You don't believe that, Alec. This is not the wind. And even if it were, why has it dropped so suddenly? It seems there's not a breath of it, now.'

'It rises and falls quickly, Joseph. We know that, too,' I said, and as I spoke the words, I hated myself; for I was hiding from the strangeness because I could no longer stand it, and agreeing with Milne because I did not want any discord between myself and the Principal. But Milne was hiding from the strangeness also: I could see it in his face, in the deep furrows of his forehead, in the wideness of his eyes as he gazed out at the distant, impossible columns of cloud. I felt that I was betraying poor Joseph, who alone among us was giving voice to what we were all thinking.

Anywhere in the world, clouds could not do what those clouds had done.

We all made a slow circuit of the lightroom, looking in every direction out from the island. The columns surrounded us, but though we had an unobstructed view of the ocean out to the horizon, I could not decide where the columns met the surface of the water, nor where their upper reaches ended. They were dark and furious grey in colour and stood perfectly still upon the world.

'I can see clouds between them,' said Milne suddenly, grabbing my shoulder and pointing. 'Look, do you see?'

Peering into the distance, I saw that he was right. In the narrow vertical spaces between the columns, the wispy forms of clouds drifted through a distant sky – a sky of normality and sanity: the sky of the world we knew. It seemed to me that the impossible columns were like the bars of a gigantic cage or prison, keeping us inside a smaller world where things were not as they were outside amidst the run and gyre of mankind; as if they were the visible boundary between the two worlds, defining and separating them. And I felt my heart tense and quicken in my chest, and I felt wonder and despair flooding my mind in equal measure, for surely we were at the mercy of powers beyond the imagination of man.

And yet, in those moments of dire extremity, I found myself wondering whether we were somehow being *told* or *shown* something that might help us in our understanding. Thinking on what I remember of that day, I am forced to admit that this could have been nothing more than wishful thinking: a desperate desire for the presence of someone or something benign; for in those terrible moments it occurred to me that strangeness could reach an intensity that was lethal to the human mind, that we were in the presence of something that might well annihilate us by its mere proximity to us.

For a moment, I wondered if the columns were angels.

And then the wind rose again in a sudden torrent of sound that was like no sound we had ever heard. And then it fell, and rose again, and fell again. There was something mechanical in the sound, shimmering and metallic, and something else akin to wailing voices, and the speed with which it rose and fell increased, as did its volume and intensity, so that I felt the floor tremble beneath my feet, and the tower crack and strain with the pressure.

Joseph whimpered and clapped his hands to his ears in a pitiful attempt to shut out the monstrous, shimmering wail of that grinding, unnatural wind. He fled the lightroom, hurling himself down the stairs into the house below.

Milne had shut his eyes and was muttering to himself, and it was only after some moments that I realised he was praying:

'Lord have mercy... Lord have mercy... Lord have mercy...'

'Look,' I said, pointing through the windows, though I knew that Milne did not see. 'Look at the clouds!'

'I won't look,' he said. 'I can't look!'

'They're changing.'

'I can't look, Alec!'

I glanced at him and saw that he was standing perfectly still, with his eyes tightly shut, his arms straight at his sides, his hands balled into great fists, the veins standing out hard and blue. And so like a terrified child did he seem that I felt tears of compassion flooding my eyes, and sympathetic love rose in my breast; love for him and for Joseph – for it was deeply, terribly wrong that men should be so afraid.

And so I let him be: I did not force him to open his eyes and see what I was seeing; I was not so heartless. Instead, I turned back to the windows and watched as the columns of cloud continued to twist and collapse, and then to rise again in different shapes, surging and intertwining like the roots of some colossal grey tree. Whether they were doing this under the influence of the chaotic, unnatural gales, or of their own accord, it was impossible to know.

I felt rather than saw Milne come to stand beside me, and I knew that he had overcome his terror at least enough to open his eyes and watch with me, as the great grey cords continued to writhe in the moaning firmament.

Milne placed a hand gently upon my shoulder, and said, 'I won't let you see it alone.'

I put my hand upon his and clasped it tightly, for I believed that whatever was about to happen would put an end to us. I thought of Mary Ducat and how I had assured her that I would discover the truth of what had happened to her husband and to the other keepers.

'Dear Mary,' I said, my voice no more than an abject trembling, 'I have kept my promise.'

The sky continued to surge and pulsate with the vast grey cords as they moved and swelled and rose and fell with the wailing metallic wind. And yet they kept their distance from the island and the lighthouse – if distance had any meaning in this uttermost place.

And then, as John Milne and I continued to watch, our breath coming in quick, short gasps of frighted expectation, the grey cords gradually ceased their convulsions, and slowly, very slowly, began to dissipate, growing hazy and indistinct, until finally they vanished altogether, leaving the sky in blessed normalcy. The unnatural gales likewise faded from our awareness, leaving in their wake the soft sigh of the ordered world.

John Milne and I stood in the lightroom for many minutes, neither moving nor speaking, hardly believing that we were still alive, and that the world had returned to its natural state.

Presently, I said, 'I think it has ended.'

'Yes,' Milne replied. 'But what has ended, Alec? *What* has ended?'

SEVEN

Max stopped reading and looked at each of the others in turn.

'So, the same thing *did* happen to them,' said Jennifer.

'Not quite,' Nick said. 'But it was definitely similar. There was definitely something badly wrong with the sky…'

'Look,' said Max, 'whatever's going on here, I think we've outstayed our welcome. We saw the sky doing something it's not supposed to do. Whether it was something rational and understandable – an unusual atmospheric phenomenon – or whether it was something else, I don't care. I'm from Florida, and believe me, I've seen enough hurricanes to know that you treat this kind of thing with respect and get the hell out of the way when it shows up. I think we should radio the mainland and request an evacuation.'

'And what do we tell the JNCC?' asked Jennifer. 'This research programme isn't cheap to run…'

'Jennifer, they can bill me!'

'I think Max is right,' said Nick. 'This isn't worth risking our safety over. We can tell the JNCC that we've observed an unusual meteorological phenomenon which we believe to be potentially hazardous. If they want, they can send out someone else to investigate.'

'I agree,' said Jennifer. She gave Max a smile. 'I just thought I had to mention that it's going to be a bit difficult when we get back.'

Max reached out and gently squeezed her shoulder. 'Don't worry, they'll believe us. And we've got the recordings from the hydrophones and transducer; we've got *proof* that something weird's happening here.'

'What about Donald?' asked Rebecca. 'He's not going to be too pleased.'

Max frowned at her. 'Donald can kiss my ass. And if he wants to stop me from calling the mainland, he's welcome to try.'

'I'm sure it won't come to that,' said Jennifer. 'But will you please let me tell him?'

Max said nothing, merely gave her a humourless smile and indicated the door of the tent. Jennifer nodded and crawled out with as much dignity as she could muster. Rebecca suddenly felt terribly sorry for her. She hated confrontations of any kind and didn't relish the prospect of watching Donald's reaction to what was essentially a mutiny.

Max followed her out, then Rebecca and finally Nick. They paused for a moment to look at the sky, which was normal, thank God.

Max quickly scanned the island. 'Can't see him. Must be on the platform,' he said and began to walk down the slope towards the stairway leading to the West Landing.

They descended the stairs as quickly as they could. The crane platform appeared to be deserted. *He must be in the equipment tent*, Rebecca thought. Max was first onto the platform and was making straight for the tent.

'Max,' said Jennifer.

He halted suddenly and nodded to her. 'Okay, go ahead.'

'Thank you.' Jennifer walked past him and into the tent. 'Donald, there's something we have to… Donald?' She came out a moment later. 'He's not there.'

Max sighed loudly and poked his head into the tent. 'Donald? Donald!' He turned to the others. 'All right, he must be somewhere else up there. Must have missed him.' Without another word, he stalked back to the stairway and began to climb.

When they reached the top, Max cupped his hands to his mouth and shouted: '*Donald! Where are you? We need to talk!*'

Nick shouted, too.

There was no reply, other than the soft hiss of the sea and the cries of the birds.

'Where the hell is he?' said Max. 'All right, fine!' He turned back to the stairway. 'We'll call the mainland anyway.'

'Wait,' said Nick. 'We have to find him first.'

'I don't need his permission, Nick.'

'That's not what I mean.' Nick looked all around him. 'I can't see him anywhere. He might be in trouble, and if that's the case, then our first responsibility is to find him – before we make the call, before we do anything. Okay?'

Max sighed and nodded. 'Yeah, you're right. Of course. Okay, let's… let's spread out and look for him.'

Rebecca and Jennifer immediately started to walk away in opposite directions. Nick stopped them. 'I appreciate your enthusiasm, ladies, but I don't want anyone going off by themselves. Max, you go with Jennifer. Becks, you stay with me.'

Max nodded. 'You got it.'

He and Jennifer began to walk northwest along the edge of the island.

As she walked with Nick in the opposite direction, Rebecca felt relief flooding her like a soothing drink. As soon as they had found Donald, they would be getting off the island, leaving its strangeness and tragedy behind forever. She carefully scanned the slope rising to the north towards the lighthouse, hoping to catch a glimpse of Donald. Nick kept an eye on the precipitous edge along which they walked, in case he had slipped and was clinging to the steep sides. That was unlikely, of course, since if he had, he would undoubtedly have been calling for help.

Christ, Rebecca thought. *I hope he hasn't fallen into the sea... or jumped!*

'You okay?' said Nick.

'Yeah.'

'I'm sorry about this... I'm really sorry.'

'It's not your fault.'

'All the same... I was hoping this trip would end differently.'

'We're going to get out of here, Nick. That's all that matters.'

He took her hand and held it gently.

'And the next time we go away together,' she added, 'we're going to my parents' place in the south of France, okay?'

He gave a soft laugh. 'So... you *want* there to be a next time?'

She stopped walking, drew him to her and kissed him. 'Yes.'

They kissed again, more deeply, and hugged each other tightly.

'I'm scared of this place,' she whispered. 'I don't know what's happening, or why, and I don't think it's even *possible* to know what's happening. None of it makes any sense.'

'I know,' he whispered back. 'Come on. The quicker we find Donald, the quicker we can get out of here.'

They walked on, following the curve of the island's southernmost edge, turning northeast.

'We'll check the East Landing,' said Nick.

'How well do you know Donald?' Rebecca asked.

'Fairly well.'

'He's strange.'

Nick gave a brief chuckle. 'On the basis of this trip, I can see how you'd think so.'

'He's very religious, isn't he?'

'Yes, he has a strong faith.'

'I still can't figure out how a scientist can also believe in God.'

'Well, lots of them don't, of course... but lots of them do. Donald is one of those who have no problem attributing the universe and all its phenomena and laws to a single causative agent. For him, science is all about the search for understanding of God's creation. I'm not sure *why* he has that view... maybe he had a religious upbringing – that can influence a person for the whole of his life, you know.'

'Yeah... and what about you?'

'What about me?'

'Do you believe in God?'

'I'm not sure.' He chuckled. 'Not much of an answer, is it?'

'Not much. But it's honest.'

'I can accept the idea of a First Cause, a supremely powerful entity with the ability to create space, time and matter – to create *universes*. But what I can't accept is that human religion has come anywhere near describing or understanding it, or ever could.'

'Why not?'

'Think about it. A being of infinite intelligence, infinite power, eternal and uncreated... how could finite beings like humans ever hope to understand it? Have you ever read Rainer Maria Rilke?'

'Yeah – I mean, I've read a few of his poems, not many.'

'Ever read the *Duino Elegies*?'

She shook her head. 'No.'

'I'll give you my copy when we get back to Aberdeen. The Second Elegy expresses it perfectly.'

To Rebecca's surprise, he began to quote the poem from memory.

'"Every angel is terrible./And still, alas/knowing all that/I serenade you/you almost deadly/birds of the soul.

'"If the dangerous archangel/took one step now/down towards us/from behind the stars/our heartbeats/rising like thunder/would kill us."'

'That's beautiful,' said Rebecca. 'And frightening.'

'If angels exist, then I think that's what they are. And God. If God and angels exist, then I don't think we could survive an encounter with them. They'd be too powerful, too *magnificent*... I think that their presence would annihilate us. We could never hope to have a direct, personal relationship with them.'

'That's a sad way of looking at the world. To believe that there might be a supreme being, but to be forever apart from it...'

'Maybe not forever. If you believe in the soul, it has to be made of less perishable stuff than the body...'

They had reached the top of the flight of steps leading down to the East Landing, which they could see from their vantage point.

'He's not there,' said Nick.

'Do you think he could have fallen into the sea?'

Nick lowered his head. 'It's possible. Damn it!'

'Or maybe... something else happened to him,' Rebecca said in a very quiet voice.

'I was thinking that too, but I didn't want to say anything.'

They looked at each other in silence for a long moment.

'Come on,' said Nick. 'There's still the north part of the island.'

They continued their search, but could find no sign of Donald. Away in the distance to the west, they saw the figures of Jennifer and Max approaching slowly – almost mournfully, Rebecca thought.

'You know,' she said, 'the one place we haven't checked is around the lighthouse.'

'What's the point? That's where our camp is, and Donald said he was going to carry on working. There's no reason he'd still be there.'

'All the same…'

Nick nodded. 'Okay, let's head back.'

As they approached the lighthouse, Rebecca said: 'Wait. Let's check the chapel first.'

Nick looked at her askance. 'You think he might be in *there*?'

'Remember what happened to Dalemore?'

'Oh… okay.'

They detoured to the south, towards the tiny heap of stones that lay a few yards from the wall of the lighthouse enclosure. Nick called out Donald's name, but there was no reply.

They reached the entrance, and Nick bent down to look inside.

Careful, thought Rebecca. *Careful…*

'*Christ!*' Nick recoiled, launching himself backwards away from the entrance. He fell heavily onto his back, his legs splayed apart. His eyes darted to Rebecca. 'Get away! *Get away!*'

She looked from him to the entrance, and her eyes widened and she sucked in her breath.

Slowly, almost tentatively, the white fox emerged from the darkness inside the chapel. It looked at Nick, and then it looked at Rebecca.

With its five eyes.

'Oh no,' Rebecca whispered. 'Oh no... no.'

Nick scrambled to his feet and rushed to place himself between Rebecca and the animal. 'Back away,' he said over his shoulder. 'Just... back away.'

The fox stood perfectly still, watching them.

A distant voice found its way into Rebecca's awareness, calling her and Nick's names. Max. She wanted to turn and look at him and Jennifer, but she couldn't take her eyes from the white fox.

She heard the sound of running feet, approaching rapidly. They slowed as Max and Jennifer drew up alongside them. She heard Max saying: 'Oh man... oh what the *fuck!*' And still she couldn't stop looking at those five eyes, glinting like pieces of obsidian in the sunlight.

'It should have run away,' said Jennifer. 'Why hasn't it run away?'

'Because it isn't afraid of us,' Nick replied.

The fox looked at each person who spoke.

It understands us, Rebecca thought. *It understands what we're saying!*

Max rummaged in his pocket and brought out a small digital camera. He switched it on, pointed it at the fox and took several pictures. The fox looked at him, but remained still.

Nick crouched down on his haunches and edged his way very slowly towards the animal.

Max lowered his camera. 'Nick, buddy, what are you doing?'

'Nick, please don't!' said Rebecca.

'I just want to get a little closer. I want a closer look at... at its eyes.'

Very slowly, an inch at a time, Nick reached out towards the fox. His hand drew closer and closer to the animal's muzzle. The fox remained perfectly still, watching him.

161

When his hand was no more than an inch away, a scream echoed faintly across the island. They all jumped, and Nick stood up suddenly. The scream was followed by another, much louder.

'Donald!' cried Jennifer.

'Where's it coming from?' said Max.

'That way,' said Nick. 'The lighthouse. Come on!'

They ran up the slope towards the gate in the low wall surrounding the lighthouse and its outbuildings. Once inside the courtyard, they hurried around the lighthouse, calling out Donald's name again and again.

They came to a halt in front of the two outbuildings. The door to the larger one was standing slightly ajar.

'That was locked,' said Nick. 'They're always locked – the lighthouse, the outbuildings.'

'Not this one,' said Max. 'Not anymore.'

Nick approached the door, his eyes fixed on the sliver of blackness which partially framed it. 'Donald?' he said.

A faint whimper drifted out to them.

Nick pushed open the door and stepped inside. Max moved forward quickly to accompany him. Rebecca and Jennifer waited outside.

Presently, Max's voice said: 'What the hell?'

'What is it?' Jennifer called out. 'Is he there?'

'Yeah, he's here,' Max replied from the darkness.

'Come on, give me a hand,' Nick muttered.

A few moments later, he and Max emerged from the outbuilding, carrying Donald between them.

'Oh God!' said Jennifer, rushing forward. 'What happened to him?'

'I've no idea,' Nick replied as he and Max gently laid Donald down on the cobbles. Donald stared up at the sky, his eyes wide. A thin line of spittle inched down from the corner of his mouth.

'God protect me,' he whispered. 'God protect me...'

Max leaned over him. 'Don... Don, what happened?'

Donald didn't reply; he simply kept repeating the same phrase, over and over again.

Rebecca looked at the open door to the outbuilding. 'Something happened to him in there,' she said.

Max glanced at Rebecca, then at the door. He stood up. 'Whatever happened to him, he needs medical attention. I'm going down to the platform... gonna call the mainland and request an immediate evac.'

'Want me to come?' asked Nick.

'No. You stay here with Becks and Jennifer and...' He indicated Donald's prone form.

'Okay,' said Nick. 'Make the call, and get right back up here.'

'No problem.'

'Wait!' said Jennifer suddenly. 'Listen.'

Max sighed. 'What?'

'The sea...'

'What are you–'

'Shh!'

They all listened.

After a few moments, Max whispered: 'What the hell is that?'

'Sounds like... boiling liquid,' said Nick.

Rebecca realised that he was right: there was a bubbling sound, heavy, rumbling, immense, and growing steadily louder. It sounded as if the entire ocean were boiling.

'Where's it coming from?' asked Max. 'I can't figure the direction...'

'Come on,' said Nick as he walked out of the courtyard. Rebecca took hold of his arm and walked alongside him, with Jennifer and Max following behind. When they reached the west side of the lighthouse, Nick stopped and pointed down to the sea.

'Dear God,' said Jennifer.

About a hundred metres beyond the ragged edge of the island, the ocean was foaming and bubbling as if in response to some vast heat source beneath the surface. The water roiled and twisted, splitting apart and disgorging thick white gouts of spume high into the air. The gouts hung briefly against the blue sky before slapping loudly upon the sea's tortured surface, to be absorbed in the churning mass and then flung out again.

Max stared open-mouthed at the boiling ocean. 'Holy Christ… what's causing that? What's *causing* that?'

Jennifer shook her head. 'It doesn't look like water… it looks more like mud… thick, viscous…'

'It could be sediment from the seabed,' said Nick.

'What could churn up that much sediment?' said Max. 'And anyway, ocean sediment isn't *white.*'

At that moment, a vast plume of foam erupted from the bubbling mass, arcing high into the air. Nick watched its trajectory, then grabbed Rebecca and dragged her back towards the wall. 'It's going to hit the island. Get back. Back! Back! Back!'

They clambered over the wall as another eruption flooded the sky, its vast tendrils of spume cartwheeling towards them. Some of the tendrils struck the lighthouse, exploding in thick white showers that fell all around them.

'Get Donald! Into the tents, quick!' said Nick.

'Screw the tents!' shouted Max, as he made for the front door to the lighthouse. He tried the door handle, found it locked, and then began to kick it repeatedly. After four or five kicks, the lock gave and the door opened with a loud crack of splintered wood. He turned to the others. 'I'm not staying out there in a goddamned tent. We'll be safer in here.'

'All right,' said Nick, pushing Rebecca towards the door. He glanced over his shoulder in time to see an enormous tendril of foam land on the two tents, crushing them beneath its weight.

He and Max took hold of Donald and carried him through the door. Max slammed it shut behind them. They stood in the dark hallway, breathing heavily and listening to the boiling of the ocean and the loud slaps of the viscous water and foam hitting the cobblestones outside.

'How the hell are we going to get to the crane platform in this?' asked Max.

'We aren't,' Nick replied. 'You saw what happened to the tents. It'd be suicide to go out there now.'

From somewhere above them, they could hear the sounds of wet impacts against the lighthouse tower. Each heavy thud sent reverberations through the entire building.

Max looked up at the ceiling, his eyes wide and filled with fear. 'Oh crap!'

'Listen,' said Nick. 'We have to stay in here until that... whatever it is finishes. Then we'll go down to the platform and radio the mainland.'

'Yeah,' said Max. 'I only hope to God our equipment's still there...'

EIGHT

Rebecca paced back and forth along the corridor leading to the front door. Jennifer was in the sitting room, or what had once been the sitting room, where they had placed Donald. He had been fading in and out of consciousness, and his moaning and whimpering had become so unbearable to Rebecca that she'd had to leave the room.

The eruptions had ceased more than an hour ago, and Nick and Max had gone outside and reported that the ocean appeared to have settled back into its normal state. Jennifer had suggested that they go down to the crane platform, but when they had gone to the head of the rock-hewn stairway, they had found it to be completely covered with the thick foam. They had decided that it would be far too dangerous to attempt to negotiate the stairway just then and had agreed to wait for a while in the hope that the material would dissipate.

Rebecca went back to the sitting room to see how Jennifer was doing. The room was empty of furnishings, except for a few metal shelving units containing various tools and bits and pieces of equipment; Rebecca assumed that they had something to do with the maintenance of the lighthouse. She was tired and hungry and was still profoundly shaken by what had happened in the last few hours. She had no idea what could possibly have caused the ocean to do that... and she had no idea what Donald could possibly have seen in the outbuilding to unhinge him so suddenly and completely.

'How is he?' Rebecca asked as she entered the room.

'The same,' replied Jennifer. She was dabbing Donald's forehead with a handkerchief. 'He's feverish. We have to get him back to the mainland. Where are Nick and Max?'

'They've gone outside again, to see if... if that stuff has cleared. Can I do anything?'

Jennifer gave her a weak smile. 'No, thank you.'

Rebecca walked slowly towards Jennifer and Donald. 'What happened to him? What did he see in there?'

Jennifer looked down at Donald, whose mouth was working continually and silently. 'I don't know.' Tears began to roll down her cheeks.

Rebecca knelt beside her and put an arm around her shoulders.

They heard the front door creaking open and footsteps along the corridor. Nick appeared in the sitting room doorway. He beckoned silently to them. Rebecca looked at Jennifer, who nodded and said, 'You go on. I'll stay here with Donald.'

'No,' said Nick. 'You come too, Jennifer. We won't be long.'

Jennifer hesitated, then stood up. They left the sitting room and walked along the corridor to the front door. As she stepped outside, Rebecca was both surprised and relieved to find that there was now no trace of the strange foam that had rained down upon the island and the lighthouse. There was nothing but pools of water here and there on the cobbles. She crouched down and tentatively touched one of the pools.

'It's just seawater,' said Max, who was rummaging around in the wreckage of the crushed tents. 'There's no sign of any of that other stuff.'

Rebecca turned and looked up at the lighthouse tower. It appeared to be quite clean and undamaged. The sky had become overcast, heavy with thick, grey clouds that stretched all the way to the horizon, and there was a curious quality to the air: a cloying humidity she hadn't felt before – at least not this far north.

'How are we doing?' Jennifer asked.

'Well, the good news is that we can salvage pretty much everything up here. Tents are a write-off, but our supplies, clothing, and sleeping bags are all okay. Even Rebecca's book made it.' He handed Dalemore's testament to her.

'And the bad news?'

'Everything we left on the crane platform is gone: equipment, radio, the works. There's no way to contact the mainland now.'

'What about our mobile phones?' said Rebecca. 'Couldn't we…?

Max shook his head. 'Sorry, Becks. No signal out here.'

'Max and I made a circuit of the island,' said Nick.

'And?' said Rebecca.

Nick hesitated. He and Max glanced at each other.

'Come on, guys, let's hear it.'

'I'm not quite sure how to describe it,' said Nick.

'Maybe it's better if you just come and take a look for yourselves,' said Max. 'It's on the north side of the island.'

'"It"?'

'Come on.'

They left the enclosure and walked down the slope towards the island's edge. The grass was damp and slippery underfoot, and Nick held Rebecca's hand tighter as he came to a halt a few metres from the cliff. 'What do you make of that?'

They stood in silence for some moments, and then Jennifer said, very quietly, 'That wasn't there yesterday.'

The extrusion of rock extended perhaps fifty metres out from the island's flank into the sea. It was about ten metres wide; its top was smooth and flat, and a dull ash-grey in colour. It ended in a perfect semicircle, around which the sea churned and foamed.

'What is it?' asked Rebecca.

'Whatever it is, it shouldn't be there,' Jennifer replied. 'It isn't part of the island.'

'It doesn't look natural,' Max said. 'The top's too flat, too regular. It looks like it was... built.'

'Yes,' agreed Jennifer. 'But by whom?'

'Could the sea level have changed?' asked Rebecca, glancing at each of them in turn. 'I mean, with changing tides...'

Nick shook his head. 'This thing was never part of Eilean Mòr. It's as if... as if the island *grew* it.'

'But that's not possible,' Rebecca whispered.

Nick put his arm around her and held her close. 'No... it's not.'

'What are we going to do?'

'I'll tell you what we should do,' said Max. 'We should read the rest of that book. Dalemore and the others got off the island at the end of their duty – they made it back to the mainland after a whole *month* here. Maybe the book will tell us how they managed it.'

'Agreed,' said Nick. 'But first, we need to get all the stuff from the tents into the house. It's going to be our home for the next few days, so we might as well get comfortable.'

'I don't know if "comfortable" is the word I'd use,' said Jennifer. 'But yes, you're right, let's do that first.'

*

They transferred their belongings from the tents into the sitting room. Rebecca made some porridge for them on the gas stove, while the others discussed what they had seen. Jennifer was leafing through Dalemore's testament, apparently looking for something. Presently, she found the passage.

'Listen to this,' she said. 'This is what John Milne said to Alec Dalemore: *Do you really know what Nature is? Are you really so familiar with all of the parts that make up the whole of the world? Can there be such a thing as the "supernatural"... or are such things simply parts of Nature which we don't understand?* I think he was onto something when he said that.'

'What are you getting at?' asked Max.

'Physicists have speculated that there might be other dimensions of existence parallel to this one. What if we've been seeing and detecting things that exist in one of those other dimensions? The white fox, the thing in the ocean, the way the sky behaved...'

'I don't know, Jennifer,' said Nick. 'I've read some of the literature myself... but those physicists also say that the various dimensions are forever isolated from one another: communication between them is impossible, even in principle.'

'What if they're wrong?' said Jennifer. 'What if communication *is* possible under certain circumstances? What if this location in our spacetime is... is a kind of *focal point*, a place where the barrier between dimensions is weak, and able to be breached?'

'But Dalemore and the others got off the island safely when their tour was over,' Nick reminded her. 'And no other strange events were ever reported by later crews, right up to the lighthouse's automation in '71.'

'Maybe it goes in cycles,' Max suggested. The others looked at him. 'Maybe conditions are the same now as they were a century ago. Maybe they'll be the same again a century from now.'

'Another dimension impinging periodically on this one,' said Nick. 'Is it possible?'

'That thing we saw just now,' said Max. 'That… promontory, whatever you want to call it… it appeared out of thin air. *It shouldn't be there.*'

'But what's its purpose?' said Rebecca. 'What's it *for*?'

Max regarded the book lying on the floor close to her. 'Maybe Dalemore and the others found out.'

Jennifer returned to Donald, who appeared to have lapsed into unconsciousness. 'We need to read the rest of the manuscript,' she said.

12
FROM THE OCEAN

For the next few days, we hardly said a word to each other beyond what was necessary to our maintenance of the light. I was both glad of this and discomfited by it: on the one hand, we all knew that there was nothing that could be said beyond wondering what we had seen, and admitting that we could form no conception of an answer, and yet, on the other, I felt a profound need to give support to my companions and to receive support from them. I sensed a desperate need to speak of it, so that we might reassure ourselves that it had actually happened, that we were not losing our minds, and that we could find refuge from the unknowable in our shared humanity and fellow-feeling.

It had become obvious to me that Ducat, Marshall and MacArthur must have experienced similar things, and that they had been utterly undone by them. Once again, I entertained the theory that one of the keepers had become completely unhinged, and had done away with his fellows and then himself, although the precise nature of the final extremity which they had confronted remained unknown. Of course, it could not have been anything we ourselves had experienced thus far: for we were still alive and in possession of our faculties. This thought depressed me considerably, for we had many more days to spend on Eilean Mòr, during which something might well happen to rob us of our sanity and cast us to perdition.

I had decided one thing already: I would indeed follow Milne's wishes and throw the carved stone into the sea, and I would ask Milne and Moore to watch me doing it, so that they would be free of any suspicion that I was being untruthful with them, that I might keep the thing in secret without their knowledge (which, of course, is what I had initially planned to do).

This I did on the 14th of January. Milne came with me to the cliff's edge on the eastern side of the island, a few yards from the light, while Joseph watched from the lightroom; thus we obeyed the rule that all three keepers should never go outside at once. I hefted the strange object in my hand and hurled it as far as I could, and we watched it tumble end over end through the grey air, down towards the waiting sea. It hit the surface with barely a sound and vanished from view beneath the rolling waves.

'There,' I said. 'The thing is gone, and with it, I hope, all the strangeness we've seen.'

Milne glanced at me. 'So the same thought occurred to you, Alec. The thought that that thing was to blame.'

I nodded. 'Aye, I'll confess to that, John. It was here on the island all the time, buried beneath the floor of the chapel. Don't ask me how such a thing could be, but right now I'd wager all I have that, somehow, the stone was to blame.'

'Thank you, Alec,' he said.

'For what?'

'For doing as I asked: for getting rid of it. I feared you wouldn't.'

'Then I'll confess something else,' I replied, turning to him. 'I was considering hiding it in my room and telling you that I'd thrown it into the sea…'

Milne nodded, and half-smiled. 'I had an idea you might.' He hesitated before asking, 'What changed your mind?'

I was on the point of laughing and asking how he could possibly ask a question to which the answer was so obvious. But then I realised that this was Milne's way of broaching the subject we had been so carefully avoiding for the last two days.

'What happened to the clouds,' I replied. 'When they became alive, or whatever it was that they did... I didn't think that the stone was in any way responsible, at least not then. But when it ended and we were left alive and sane, I realised that the stone was a kind of emblem in my mind...'

'An emblem?'

'Yes, of all that has happened here – to us, and to Ducat, Marshall and MacArthur. Whether it has any more significance than that, I can't say, but after what happened two days ago, I didn't want to look at it any more – nor even to have it with us on the island.'

'And the clouds,' said Milne, looking up at the cold, flat slate of the sky, at the sullen, featureless vault hanging far above us. 'And the sound of the wind. What in God's name happened?'

'How can anyone say?' I remained silent for some moments before continuing, 'All I *can* say is this: we are in the hands of something we don't understand. Something is here, John. What it is, I don't know. What it wants, I can't say. But it *is* here.'

'Do you think we'll go the same way as Ducat, Marshall and MacArthur?' Milne asked, still looking at the sky.

'Let's make an agreement, John, you and I. Let's do everything in our power to avoid it!'

Milne looked at me, and then smiled and nodded. 'Aye, agreed.'

We turned our backs on the sea and began to walk towards the light.

'Can I ask you one other thing, Alec?'

'Of course.'

'While the clouds were... well, while it was happening, I heard you say something. "Dear Mary," you said, "I have kept my promise." What did you mean by that?'

'It's the reason I volunteered to join the relief crew. I received a letter from James Ducat's wife, informing me of what had happened. She asked me to try to find out what had befallen her husband and the other keepers, and I vowed to do as she asked, somehow. Two days ago, I thought we were lost; I thought our ending was upon us and that I had answered her question – though I would never be able to tell her.'

'I see. You knew Ducat well?'

'He saved my life,' I replied and told Milne of how my ship was wrecked off Gallan Head a year ago, and of how Ducat had saved me from death upon the rocks. I told him of the unpayable debt I owed that man, of how I had become a friend to him and his family in the months that followed, and how I considered it my duty at least to attempt to find an answer to the mystery of his disappearance, for the sake of Mary and the children.

'I didn't know that,' said Milne, and in his voice I detected something that might have been a new respect. I certainly hoped so, for Occasional Keepers are not always held in high esteem by their full-time colleagues, and I had the additional disadvantage of having replaced a man who was unable to do duty on the island – just as Donald MacArthur had done.

At that moment, I thought of broaching the subject of the conversation I had overheard Milne and Moore having in the kitchen soon after we arrived. But then I realised that there was no longer any need. To their great credit, they had tried to ignore the ill omen of my presence, and now I was glad to reveal something of my character to Milne, to reassure him that I was a man who could be trusted in matters of importance.

I also noticed a new lightness in Milne's step as we walked across the yard to the kitchen door, as if he were happy to be returning to the light and to the resumption of his duties, and for the first time I realised how important my action had been in ridding us of the carved stone. I had the impression that we were beginning again on Eilean Mòr, that we had rid ourselves of fear and brooding mystery, and that now we would be able to discharge our duties cleansed of the dark strangeness that had so hideously besieged us over the past week.

Although I cannot say for certain, perhaps somewhere in my mind there was a dim awareness of how naive such thoughts were. With hindsight, it seems obvious that I was merely seizing on my disposal of the stone as a harbinger of better fortune, which is understandable enough.

At any rate, I was profoundly, terribly mistaken. Four days later, on the 18th of January, there occurred an event that was to mark the beginning of a new phase of our strange torment on Eilean Mòr.

*

On the night of the 18th, Milne was doing duty in the lightroom. Joseph had already transferred the meteorological and other information from the slate to the logbook, and he and I played a couple of hands of cards in the kitchen and then went into the sitting room to read. Joseph chose a book of history, while I took up a copy of one of Walter Scott's stories. I had briefly considered taking Martin Martin's *A Description of the Western Isles of Scotland* again but decided against it, for now I had no desire to acquaint myself further with the mysteries of ancient folklore and superstition.

I took a pipe and puffed happily upon it as I settled back with my book, listening as I lost myself in its pages to the rising wind and rattle of rain outside. Presently, I felt my eyelids drooping and a pleasant fatigue gently overcoming me. I rested the open book upon my chest and allowed myself to drift towards sleep. I began to dream vaguely of a great dark sea, above which a lone seabird flew on slowly flapping wings. The seabird shrieked – a strange, almost human sound…

And then I was shaken awake by Joseph. I opened my eyes to see him standing over me, a look of great fear and confusion on his face.

'What is it?' I mumbled, sitting up straight.

At that moment, I realised the origin of the cry I had heard in my brief dream, for it sounded again, from somewhere above.

In the lightroom, John Milne was screaming.

Joseph and I ran from the sitting room. As we hurried up the stairs, another cry filled the tower. The sound of a man screaming is one of the most tragic and horrible things, and I could not begin to guess at what was happening to make Milne cry out so. There was such a pitiful despair in his voice that my heart withered in my chest.

'John, we're coming!' shouted Joseph behind me.

We entered the lightroom to find Milne standing at the windows, shuddering and moving to and fro, like a child swaying to the strains of a lullaby. He was hugging himself with his powerful arms, as if he were freezing cold. And all the while, he was gazing out through the windows – out and down towards the sea.

I went to him and laid a hand on his shoulder, and he flinched and groaned at the contact. 'John, what is it?'

Milne shook his head. 'I can see it. Look there… look! Can't you see?'

'See what?' I followed his pointed arm and looked out into the darkness.

'Down there, Alec. Down there in the sea. It's there!'

'There's nothing there, John!' I said firmly, for in truth I could see nothing but the whirling of the rain, driven to frenzy by the constantly rising wind which threw it upon the windows in crackling bursts, and the great, dark, moving mass of the ocean beyond.

'Wait for the light,' he said. 'Wait for the light to come around, and then you'll see!'

A few seconds later, the lens assembly brought the white beam around and cast it before us into the night, etching the sea's heaving surface with bright silver and making diamonds of the flying rain. Still, I could see nothing but the world, nothing that could make a man scream.

'Joseph!' I shouted. 'Can you see anything out there?'

'No,' said Milne. 'Don't let him. Please don't let him.'

But the lad came up behind me, and together we waited for the next passing of the light. When it came around, Joseph jumped back from the windows and cried out, 'Oh, Jesus Christ save us!'

Milne turned to him. 'Get out of here, Joseph. Go back downstairs.'

'No.'

'Get downstairs, laddie, *now!*'

'I won't!'

'You mustn't see it,' Milne said, and I saw tears flowing down his face.

I shook my head furiously. 'There's nothing out there. I can't see anything out there but the sea and the rain.'

'Why can't you see it?' Joseph whimpered, still backing away from the window.

'Please go downstairs,' repeated Milne.

'I don't want to be alone,' said Joseph.

The light came around again, and again I pressed my face to the glass and tried to see, but again I could discern nothing but the fierceness of the wind and rain and ocean. Why couldn't I see what the others were seeing? My fear was compounded by confusion and desperation.

I turned to Milne. 'All right, John – describe it.'

He shook his head. 'I can't.'

'What do you mean you can't? What is it? What does it look like?'

'It's moving in the ocean,' he said, his voice thick with terror and revulsion. 'It's coming up out of the sea. Coming closer now… oh God!'

Joseph went again to the windows and waited for the light to swing round, and I marvelled at the perversity of his action, for the sight of it had smitten him like a physical blow, and yet, against all sanity and logic, he strained to see it again. He was as one hypnotised by some immense and malign power, held helpless in its grasp, or perhaps forced by his own disbelief to look upon it again and again.

Without warning, Milne lunged at him and threw him violently to the floor. '*No!*' he screamed, as I seized him and drew him back, fearful of what else he might do in the chaos of his terror. Under normal circumstances, I was perhaps his equal in strength, but panic lends a man greater strength, and I thought again of my speculation that one of the missing Keepers had gone violently insane and murdered his fellows.

'John,' I whispered into his ear. 'Be calm, now. Be calm.'

'I can't let him see,' Milne said softly through his tears. 'It'll be the end of him.' Another glance through the flood of the white beam, and Milne collapsed in my arms, and gently as I could I eased him to the floor.

'It's on the island now,' he whispered.

'THIS NIGHT WOUNDS TIME'

I awoke in my bed, and immediately I was seized with confusion and panic. The last thing I remembered was John Milne collapsing to the floor in the lightroom, and me cradling his trembling form in my arms. Grey light seeped in through the window, and as I sat up suddenly, I saw a figure rising from the single wooden chair in a dim corner of the room.

'What's happening?' I cried.

The figure came into the watery light, and I saw that it was Milne. He had a frown of deep concern upon his face as he said, 'Rest easy now, Alec. You're all right…'

'I *know* I'm all right,' I said loudly. 'But you, you…'

Milne retreated a little way, took up the chair from the corner and brought it to my bedside. He sat down and leaned forward, resting his elbows on his knees, and looked at me with great intensity.

'How are you feeling, Alec?'

'I don't understand what's happening,' I replied. 'The last thing I remember, I was up in the lightroom with you and Joseph. You'd cried out, and we'd gone up to see what was wrong. And then… then…'

'What? Tell me what you remember,' he said very gently.

I spoke in a swift, frantic whisper, while Milne sat and listened. 'You and Joseph saw something coming out of the sea. You were both terrified, pointing through the windows, saying it was coming towards the island. I looked, but I couldn't see anything – nothing but the storm, the rain, the wind. I couldn't see what you were seeing… and then you threw Joseph to the floor because you didn't want him to see it, and I took hold of you because I didn't know what else you might do, such was your fright. And then you seemed to collapse, as if overwhelmed by what you saw.'

'And then?' he said.

'And then… I woke up here. Is it really morning?'

'It is.'

'What's the time?'

'Half past ten. You've been asleep for nearly thirteen hours…'

'Thirteen hours! It's not possible.'

'I can assure you it is, laddie, for here you are, and half past ten is the time.'

I lay back against my pillow, still hardly believing what Milne had said. I recalled the strange and frightening lapse in consciousness I had experienced some days before, when I had suddenly and unaccountably found myself inside the ruined chapel, and again I feared for my reason and sanity. But it was Milne and Moore who had been pushed to the point of madness last night; it was *they* who had seen something in the ocean which I could not see. Could I be the victim of lunacy, when I had been the one to see nothing but the natural elements?

I sighed and met Milne's gaze squarely. 'What did you and Joseph see, John? What was out there to cause you to cry out and weep so?'

Very slowly, John Milne shook his head. 'Alec… we saw nothing. It was *you* who was raving about something coming out of the ocean.'

'Me?'

'Joseph and I have been very concerned about you, laddie. Joseph, in fact, wondered if you would last the night. I don't mind telling you I'm glad to see that you have.'

I felt the room sway around me, and my breath began to come in gasps. What Milne was saying was not possible. I had seen nothing! But after all, I was the one lying in bed after spending thirteen hours in oblivion, not Milne, and not Joseph.

'I don't understand.'

Milne shrugged and gave me a smile which, I supposed, was intended to encourage me. 'Neither do we. But you seem to have regained your senses.' He shook his head again. 'We were *very* worried about you.'

'All right then, John. It seems clear enough that I have no memory of what really happened last night. So, will you please do me the favour of telling me?'

Milne hesitated, and then he sighed and said, 'Very well. I was on duty in the lightroom. Everything was normal. You and Joseph were downstairs. At about half past nine, you came up with a mug of tea for me, and we talked for a few minutes. Then you went to the windows and looked out to the north. You made some comment about the weather, the rising wind, the rain… then you looked down at the sea, and you cried out…'

'*I* cried out?'

'Yes. I came over and asked you what was wrong. The look on your face, Alec… well, I looked where you were pointing, but I couldn't see anything out of the ordinary. But you said there was something there, moving in the sea. I tried to calm you. I reminded you that a stormy sea plays tricks on a man's mind, that sometimes one sees things that aren't really there.'

'I understand that well enough,' I said.

'I know, but last night you wouldn't accept it. You kept shouting that there was something out there – something you wouldn't or couldn't describe. But there was panic in your voice, and I was afraid, and I called down to Joseph to come up and help, because I didn't know what you might do – break the windows and injure yourself, perhaps, or…'

'Or injure you?'

'Aye,' Milne nodded. 'I'm afraid of no man, Alec, but a man seized with fear and panic can be difficult to manage – I've seen it before. And so Joseph came up to the lightroom, and immediately you began screaming at him to get out, to go back downstairs, and that you didn't want him to see what was out there, that it would be too much for him, that to see it would be too much for any man. To his credit, the lad stayed calm, and we tried to get you away from the windows, but you kept screaming and pointing, and saying strange things…'

'What things?' I asked. 'What was I saying?'

'Ach, I'm not sure I remember precisely. Jumbles of words that didn't mean anything.'

'Please try to remember, John.'

'Well,' he sighed, 'you talked of a shadow… "it's a shadow," you said, "a shadow of something no longer here… but still it moves and lives. And the sea knows and is afraid of it, the cause of all storms."'

'What else?' I asked, trying to remember these events but failing utterly. It was as if Milne were describing a scene at which I had not been present, and again I experienced a vertiginous feeling of shock, confusion and disbelief.

'You…' His voice trailed off, and he looked at me, and for the first time since I had woken, I saw fear in his eyes, and it seemed that it was not felt for me, and I believed then that he remembered far more of what I had said than he was prepared to admit.

'You must tell me what else you remember, John,' I said, leaning forward. 'It's my right to know!'

'Your right?'

'Yes. If what you say is true, then there is something wrong with me, with my mind. If so, then I am owed the facts by a fellow man!'

Milne gave another sigh. 'It's true you said other things, but they were things no Christian man would say…'

'Blasphemies?'

'No, not as such… but such strange things! About what you were seeing outside. Nothing of which a Christian mind could conceive. "The coming together of past, present and future," you said. "The primal night… the first thought in the great outside… the shadow of that which thought first, in the night which was, and which will be. It is here," you said. "It is still here, and it is still alive."'

And then Milne stood up suddenly and went to the window. For many moments he stood there with his back to me, gazing out silently across the island to the sea beyond.

'"It breathes our dreams," you said. "It forged the cross and the star and the crescent in our minds, and all are shadows of its shadow. It lives on the land and in the sea… and in the seas of space and time, and the minds which live in space and time. And God is the shadow of its shadow, for it is not God."

'And then you began to weep, Alec. And you moaned with such despair that I thought my heart and mind would break, as yours appeared to be breaking. And then you laughed when Joseph began to pray. "It's coming closer," you said. "It's coming onto the island now. What is it made of?" you asked. "Why can't you see it?"'

Milne turned away from the window and stood facing me, his hands clasped behind his back. 'And then you collapsed to the floor, and Joseph and I held you while you wept.'

'Did I… did I say anything else?' I asked quietly.

'One more thing. Just before you fell unconscious, you said, "This night wounds time."'

'What does that mean? What does any of it mean?'

'I don't know, Alec. I truly don't know.'

*

Milne left my room, and I lay in bed for a while trying to make sense of everything he had said. But of course, it *didn't* make sense. I felt fine, apart from the slight headache and that certain fuzzy feeling behind the eyes which one gets after too much sleep. I truly did not think I was losing my mind. Of course, who knows what madness feels like, except the mad? But I felt in full control of my faculties, and I was still confident that my own memory of the previous night's events was accurate. In fact, had Milne not described to me what *he* recalled, I would have gone to him and Joseph with the same concern they evidently felt for me, with not the slightest suspicion that my memories were anything but true.

And the things Milne told me I had said! They were not the products of *my* mind, for I could never have conceived of such bizarre notions. Bizarre and *blasphemous*, in spite of Milne's reluctance to call them that. Living shadows in the seas of space and time... the primal night... breathing dreams and forging the Cross. Such concepts completely passed my understanding, and I wondered whether, even in madness, my mind would be capable of producing such abnormalities of thought. The more I pondered the matter, the more outrageous it seemed.

And then, I found myself asking the obvious question – one that, perhaps, I had been avoiding, such were the frightening implications.

Was John Milne lying to me?

But why *would* he lie? Had he and Joseph seen something so awful that their own minds refused to retain any memory of it? Or perhaps they did remember. Perhaps Joseph had come up behind me while I was holding Milne in my arms and struck me, rendering me unconscious. Perhaps they had then brought me here to my bed, and created this story between themselves while I slept. If their memories of last night were too strange and horrible to contemplate, they might have wished them upon me, convincing themselves that it was *I* who had seen whatever it was that had come out of the ocean.

Perhaps… perhaps. But still it didn't make any sense, for Milne had seemed perfectly calm and rational just now. He didn't seem like a man who had been driven by extremity to twist the truth so. And what I knew of him, of the kind of man he was, prevented me from accepting that he could have done anything like this. And Joseph, too: surely he would never have stooped to such a thing.

I lay there in misery for some time, not knowing what to think. The alternatives all seemed equally dreadful. And then suddenly, like a flash of lightning, another thought occurred to me: a thought that was difficult to grasp, such was its outrageousness. Was it possible that *both I and Milne remembered correctly?* That last night's events had happened just as I recalled, *and* just as he recalled? Of course, I had no idea how this could be so, and yet, perversely, it seemed the most rational explanation – or at least, more rational than what I had previously been contemplating.

I felt immense relief as I got out of bed, dressed and went to the kitchen. I wasn't sure if I should mention my theory to the others (perhaps they would merely consider it further evidence of my mental frailty). Nevertheless it had the ring of strange truth to it, and I clung to it for what it offered: a way to avoid the thought that either I was the victim of a solitary madness, or that my fellow Lightkeepers were conspiring against me.

'Good morning, Joseph,' I said.

The lad was sitting at the kitchen table, and he looked up sharply as I spoke. 'Alec!' he cried. He stood up and hurried over to me and gave me a powerful hug. 'You're all right, thank God!'

'Yes, I am all right. I'm sorry if I caused you concern last night.'

'That's putting it mildly. I thought… well…'

'A stormy sea plays tricks on a man's mind,' I said. 'Last night, it played those tricks on me. I should have known better. I apologise.'

'That's all right, Alec. I'm glad to see you're back to your normal self. You gave John and me a nasty fright, I don't mind telling you.'

'So John said. Where is he?'

'Outside, making an inspection. Will you have some tea?'

'Yes, please.'

I sat at the table while Joseph poured me a mug.

'The strange thing is,' I continued, 'I have no memory of what happened… what I said and what I thought I saw.'

Joseph hesitated. 'Aye… John mentioned that.'

There was something in his bearing that caught my attention, although I couldn't quite define it: some slight agitation that made me sit forward and regard him carefully.

'And the things I said…'

'Aye, strange things.'

'Strange, too, that I should faint away so completely.'

Joseph stopped what he was doing.

Another thought had occurred to me: if my memories of the previous night were at such variance with Milne's, then what did *Joseph* remember? Would his account corroborate mine, or Milne's – or did he remember something entirely different?

'What else did John say?'

Joseph didn't answer.

'Did he tell you that I remember events differently? That I'm certain it was *he and you* who saw something that I couldn't see?'

Joseph gave me a strange look, and I stood up and went to stand beside him.

'Joseph,' I said, 'what do *you* remember of last night?'

Again, Joseph made no reply. He merely shook his head, and I could see that he was struggling to remain calm, as if he were wrestling with some unknown inner turmoil.

'Tell me, Joseph… please.'

'Why?' he whispered. 'Why do you want to know?'

'Because your memories might hold the answer – or at least some clue as to what really happened. I don't trust my own recollections, nor do I trust John's. If you remember something different, you must tell me.'

'But that's it, Alec,' he sighed and looked at me, and there was such a haunted look in his eyes that I felt my heart stall in my chest. 'That's the strange thing. I can't tell you what I remember of last night… because I *have* no memories. I can recall nothing of what happened. Absolutely nothing!'

14

Strange Traces

I looked at Joseph for a long moment. 'No memories? None at all?'

He shook his head.

'How can that be?'

'I don't know.'

'What's the last thing you do remember?'

'I remember playing a couple of hands of cards with you, here in the kitchen, and then going into the sitting room... after that, nothing. I woke up in my bed, and I have no idea what happened in the hours between.'

'And John knows about this?'

'Of course he does. I was frightened when I woke up; I couldn't hide that from him.'

'And what did he say?'

Joseph shrugged. 'What *could* he say? He had no answer for it. But,' he gave a small, rueful smile, 'he asked me not to say anything about it to you.'

I put my hand on his shoulder. 'Thank you.'

'You won't mention it to him, will you? I don't like going against the wishes of the Principal.'

'No, I won't say a word.'

'You said you remembered things differently from John. What do you mean, Alec?'

So that was the reason for the strange look Joseph had given me a few moments ago: Milne had told him nothing of my belief that it was he and Joseph who had experienced something strange and terrible last night. And in that moment, I felt a sudden and profound sympathy for John Milne. Something inexplicable had happened, and for each one of us, it had been different: according to my memory, Milne and Moore had experienced it; according to Milne's memory, I alone had experienced it, and from Moore's perspective, the entire night was shrouded in the fog of total amnesia.

This was surely more frightening to Milne than anything we had hitherto experienced on Eilean Mòr, for he was the Principal Keeper, who had responsibility not only for the light, but for the safety of the men in his charge. He was answerable to the Northern Lighthouse Board, and in view of the tragic circumstances which had led to our being here, the Board would perhaps require an even more detailed account of our month's duty than would normally be the case. Superintendent Muirhead would want to speak with him at length, I had no doubt, in the hope of revealing some piece of information – however seemingly insignificant – which might lead to a solution to the mystery of the disappearance of Ducat, Marshall and MacArthur.

What would Milne be able to say about any of this? I could imagine how his report would seem, even to one as sympathetic as Mr. Muirhead, who would read it in the peace and safety of his office in George Street in Edinburgh. Would he believe any of it? Or would he recommend the dismissal of Milne and Moore from the service, judging them to be no longer trustworthy in the discharge of such an important duty? It would be unjust in the extreme, of course. But would the Superintendent have any alternative, were he to read a true and honest account of all that had befallen us so far on Eilean Mòr… and of what might yet befall us?

Milne had obviously decided that it would be better if Joseph were not told of the strange discrepancies between what he and I remembered of last night. I could well imagine the turmoil of his thoughts, the helplessness he must be feeling, for I felt exactly the same – as if the fabric of reality had come undone, revealing something frightening and impossible to understand beneath. Perhaps Milne wondered whether James Ducat had faced similar fears and uncertainties, whether recent history was, even now, in the process of repeating itself.

Joseph's voice took me away from my thoughts.

'Please answer me, Alec.'

'What?'

'You said you remember things differently from John. What did you mean by that?'

There was no point in lying to him, as Milne would doubtless have had me do. And so I told him everything I recalled from last night. When I had finished, he sat down at the table in silence. When he finally spoke, it was to echo the thought that had occurred to me earlier, and I looked at him in surprise.

'It's as if the world were split into two, with you remembering one thing, and John another,' he said.

'It seems that way.'

'But how could that be? It goes against all reason!'

'I don't know. But the alternatives are equally unsettling, I have to say.'

'Alternatives?'

'Either I am losing my mind, or John is losing his. There's no way of knowing which it is, since…'

'Since I remember nothing. If I had, I might have known the answer.'

'Yes.'

'But that still doesn't explain why I can't remember anything, does it? In fact, I'd say it puts me in the same boat with you and John.' Joseph shook his head. 'I don't know, Alec. *One* of us losing his reason and faculties, that I can accept, horrible as it is… but *all three of us?* At exactly the same time? I can't believe that. This isn't madness, Alec. It's something else.'

'What else could it be?'

'Both you and John saw something come onto the island last night. Each of you thinks it was the other who saw it, but the fact remains, *you saw the same thing*. What was it, and why couldn't you describe it? Was it the same thing that ripped away part of the safety rail down by the West Landing, which we saw when we arrived? Did it take away Ducat, Marshall and MacArthur? And if it did, why didn't it take us?'

'I don't know.'

'This is not madness… it is *not*.'

'Joseph is right.'

We both jumped in shock and turned to see Milne standing in the doorway leading to the sitting room.

'This is not madness. It *is* something else.'

'How long have you been standing there, John?' I asked.

Milne entered the kitchen. 'Not long. I've just been inspecting the buildings – and the north part of the island.'

'Why?' asked Joseph.

'Because that's the direction it came from, according to Alec – and apparently according to you and me as well.'

'Then you accept that something really did happen last night?' I said.

Milne walked across the kitchen in silence, and stopped at the door leading outside. Then he said, 'Will you come with me please, Alec?'

I stood up and went to the door. 'Where are we going?'

'There's something I want you to see. And when we've finished, I'll show Joseph.' He turned to Moore. 'We won't be long, laddie.'

Joseph looked from Milne to me and said, 'Understood, John.'

I took my oilskin from the peg, put it on and followed Milne outside. The air was icy and still, the high winds of last night having blown themselves away to nothing. The cobbles of the yard were slick with fallen rain, while the sea continued its incessant whisper. As we passed through the gate and walked around the low wall surrounding the light and its outbuildings, I glanced at the tower and the house.

'Any storm damage?' I asked.

'No, none.'

'What's this about, John?'

'You'll see.'

'Why can't you tell me?'

'You'll see.'

We walked the few yards up the slumped shoulder of the island to the summit. The Flannan Isles Light is constructed near to the highest point of Eilean Mòr, where the slope meets the island's northern flank, which plunges at a forty-five-degree angle into the sea. Here, one has the uncanny impression of standing upon the knuckle of an enormous, clenched fist. To the west, three more 'knuckles', formed by inlets cut deep into the island by countless millennia of the sea's action, fall away into the near distance. The ground is covered by tough grass, mottled here and there with patches of exposed rock. To the east-northeast, the tiny islet of Dearc na Sgeir crouches upon the ocean's surface in a faint haze of spindrift.

I slowed my pace as we approached the sharp drop – and came to a sudden halt when Milne pointed to the ground between the tower and the island's edge.

'There,' he said.

For several moments, I looked at the ground, not knowing what to say or even what to think.

Across the narrow patch of ground, there were patterns formed of bright yellow – almost white – grass, as if some corrosive substance had been poured there. I crouched down for a closer look. The short, tough blades of grass seemed undamaged, apart from the strange leeching of their colour.

Gingerly, I reached down towards the nearest patch, but Milne stayed my hand.

'Don't touch it, Alec.'

'Is it some kind of chemical burn, do you think?'

'Perhaps.'

'Caused by what?'

'Isn't it obvious? By whatever came up out of the sea last night.'

'But I've never heard of any kind of animal that leaves traces like this.'

Milne gave a short, humourless laugh. 'Aye, I'll go along with that. And I've never heard of any kind of animal that can mess up a man's memories and make him think that those memories belong to someone else!'

'So it wasn't an animal,' I said.

Milne thrust his hands in his pockets and stood stiffly beside me, gazing sternly into the north. 'I owe you an apology, Alec.'

'Why?'

He glanced down at me and smiled a slight, sad smile. 'I thought you were losing your mind. Last night, and this morning, I cursed Muirhead for allowing such an undependable man to come to Eilean Mòr with Joseph and me. I'd thought you just a weak-minded Occasional who had no business doing duty at a rock light. I was wrong. I'm sorry.'

'And what of the other things we've seen? The light, the fox, what happened in the store room, the sky. We saw them together.'

'Aye, that's true enough, but I believed that there was some ordinary explanation for them, even for what happened to the sky, though I couldn't think of it. Even now, I want to think that. But it's not possible any longer, is it? What happened last night... and this... well, I don't know, Alec.'

I stood up. 'There's no need to apologise for thinking me weak-minded, John. I confess, I was thinking the same about you.'

He gave me a sharp glance, saw the expression on my face, and smiled again. I offered him my hand, and he shook it.

'Look at the shapes,' he said then, indicating the patches of strangely-coloured grass.

The patches were curved in thin crescents and 'S' shapes, and I had the impression that they had been made by something like a heavy cord or rope: something long and flexible that had whipped across the ground.

Milne turned away, and pointed down the steep rocky incline that plunged into the foaming sea. 'And look there,' he said.

I followed where he was pointing, and saw the same discolouration on the bare rock face of the island's northern flank. 'Something was here,' I said.

'Aye... something.'

We stood in silence for some moments, listening to the murmur of the ocean.

'Did Joseph tell you that he can't remember a single thing about last night?' Milne asked.

I said nothing.

'It's all right, Alec. I know I asked him not to mention it, and I don't mind if he went against my wishes. That was before I came outside and saw this, before I realised that you weren't deluded.'

'Yes, he told me.'

'Why do you think that is?'

'How can I say? I'm not a doctor.'

'But you are an intelligent man, and any thought you might have – any suggestion, however wild and vague – might help me...'

'Help you to do what?'

He hesitated and then said, 'To keep us alive until the *Hesperus* returns.'

I turned to face him. 'You think we may well die here.'

'Ducat, Marshall and MacArthur are dead – at least, I hope they are, for the alternative doesn't bear thinking about. And so help me God, I think we'll have our work cut out to get off the island alive, and with our reason intact.' Suddenly, he seized my arm tightly and leaned close to me. 'We can do it, Alec – we *can* survive. But we'll have to keep our wits about us, and not fall prey to fear or mistrust: fear of what's out there, and mistrust of each other.'

'Aye, agreed,' I said.

'Good. And so I'll ask you again: why do you think Joseph has no memory of what happened last night?'

'I can think of three reasons,' I said.

'And what are they?'

'One: he does remember, but he's lying for some reason.'

'Do you think that could be true?'

'Perhaps... perhaps his fear is too great, and so he's denying that he remembers. But I doubt it.'

'As do I. Two?'

'Two: he was so shocked by what happened that his mind really did refuse to retain any memory of it.'

Milne nodded. 'And three?'

'Three... something doesn't *want* him to remember.'

Milne regarded me through narrow, thoughtful eyes. 'And why do you think that could be?'

'Perhaps, John,' I said, looking out upon the rippling grey ocean, 'we will have to wait for the answer to that question.'

15
Dream of a Strange Place

Like the light and the fox, whatever came out of the ocean on the night of the 18th of January, we never saw again. It was as if, having revealed itself to us once, it vanished from the world, leaving us to ask ourselves what it was and why it had appeared. For the next two days, things returned to normal, just as they had following previous events. But for us, of course, nothing about Eilean Mòr could ever be called 'normal' again. We looked at the island and the sea and the sky in a different way, as men who knew something of their unfathomable mysteries that no one else in the world knew. No one else, that is, but the three Lighthouse Keepers who had vanished.

Yes, our tasks were normal ones, but our state of mind was not, and I wondered if it ever would be again. In an effort to return to that form of mentality which I feared I had lost forever, I threw myself into my allotted duties with yet more diligence and attention to detail. At night, when I was on duty in the lightroom, I walked restlessly around the confined space, repeatedly checking the great lamps and the mechanism, making sure it was moving freely. I lost count of the number of times I checked that the oil canteens were full, and when the fountains needed filling, I made a careful note of how much oil we would need to bring up from the store room to renew the supply. I listened attentively to the sound of the mechanical escapement mechanism which kept the lens assembly rotating – even though I knew how much time would elapse before it needed to be re-wound. And while I was there, I refrained from looking out of the windows and into the darkness beyond.

While I was off light duty, I cleaned the entire house from top to bottom, dusting and wiping, mopping and dusting again; I swept the yard outside more than it needed to be swept, and when seabirds dashed themselves to death against the tower, as they are wont to do when the light is in operation, I did not curse them as usual, but carefully picked up their bodies one by one and threw them into the sea. Of course, I was well aware that I was attempting to escape from my thoughts; for those thoughts, if left unchecked, would turn again and again to that vast and terrible Unknown that had gathered upon Eilean Mòr. By throwing myself into ceaseless, even needlessly repetitive action, I was at least holding them at bay.

Once, I caught Joseph watching me while I was briskly mopping the kitchen floor, and I wondered whether he thought me foolish or, worse, strangely obsessed, in the manner of a madman endlessly engaged upon some bizarre and pointless task. But then, not long after, he too began to fall with increased enthusiasm to the various small but important jobs that keep a rock light functioning properly. And when it was my turn to cook, he came into the kitchen and asked if he might help, and when I turned to him, I saw such hope in his eyes that I was moved almost to tears, and I readily agreed, and together we prepared a good and wholesome meal for the three of us, which we rounded off a little extravagantly with a dram of whisky each.

I'm quite sure that Milne noticed all this, and more than once I saw him smile to himself, such was the man's wisdom. He knew what we were doing and why, and he approved, for he was the Principal, and our welfare and that of the light were in his hands. We were three men against that great and terrible Unknown, twenty miles out into the rolling sea with no help at hand, far from the comfort of friends and family and home. It would still be more than a week before the *Hesperus* came to relieve us, and we were facing a fathomless darkness, with nothing to guide us save the knowledge that three other men had also faced it and were now gone from the world.

*

Late on the evening of the 23rd of January, two days after Milne had discovered the traces upon the grass and the rocks of the island's northern side, I left Joseph in the lightroom, said goodnight to Milne and went to bed. Nothing untoward had happened for the last two days, and the tiredness I felt was that pleasant sort which comes from prolonged physical activity.

I got into bed and put out the oil lamp on the bedside table. The room faded into darkness periodically broken by a brief flaring behind the curtains as the light swung around above the house. There was no rain that night, and the wind was low and soothing, as if the world were whispering a lullaby. Sleep came quickly. My awareness, so filled with care and trepidation, retreated without my realising it, and I plunged into that state of nonbeing where time and space no longer have any meaning, through vast regions into nowhere.

Having completed that timeless journey which no man understands, my mind emerged into the realm of dreams, and almost immediately I experienced that curious sensation, which happens to people on occasion, of becoming aware that I *was* dreaming.

I found myself standing outside the lighthouse, on the southern slope of the island, so that the tower loomed tall above me. The light flashed twice every half-minute against a black sky devoid of stars. The air was bitter, and rain fell unnaturally slowly in great freezing torrents. I marvelled at the cold deluge coming from out of that starless sky, for there were no clouds and no winds to drive it so relentlessly into my upturned face.

As I looked south across the ocean, I saw that it was perfectly still – though not in the manner of a flat, calm lake.

The foaming crests and deep, dark troughs of its natural movement had been curtailed by the strange power of the dream, so that now it appeared as a rolling grey landscape of hills and valleys, complex ridges and narrow plains. And then the island itself began to move and sway, the rock turning to cool, grey liquid and the grass becoming fronded crests of pale green upon the surface of the waves. I sank to my waist and then further to my chest in this moving mass of liquid, and I was filled with fear and wonder at this reversal of the essential natures of the sea and the land.

And then stars appeared from out of the black sky, and it seemed that they were not stars at all, but living, moving bodies that rippled through the firmament, seething and flexing and breathing with strange life, like creatures of some limitless, lightless ocean. But it seemed to me that they were not merely inhabitants of this ocean: they were *part* of it, a visible expression of the unending depth of its eternity.

As they gathered together in groups far above me (and yet, it seemed, directly over my head), the cold rain altered its course and moved upwards, away from the frozen sea and the unfrozen land, into them. And then, as if my awareness were settling into the dream to the extent that I became conscious of my own physicality within that non-physical realm, I began to feel coldness seeping into my body, from skin to flesh to bone, and it was a coldness the like of which I had never felt before: it was the coldness of the space between worlds, where no warmth of human life could ever reach, and where human thought, feeling and awareness were eternally and irredeemably foreign and unbelonging.

I felt the terror of those spaces flood my being along with the cold, and in desperation I turned towards the lighthouse. There I saw three figures standing upon the balcony surrounding the lightroom, two dressed in heavy oilskins and one without. All were looking up into the firmament, at the bright shapes that were moving there, but as my gaze fell upon them, they all turned to look down at me, their forms periodically thrown into dark silhouette by the turning of the great beam.

I cried out to them, begging for help, shouting for them to come down and gather me out of that relentless, infinite cold. But they slowly shook their heads, and their faces were etched in such sadness, such monumental despair, that I thought I would die beneath their gaze.

In the midst of the dream I thought of Mary Ducat and of the dream she had described to me outside the Shore Station at Breasclete. And as if in response to this thought (I say 'as if', but who is to say that it was not indeed in direct response to it?), I sensed the approach of something vast and unseen, something that had no shape, but which was alive in some greater, more profound way than all the fragile life on God's earth.

And then I understood what Mary had said when she described her feeling that her dream had been stolen from her, for as I tried to claw my way out of the immense, eternal cold, I perceived the scene retreating from me: the frozen sea, the liquefied mass of the island, the sky full of strange, living stars, the lighthouse and its three lost, forlorn keepers, all seemed to be *gathered up in folds of living darkness and carried away* into the nothingness that surrounded my dreaming mind.

I was alone, drifting in a featureless void of sleep – and yet still aware that I was asleep. For how long I remained in this state I do not know. But when I awoke, it was to the sound of the fog horn and a world of thick white mist beyond my window.

NINE

Rebecca awoke suddenly. She was curled up in a corner of the sitting room, her arms wrapped tightly around herself, the cold hard floor pressing painfully against her left shoulder. For some moments, she lay still, her eyes wide open in the darkness, her mind racing.

What happened? she thought. *Oh God... what happened?*

A ghost of illumination flared briefly and dully as the automated light flung its beam out beyond the window into the night.

An impossible, premature night.

She heard someone nearby move and groan; someone else muttered something unintelligible. There was a gasp, which she thought came from Jennifer.

'Jesus Christ!' That was Max.

She felt someone leaning over her. She gave a soft whimper.

'Becks... Rebecca.'

She turned over and looked up into a dark-shrouded face. 'Nick...'

'Are you okay?' He placed a hand on her shoulder, and she seized it in both of hers and held onto it as tightly as if he were trying to pull her out of some bottomless abyss. She felt tears welling in her eyes.

'Nick… what the *fuck* just happened?'

'Whatever happened, I think we missed it,' said Max from across the room. He was fiddling with one of their battery-powered lanterns, a small quartz-halogen torch clenched between his teeth. He switched the lantern on and sat cross-legged on the floor. 'Anyone got any theories?' He heaved a great, ragged sigh. 'Any at all?'

Rebecca sat up and leaned back against the wall, drawing her legs up to her chest and wrapping her arms around them. She looked at the others. Jennifer had stood up and was looking comically around the room, as if she had never seen it before. Her hair had come loose from its neat bun and was hanging in grey strands over her face. Her gaze fell on Donald, who was still lying by the wall, and hurried to him.

'How is he?' asked Nick.

'Asleep,' she replied. 'Still alive… but asleep.'

'What time was it when Becks started reading?' asked Max.

'I think it was about three thirty,' replied Nick, still looking at Rebecca.

'Three thirty in the afternoon,' Max repeated. He looked at his watch. 'And now it's one fifteen a.m.'

Rebecca looked up at Nick. Suddenly unable to utter a sound – even a whisper – she mouthed the words: *What happened?*

Nick shook his head, and the fear and confusion in his eyes was so unbearable that Rebecca shut her own and turned away.

'I can't believe this… I mean, I can't friggin' *believe* this!'

'Calm down, Max,' said Nick over his shoulder.

'Calm *down?* What the fuck? I mean, one minute we're sitting here listening to Becks read from that goddamned book, and the next…' His voice trailed off, and he put his head in his hands. 'Jesus… Jesus.'

'Max is right,' said Jennifer. 'I can't believe we've been unconscious for nearly ten hours. I can't imagine what could have caused it.'

'Where's Whitley Strieber when you need him?' said Max.

'What do you mean?' asked Jennifer.

Max shrugged. 'You know… that whole missing time thing.'

'You think we were… *abducted* by something?' said Rebecca.

'Hell, *I* don't know. All I know is, you don't just fall asleep for ten hours without warning – unless we've all suddenly got narcolepsy or something.'

'Unlikely,' said Nick.

'Perhaps we weren't unconscious,' said Jennifer. 'Perhaps nothing happened.'

Max glanced at her. 'Huh?'

'We know that whatever Dalemore and the others encountered here had the ability – whether consciously intended or otherwise – to alter their perceptions of reality. Think about the discrepancies in their accounts of that thing coming out of the ocean and onto the island. If we're correct in our assumption that we're witnessing the intersection of another dimension – another aspect of reality – with our own… then it may affect our perception of time. Or it may affect time itself…'

'You mean,' said Nick, 'that nothing happened during those ten hours… because those ten hours *didn't exist?*'

Jennifer nodded. 'A disruption in the flow of time – or our *perception* of the flow of time. A momentary dislocation in the way we experience reality.'

Nick gave a despairing sigh. 'My God, Jennifer. Do you know what you've just described?'

She frowned at him. 'I'm not sure I follow.'

'You've just described madness – only not as a phenomenon occurring within the human mind, but in the external world. *We're in a region of the world that has lost its sanity.*'

Rebecca was about to say something but then suddenly recoiled from the wall against which she had been leaning. She scrambled to her feet and moved quickly to the centre of the room. Everyone jumped. Max immediately got to his feet.

'What's wrong?' Nick demanded as he went to her.

'I'm not sure,' she said. 'But for some reason, I don't want to be close to that wall.'

'Why the hell not?' said Max.

'I don't know!' she shouted, and suddenly the tears came, and she turned to Nick and held onto him tightly as she began to sob.

'It's all right, Becks,' he whispered as he stroked her hair. 'It's all right.'

'No it's not!' she said, her voice muffled against his chest.

'Wait,' said Max. Slowly, with immense reluctance, he took a step towards the window. 'Do you hear that?'

Rebecca shut her eyes and held her breath, listening along with the others.

'What is it?' Jennifer whispered.

His voice oddly calm and uninflected, Max replied: 'Movement. Something's moving outside.'

'The wind,' whispered Jennifer.

'There is no wind.' Max turned and looked at them all. 'No wind…'

Nick went and stood beside him, and together they listened. After a few moments, Rebecca wiped her eyes on the sleeve of her sweater and joined them. She listened intently, breathing as quietly as she could, her breath coming in quick, shallow gasps. She struggled to identify the sound, but all she could do was decide what it was not.

It was not the sound of footsteps, nor was it the sound of an animal. It was not the fluttering of a night bird's wings, nor was it the soft rattle of a bat's. *Do they come this far out?* she asked herself. *Do bats fly over the sea?* She tried to compare the sound to something with which she was familiar, tried to imagine what might be making it.

It seemed to contain several elements: sounds *within* a sound that were being constantly repeated. They reminded her of the soft crackle of a sheet of paper being wadded up into a ball; of something tapping very gently on a distant drum; of the low, fitful moan of something sleeping uneasily; of the breathy hiss of a gas lamp brought suddenly to life. And beneath all those sounds, a soft, wet movement, viscous, shuffling, *alive*. She could not imagine anything making a sound like that.

She recalled her sudden, uncontrollable desire to get away from the wall, and she knew that her unconscious mind had reacted instinctively to the presence of something on the other side, outside the house. The reptilian core of her brain had recoiled from it, as wild animals do from predators.

'What should we do?' Jennifer whispered, looking at each of them in turn. 'What should we do?'

'Screw this!' said Max, and he strode purposefully towards the window.

Nick reached out with one hand. 'Max!'

'I wanna see what's making that *goddamned* sound.'

He leaned in close to the window, his face reflected in the obsidian mirror blackness beyond. The others watched his face as it turned to left and right, as he craned his neck trying to glimpse beyond the window frame. His reflection was briefly overwhelmed by the beam from the light above, before reappearing in the window.

'There's nothing out there,' he said. 'At least, nothing I can see.'

'Max, please come away from the window,' said Jennifer.

Max turned around. Rebecca couldn't look at his face, couldn't bring herself to stop looking at the window, in which the back of his head was now reflected. She was waiting for something to come through, waiting for something unimaginable to smash the glass, reach in and drag Max outside.

For fuck's sake, come away from the window!

'Nick,' said Max. 'What do you say to taking a look around out there?'

'*What? Are you crazy?*' Rebecca cried. She clutched his arm. 'Nick, don't.'

'I'd rather not,' Nick replied. 'But...' he smiled at Max. 'If I don't, you're still going to go, aren't you? I mean, you really are that much of an arsehole.'

Max chuckled. 'Not quite, Nicky. But I have to tell you something. I've never run away from anything in my life, and I never hid from anything or anyone. That just ain't my style. I wanna see what's out there, right now. If it's dangerous and wants in, then it'll get in, and we're not as safe as we might think we are. And if it's nothing – if what we're hearing is just some trick of acoustics or some such – well, then we'll know that too by going outside. And we won't have to spend the rest of the night shivering like scared kids. What do you say?'

'Hurricanes,' said Rebecca.

Max glanced at her. 'What?'

'You said you've never run from anything in your life. But you've run from hurricanes.'

Max said nothing. Instead, he went to the rear wall of the sitting room and began to rummage around on the equipment shelves. Presently, he came back with two large, heavy spanners, one of which he handed to Nick, who hefted the makeshift weapon dubiously. 'Think this'll do any good?'

'Would you rather go without it?' asked Max.

'Point taken.'

'I'm going with you,' said Rebecca.

Nick glanced at her. 'Absolutely not.'

'Don't tell me what I can and can't do.'

Nick shook his head resolutely. 'Not going to happen, Becks.'

'Listen, Nick,' she said. 'I'm not going to stay in here like...' she glanced at Max '...like a *scared kid*, while you go out there. I'm just not going to do it!'

'And what about the way you came away from that wall? It was like someone had put two hundred volts through you. What's going to happen if you go outside and...'

'And what? There's something dangerous out there? Something lethal? Max is right. If that's the case, and it wants to get in here, it'll get in. Whether we're inside or outside doesn't really matter, does it?'

'I... suppose not, but...'

'No buts, Nick! And what if it attacks you and Max? Then Jennifer and... and Donald and I are left in here, aren't we... *defenceless*.'

Max looked at the expression on Nick's face and whistled. 'The girl's good.'

'All right,' Nick sighed. 'But stay close to me. We'll do one circuit around the lighthouse – *one* – and then come back inside. Shouldn't take more than a couple of minutes.'

'And what if something's out there?' asked Jennifer.

'Then we'll be back inside in a lot less than a couple of minutes,' said Max. 'But at least then we'll know what the deal is.'

'Jennifer, you stay here with Donald,' said Nick. 'We won't be long.'

Jennifer nodded.

Max picked up a hammer from the shelf and handed it to Rebecca. They all looked at each other for several moments, each expecting – hoping – that someone would say something else. But no one did.

Nick looked down at his spanner, hefted it uncertainly, then said, 'All right. Let's... let's take a look outside.'

Taking their weapons and some torches, they filed out of the sitting room and along the corridor leading to the front door. Max was leading the way. Suddenly, he stopped dead. Nick bumped into him. 'What is it?' he asked, trying to see past his friend in the gloom.

'Christ, I'd forgotten all about that,' said Max quietly.

'Forgotten what?'

Max stood aside to let Nick see.

'Oh God,' he whispered.

The front door was still standing ajar, its frame splintered from Max's kicks the previous evening. They had planned to repair it during the afternoon... the afternoon that had vanished.

Max gave a low chuckle.

'What's so funny?' Nick demanded.

'I'm sorry, man. But there we were, saying that whatever's outside could probably get into the house any time it chose. How right we were.'

'Never mind that now,' said Rebecca. 'Let's just go out and get this over with.'

'I hear you, Becks.' Max continued on to the door, slowly took hold of the handle, and pulled it completely open. Then, taking a deep breath, he stepped out into the darkness.

TEN

They huddled together on the doorstep in the still night. Although it was cold, there was no wind, and the stars ranged vastly overhead glittered like tiny flecks of silver on black velvet. All around, the sea hissed softly: a great exhalation, as if it had drawn in its breath at the beginning of the world and was now slowly letting it out, as it had always done and always would, for as long as the Sun lived and the world turned.

The light flashed out its warning every fifteen seconds from the tower above them, momentarily casting a cold, spectral light upon the flagstones of the little courtyard. They stood still and listened. For perhaps a minute, they heard nothing but the sea.

And then, gradually, the sea fell silent, and the group looked at each other.

'I can't hear it anymore,' whispered Rebecca.

'Nor can I,' Nick replied.

Rebecca clutched her weapon tightly. *Even the sea knows something is wrong*, she thought.

Max stepped away from the porch and shone his torch to the right and left. Nick followed and stood beside him, holding his gas-powered lantern above his head.

'I don't see anything,' said Max in a low, steady voice.

'All right,' said Nick. 'Let's get this over with. Which way do you want to go?'

'Does it matter?'

'I suppose not... left, then.'

'Okay.'

They moved further away from the door, treading carefully, as if the flagstones were a thin crust of ice on a deep lake.

'Becks,' said Max, glancing over his shoulder. 'Stay between us. Nick, take up the rear, and keep a watch behind us. If you see anything, holler.'

'Don't worry. I will.'

Ahead, the floor of the compound angled left around the corner of the house. The darkness was solid, palpable, unrelieved by the paradoxical brightness of the scattered stars. They continued forward, straining to catch the slightest movement, the faintest sound, but the only movement was that of the light cast by their torches, the only sound that of their own breathing.

And then they heard it, that strange confusion of disparate noises, and they stopped and held their breath and listened, as field mice listen to the flap of the falcon's wings.

'It's around the corner,' whispered Max.

The crackle of paper, the soft beat of a distant drum, the low moan of uneasy sleep, the hiss of flame, the shuffle of something wet and prehensile...

Rebecca felt her breath quicken in her chest. *It's there. Max is right... it is there. Jesus Jesus Jesus...*

Max edged forward. After what seemed like an hour, they reached the corner of the house. Max glanced back once, then took a deep breath and thrust his head around the corner.

For an instant, it seemed to Rebecca that the sounds quickened and grew louder, as if whatever was making them had been startled, and then they subsided again to their former volume, a strange substitute for the lost whisper of the sea.

Max's voice drifted back to her. 'Nothing… nothing there.'

It's playing with us, thought Rebecca. *Playing hide and seek*. Briefly, she considered voicing the thought, but decided not to. She didn't want to hear it said – not by her, not by anyone. Even though Max couldn't see anything, Rebecca still felt the presence of something abnormal and unclean. That cold, unassailable conviction was only partly the result of the sounds it made: there was another factor at work, as though the reptile brain at the centre of her head were responding *directly* to it, without recourse to her physical senses.

'Can you feel it?' she asked with a trembling, despairing voice. 'Can you *feel* it like I do?'

Max glanced over his shoulder at her, then looked at Nick.

'I don't want to be the only one who…'

'I think we can all feel it, Becks,' said Nick. She looked at his face, which was cast into gruesome pallor by the pale light from their torches, and tried to gauge whether he was telling her the truth. But she couldn't decide. She thought about her discovery of the manuscript and the carved stone. Had she unwittingly forged some connection with whatever existed here? Had it somehow *chosen* her to find those strange artefacts? She shuddered and struggled to hold back the tears that were threatening to flow once again.

'Come on,' said Max, and disappeared around the corner of the house.

The others followed, the dark wall on their left, the ocean on their right – black, limitless, silent.

They walked slowly, listening to the sounds of their breathing and their soft footfalls on the cobblestones, and listening to that other sound that seemed to come from all around them.

Why can't we see it? Rebecca wondered. *Is it because we're inside it? Has it already eaten us? Us, and the island, and the world?*

And as she thought this, the sound again quickened and grew momentarily louder, as if the thing that was making it had heard the thought.

Can you hear me? Do you know what I'm thinking?

Rebecca waited for a further response, but there was none. The sound returned to its former volume, while above them the stars twinkled mockingly in the infinite depths of the universe, and the light at the top of the tower responded like a slow and feeble pulsar.

They turned the next corner, and entered the part of the enclosure containing the outbuildings. They paused, and listened.

'Is it louder here…?' said Max.

'I'm not sure,' Nick replied. 'Why would it be?'

They looked around, and their gazes came to rest on the door to the larger outbuilding.

It's in there, thought Rebecca.

Max walked over to the building and reached for the door handle.

Shit!

He tried the handle, but the door remained shut fast.

'Locked,' he said.

Nick joined him. 'What the hell?' He tried the handle himself. 'Donald was in here… it was unlocked… how can it be locked again now?'

Max gave the door a disgusted look and then turned away. 'Goddamn it.'

'All right,' said Nick. 'Let's get going. We'll complete our circuit and go back inside.'

Max gave the door one last try. Rebecca had a vision of him throwing rocks at a sleeping tiger – except that whatever was making the sound was not asleep – and said, 'Come on, Max. Let's go.'

He sighed and rejoined the group, and together they continued around the house. As they gained the final corner, the sound that had accompanied them began to grow fainter, and by the time they reached the front door, it had ceased altogether.

'Do you think it's gone?' asked Rebecca.

'I'm not buying that,' Max replied, pushing open the door. 'Come on, let's get inside, quick!'

With a greater relief than she had ever felt before, Rebecca followed Max inside. Nick pushed the door closed and leaned against it. 'What are we going to do about this?' he asked.

'There's a couple of old wooden chairs in the sitting room,' Max replied. 'We'll jam one under the door handle.'

Rebecca frowned. 'Do you think that'll do any good?'

'I don't know.' He checked the time. 'It's one forty-five. We should stand watch until morning. We'll do a shift each. I'll go first, then Nick.'

Max brought the two chairs from the sitting room. He placed one against the front door, so that its back was wedged firmly under the handle. The other he placed a few feet away, facing the door. He sat down. The chair creaked loudly in protest.

'If anything happens…' said Nick.

Max nodded. 'I'll come wake you up.'

'And then what?' asked Rebecca.

Nick looked at the door in silence for a long moment. 'Then we'll defend ourselves,' he said.

When he and Rebecca returned to the sitting room, they found Jennifer sitting beside Donald, holding his hand.

'How is he?' asked Nick.

Jennifer turned haunted eyes to him. 'He's awake... he's been saying things...'

'What things?'

Donald's mouth started working again, a tiny strangled voice – barely more than a whisper – issuing from his twitching lips.

Jennifer shook her head. 'I don't know what to make of it. Come and listen.'

Nick and Rebecca crouched down beside them and bent close, trying to make out what Donald was saying.

'... Mother Hydra... Mother Hydra... she is coming I can feel her she is coming close now so close through the spaces filled with things that move but are not alive oh God please my God please help me the separating void is birthing that place those things they are here descending the moon ladder transfiguring the night oh dear God and Jesus Christ preserve and protect me I can see them inside my mind the rotating cylinder the carved rim Christ be with us through the void the continuum where are you Lord please where are you save me save us don't let them into the world I can see them substance without flesh they can't be they shouldn't be they mustn't exist... inside my mind the rotating cylinder here descending the moon ladder transfiguring translating now through the void the Christ – preserve and protect me I can see – are you save me save us don't let them the carved rim Christ be with us they are world I can see them – substance without continuum where are you Lord please exist but I can see them where she is coming I can see she is coming – flesh they can't be – Mother Hydra Mother Hydra Mother Hydra birthing that place...'

Rebecca looked away, feeling nauseous, and moved to the other side of the room.

'What the hell does all this mean?' Nick asked Jennifer. 'Do you think he's been... driven insane?'

'I don't know… but one thing's for sure: he experienced some unimaginable trauma in that outbuilding, and he can't get past it… he can't assimilate it.' She shook her head. 'I take it you didn't see anything outside.'

'No, nothing; we just heard the sound.'

'I was expecting something terrible to happen.'

Nick looked down at Donald, who was still muttering his incomprehensible monologue. 'It did,' he said.

ELEVEN

WEDNESDAY 22 JULY
8.25 AM

The first thing Rebecca did when she woke up was to check her watch. She had drifted into a fitful, uneasy sleep at about three o'clock in the morning, after more than an hour of huddling in her sleeping bag and listening breathlessly for any sounds of movement outside the house. The sigh of the ocean had returned soon after they went inside, and she had been reminded of the films she had seen over the years, whose titles now escaped her, in which the sounds of crickets, cicadas and bullfrogs ceased at the approach of some monster or alien. That was what it had been like last night, although it was not tiny, unseen animals that had been shocked into silence by whatever had made that noise, but the very *ocean*. How could that be?

She thought of what Jennifer had said about one's perception of time – of reality – being altered somehow. But was that true? Was it only the *perception* of reality that was altered... or was it reality itself? Had they only perceived the ocean to become silent, or had it actually happened?

She thought of her parents in Avignon, spending a few weeks of the summer in the warmth and beauty of the French countryside. *God, I wish I was there*, she thought. *I wish Nick and I were there right now*. In fact, she wished she were *anywhere* but here. When she had first set foot on Eilean Mòr, she'd had the impression that the island wanted to be left alone. Now she knew that she had instinctively perceived the essential reality of the place; she understood that there were some places in the world where human beings simply do not belong.

She thought of their fearful, trembling circuit of the house in a vast darkness unrelieved by the cold, hard light of the unsympathetic stars, and she wondered how many more places like this there were – on this world and others. *Could we ever live out there? Is there a place for us? Or do we exist in a tiny region of sanity in an infinite ocean of madness?*

She looked across at Jennifer, who was curled up and facing the wall, still asleep. She hadn't gone near Donald for the rest of the night, hadn't even wanted to look at him, so Nick and Max had checked on him periodically, giving him water from one of their canteens, which he had swallowed soundlessly.

What had happened to him? What had he seen in the outbuilding? She thought of what Dalemore had written, how he and Milne had thrown their full weight against the door that night long ago, and how it had remained firmly shut against two strong men. Whatever had been in there was powerful and dangerous... but what was it?

Jennifer moaned softly and stirred in her sleeping bag. Rebecca went over to her. 'What time is it?' Jennifer asked.

'Nearly half past eight. How are you feeling?'

'All right. Where are Nick and Max?'

'I don't know. I guess they're outside.'

Jennifer sat up and looked at Donald.

'He's asleep,' said Rebecca. 'What was he *saying* last night?'

Jennifer heaved a huge, ragged sigh and shook her head. 'I don't know. Nonsense words. At least... I *hope* they were nonsense.'

Rebecca felt the hairs on the back of her neck rise. 'He was delusional,' she said.

But Jennifer shook her head. 'I think we've seen too much for me to believe that, no matter how much I want to. Here, in this place… either everything is madness, or nothing is.'

Rebecca was about to say something but was interrupted as Nick came into the room. She saw the expression on his face and said: 'What now?'

'I think you should come outside and look at this.'

She hadn't thought her heart could sink any lower, but Nick's face and his tone of voice proved her wrong. Without a word, she and Jennifer followed him from the room and the house.

Overhead, the sky was thickly strewn with grey, consumptive clouds, as if it had been infected with some unimaginable disease, while all around the sea muttered and moaned as if wounded. The air felt unnaturally cloying and humid, the way it did in latitudes far further south than this. And Rebecca could smell something which she couldn't identify, but which wasn't the ocean brine.

Max was standing beyond the wall of the enclosure, looking down at something she couldn't see, something on the ground.

She and Jennifer followed Nick through the gate and onto the rough, sparse grass.

'What the hell is that?' she asked, gazing down at what lay at their feet.

The ground had been churned up in a long, meandering line that stretched away from them across the island and vanished over its ragged edge. To Rebecca, it looked like the track an earthmover might make, except that instead of regular, parallel grooves cut into the soil, this was composed of crazily-angled troughs perhaps three inches deep and about twelve long. And earthmovers left two tracks, whereas here there was only one.

Max got down on his haunches and touched the strangely disturbed earth, shaking his head.

Rebecca repeated her question, a little louder this time. 'What *is* that?'

'I have no idea,' said Max. 'But whatever made it was heavy.'

'It looks like it was made by a vehicle of some kind,' said Jennifer.

Max offered her a wan smile. 'Yeah, but what *kind* of vehicle? Something with only one wheel? The unicycle from Planet X?'

'Could it have been whatever was making that noise last night?' wondered Rebecca.

'It's possible,' said Nick. 'I mean, we couldn't tell which direction it was coming from... it might have been coming from here. At any rate, it certainly wasn't made by an animal. At least, no animal I've ever seen or heard of. I agree it looks like something left by some kind of tracked vehicle... like a tank or something.'

Max shook his head. 'A tank with only one track... and look at the depressions – they're all over the place! No two of them are parallel; they're skewed every which way. I'd like to see what kind of tank *this* was.'

'Would you?' said Rebecca.

Max looked at her in silence, then returned his attention to the ground.

Rebecca turned around and began to walk back to the house. 'I'm going to make some breakfast,' she said.

'I'll give you a hand,' said Jennifer, hurrying after her and leaving the men to ponder their discovery.

Together, Rebecca and Jennifer took their gas stove and pots and pans into what had once been the kitchen. The room still contained a large table and several work surfaces. They placed their cooking equipment on the table and then returned to the sitting room to retrieve their food supplies. Jennifer made coffee, while Rebecca measured out portions of porridge.

'I wonder if Dalemore and the others saw anything like that,' Jennifer said.

'We'll find out. As soon as we've finished breakfast, we'll read the rest of his manuscript.'

Jennifer stopped what she was doing and looked out of the kitchen window. 'I wonder if it will help.'

16
THE THREE

Feeling tired and ill at ease, I threw off the covers, got out of bed and drew the curtains. My room faced south, and as I looked through my window, I could see almost nothing of the island – nothing but an insubstantial smear of the palest green beneath a mantle of milk-white fog. The sea was lost in the whiteness, its presence unhinted at, save the ever-present sigh of its movement, and the other islands of the Flannans were misted into total invisibility. The fog horn sounded again, a desolate, blaring cry to warn any ships in the area that here was a lethal hazard, a place to be avoided if they wished to make port safely.

As I dressed, I thought of those ships, of their passengers and crews: men and women bound for destinations near and far for reasons I would never know. Some would be beginning their voyages, some ending them, but none would be aware of we Keepers who stood guard here for their sake. The crews, of course, would know of Eilean Mòr and the other Flannan Isles, but even they would have not the slightest inkling of the terrible strangeness that had settled upon us as completely as the fog that now wrapped the island in its thick, damp cloak.

And for a moment, I wished that I were aboard one of those invisible ships, making a firm heading away from this place, towards the world of God and humanity.

I went to the kitchen, where I found Joseph preparing breakfast. The smell of porridge and kippers was good, but I did not feel like eating, and said that I would just take a mug of tea up to the lightroom. I was due to relieve Milne, and I expected to be sounding the horn all day, for the fog was of that type that does not leave willingly.

Joseph looked very tired, and I asked him if he was all right.

'Ach, I'm fine,' he replied. 'But there was such a flaff last night that I hardly got a wink of sleep.'

'What are you talking about, Joseph?' I said with a smile. 'There was no flaff last night; the wind was hardly more than a whisper.'

He returned my smile as he replied, 'Well now! You're a heavy sleeper, and no mistake, Alec!'

In fact, I am not an especially heavy sleeper, and had there been high winds during the night, there was little doubt that I would have been awoken by them. I thought of pressing the point, of insisting that the night had been calm, but I stopped myself, and instead I nodded and went up to the lightroom. I had a strange, sick feeling in the pit of my stomach. Joseph had heard loud gales all night, and I had heard nothing. I didn't want to think about what this might mean, but when I entered the lightroom and bid Milne good morning, I couldn't resist asking him how the night had been.

'Peaceful enough,' he replied. 'No more than a wee pirr now and then.'

No more than a wee pirr: no more than a gentle gust of wind from time to time. I did not want to say anything more, but I realised that, in our present circumstances, I owed it to the Principal to make him aware of anything unusual. Over the past couple of days, I had found myself hoping that the strangeness had gone from the island. I was quite certain that Milne and Moore were entertaining similar hopes, and I wondered if Milne would hate me for saying what I was about to say.

'I've just seen Joseph in the kitchen…'

'Aye, and those kippers smell fine indeed.'

'He told me there were high gales all night.'

'What?'

'That's what he said: such a flaff last night that he hardly got a wink of sleep.'

'He's mistaken,' Milne said quickly and decisively.

'That's what I thought. I'm quite sure that high winds would have woken me, but I slept soundly. There were no high winds last night, were there John?'

He frowned and shook his head. 'No, there were not.'

I looked out through the windows at the solid sheet of white beyond. 'This is going to last.'

'Aye, it came on in the wee hours and grew and grew. I want you to keep the lamps lit today, Alec. And sound the horn at regular intervals.'

'Understood.'

Milne turned to leave.

'Are you going to say anything to Joseph?' I asked.

He halted, still with his back to me. 'What is there to say?'

'Nothing, I suppose.'

Milne carried on walking and disappeared down the stairs.

*

The day wore on slowly. Each minute of my watch in the lightroom felt like an hour, as though time itself were ensnared in the fog's thickness. I re-wound the light's escapement mechanism, sounded the horn and went to stand by the windows that gave onto the tower's circular balcony. The horn's echoes drifted away into the far distance through the unmoving whiteness. The silence all about was so great, so heavy, that it seemed uninterrupted by the whispering of the sea; as if the whispering and the silence were two separate things, born of two separate worlds that would never come into contact with one another through all the ages of the universe.

I leaned forward and put my face close to the windows, trying to see something of the world beyond, but there was nothing but the fog, vast and featureless, stretching, it seemed, into eternity. With no point of reference beyond the tower, I began to feel a little dizzy, as though floating without anchor to the earth in this sea of white air. I fancied I could feel its cloying dampness upon my skin, and its coldness seep into my lungs.

Suddenly, I had the intense desire to see something – anything – apart from the fog. I briefly considered going out onto the balcony and looking directly down onto the island's summit. But this was the north side, the place where we had seen the patches of discoloured grass and rock, and I did not want to look at them again.

I moved away from the windows and sounded the horn again, and this time I winced at its despondent blare, its thunderous declaration of loneliness and desolation. I walked across to the section of the lightroom that looked south across the island, and with some relief I saw that a small tract of land was still visible, sloping down and away into pale obscurity. This sliver of pallid green suspended in a vast, silent white world seemed at once very close and unthinkably distant, and I had the sudden, intense feeling that I was irrevocably parted from it: a poor creature, lonely and forlorn, adrift in an endless nothingness more profound than death.

I thought of Mary Ducat and the promise I had made to her. How stupid I had been to assure her that I would discover what had happened to her husband and the other Keepers. What arrogance to claim such an impossible quest as my own! For such was the power of the thing that lived here, that success could only bring the same ruin upon me as that which had visited them. Perhaps I *would* discover the truth, and would soon find myself facing the core of the mystery, but even then, I suspected that it would be nothing more than a flash of terrible understanding in the moment before oblivion.

Yes, perhaps I would be able to keep my promise to Mary, but now I was certain that it would come at a price, and the price was that she would never know.

I stood still for many minutes and watched the fog upon the island, watched and waited, without knowing what I waited for... until a single shout drifted up to me from downstairs.

I closed my eyes and listened. There was silence for a time, and then another shout. I recognised Joseph's voice, barking out Milne's name. Again he called, and still I stood motionless, with my eyes tightly closed.

Another shout, and this time it was met with a reply. I heard chattering voices, raised in alarm, and then the sound of footfalls upon the stairs leading up to the lightroom.

I opened my eyes and turned, and I saw Milne and Moore emerging from the stairwell. They hurried past me without saying a word and came to a halt before the windows facing south over the island. Joseph then ran to the door leading to the tower's balcony, and before Milne could stop him, he flung it open, stepped onto the balcony, seized the iron railings and leaned out into the white nothingness. Milne shouted at him to get back inside, but then he too went out, and together they stood there, gazing out from the tower.

Slowly I walked to the door and stood there and waited for them to tell me what had happened. I could not bring myself to ask them directly. I waited a long time, for they stood there on the balcony as though transfixed by the fog, as though it contained some strange, mind-numbing agent that had found its way into their panting lungs. Presently I realised that their minds were anything but dulled: they were as if seized with a fever, and when they glanced at each other, I saw that their eyes were wide and clear and were bright with an emotion that might have been excitement, hope, or terror.

'Can you see them?' cried Joseph.

Milne shook his head, but then he grasped Joseph's arm and pointed. 'Yes! There!'

'How many?'

'Three.'

'Three!'

Milne glanced over his shoulder at me. 'Alec! Get out here and look at this.'

I did as he ordered and stood beside them on the balcony, feeling the cold clamminess of the fog settling upon my face. For a few moments, I tried in vain to see what they were pointing at, but then I became aware of three figures standing perhaps thirty yards away upon the hazy cloud of green that was the entirety of the visible land. It was difficult to make them out: they were almost completely shrouded by the fog. In fact, they were hardly more than vague shapes of a slightly darker hue than the surrounding whiteness, and yet, as I stared at them I had the impression that the figures were shaped like men.

'What can you see, Alec?' asked Milne.

'I'm not sure,' I replied.

'Joseph and I saw them from the sitting room. They are men - I'm certain of it.'

'But how...? Joseph began.

'Could the *Hesperus* have returned early?' I wondered.

'Unlikely in this weather,' said Milne. 'And even if it had, they would have sounded their own horn or fired a rocket to let us know they were near.'

'Then who are they?' I asked.

'The lost keepers,' whispered Joseph. 'They must be the lost keepers!'

The three figures moved in the enveloping whiteness - or rather, they seemed to seep through it, like an ink stain moves across a sheet of blotting paper.

'It's not them,' said Milne, shaking his head. 'They're gone from the island, God help them.'

'You're wrong, John,' said Joseph vehemently. 'It *must* be them.'

'Think about what you're saying, Joseph,' I said. 'How could they have survived out there for three weeks, out in the cold and rain with no food and water? Why didn't they come into the house?'

'Perhaps they don't *need* food and water and shelter anymore,' Joseph replied.

'What the devil are you talking about?' Milne snapped.

Joseph looked at him. 'After all that's happened, John, is it really so hard to believe?'

'You think they're forerunners... the phantoms of those poor lost men? I won't believe that.'

'Perhaps we should go out and speak to them,' I said, tentatively.

Milne turned to look at me, and from the expression on his face I knew that he was wondering whether I had gone insane.

I avoided his gaze and looked again into the depths of the fog, at the three figures that moved there. So obscuring was the smoky whiteness that their very movement was indistinct, and I could not decide whether they were approaching the lighthouse or receding from it. It was true that their appearance was vaguely that of men, but such was the fog's infuriating thickness that it was more by analogy that I thought them man-shaped, than by direct observation. In the same way that a shape in a cloud can be said to look like a face, or patterns in a rock can be said to look like a painted landscape, I could not avoid the feeling that those three shapes only *looked* like men.

I felt a horrible combination of frustration and dread rising in me as I tried to discern more detail in the shapes.

And then Milne had the idea that should have occurred to us instantly. He went back into the lightroom, and returned a few moments later with a collapsible telescope, which he trained upon the figures.

'Can you see anything?' I asked.

He shook his head as he handed me the telescope. 'It just magnifies the obscurity. Damn this fog!'

I looked through the instrument and saw that he was right. Magnification revealed no further detail, had no effect other than to increase my discomfort at examining the indistinct forms more closely. I lowered the telescope and handed it to Joseph.

Milne cupped his hands around his mouth, and called out, *'Hello there! Can you hear me?'*

There was no immediate response from the figures. But when Milne called out a second time, they began to move slowly through the fog, towards the lighthouse.

'They're coming,' said Joseph, and he shouted into the whiteness, 'James Ducat! Thomas Marshall! Donald MacArthur! Is that you? Answer me, for the love of God!'

But there was no answer – just the continued approach of the three figures towards us.

'It must be them,' said Joseph.

Milne put a hand on his shoulder. 'Joseph.'

'Who else could it be?' the lad demanded of us both. 'Who else is out here?'

Milne looked at me helplessly. 'I wonder if he's right. Who else *is* out here?'

'No men,' I replied. 'No men but us on the island. So… it must be that these are not men.'

'What are you saying, Alec?' whispered Milne.

'It's as I said just now, John: Ducat and the others couldn't have survived out there for three weeks, and there *are no other men but us on the island now.*'

We looked again out over the balcony at the approaching figures, and it occurred to me that, very soon, they would emerge completely from the fog, and we would be able to see clearly who or what they were.

'I'm tired of this,' said Joseph very quietly.

Milne glanced at him. 'What was that?'

Joseph fixed him with a glassy, wide-eyed look. 'I said I'm tired of this, John! I'm tired of this place and the things that happen here. I'm tired of being afraid, of this sick fear that's like a disease eating away at us. It's as if something is taunting us, something that can cast us from the face of the earth if it wishes… but doesn't wish to – not yet. It's making us suffer first! Why? *Why?*'

'I know how you feel, Joseph,' I said. 'We both know how you feel. But we have no choice but to stay here, no matter what might happen…'

'I understand that, Alec. But that doesn't mean we have to wait for it, trembling on our knees! Something has come to us again, and this time we can all see it, and this time it's within reach!' He backed away from us, towards the door to the lightroom.

'What are you doing?' said Milne.

'I'm going outside to face it, to confront it, like a man!'

I took a step towards him as he went inside and stalked towards the stairwell leading down into the house. I glanced back at Milne, who was still looking down onto the island. He leant forward a little over the balcony railing, and I guessed that now, finally, he could see the three figures clearly.

'Stop him, Alec,' he said, still looking down from the balcony. 'Stop him, now! *Stop him!*'

I would have gone back to the railing, then. I would have looked down at what Milne was seeing. But the panic in his voice shook me like a hard slap across the face, and I stumbled over the threshold and ran to the stairwell and threw myself down the stairs after Joseph.

I caught up with him in the sitting room and seized his arm, but he shook me off and went into the hallway leading to the front door. I ran after him and grabbed him again.

'Joseph! Don't go out there.'

'I'm going to confront it,' he said, and there was a calmness – a tranquillity, almost – in his face that frightened me more than any expression of uncontrolled fear or madness. 'You can come with me, or you can stay here – it's up to you.'

I thought again of the panic in Milne's voice. 'The Principal has given you an order, laddie, and you'll follow it.'

'No, Alec, I won't.'

He shook me off again, turned to the door and reached for the latch.

I lunged forward and grabbed him around the shoulders, and for a few moments we struggled together in a violent, panting wrestle. But then suddenly he thrust his head back, directly into my face, and pain exploded through my head. My grip lessened enough for him to turn around and shove me to the floor. I went down hard and felt blood flowing from my broken nose.

As I crawled forward and tried to grab one of Joseph's ankles, I heard footfalls upon the stairs leading to the lightroom, and then Milne came rushing across the sitting room and into the hallway.

'Oh Christ, don't!' he screamed.

But he was too late, for Joseph had already unlatched the door and stepped out into the enveloping whiteness. He pulled the door shut behind him.

Milne glanced at me, saw the blood still pouring down my face, and was about to bend down to me, but I waved him away. 'Get him back,' I said. 'I'm behind you.'

He turned back to the door and put his hand on the latch. But then, he hesitated. I dragged myself to my feet, trying to staunch the flow of blood with my hand. Milne turned to me, and in his eyes I saw the reason for his hesitation. He was terrified – more terrified than anyone I have ever seen in my life, before or since.

'I'm with you, John,' I said.

Milne nodded, and I could see his hand trembling as he forced himself to lift the latch. 'God protect us,' he whispered, as he pulled open the door.

*

I do not know what I expected to see. I was still half stunned, my head was throbbing with pain, and my hands were covered with warm, sticky blood. I recall that in the dimness of my awareness, I was ready to face whatever might be out there, but only because my mind was still too sluggish to offer any thoughts of self-preservation.

Beyond the door there was a wall of whiteness, a ghost-wall both insubstantial and utterly impenetrable to sight. Again Milne hesitated, standing upon the threshold.

'Can you see him?' I said. 'Is he there?'

'No, I can't see him.'

'Then let's go.'

'No.'

'What did you see?'

'I can't.'

'We have to look for him.'

'I can't.'

'There's no visibility! If he walks around in this, he'll fall into the sea. Do you want to lose a man, John?'

'No I don't. But… dear God! You didn't see them, Alec, not properly.'

'I don't care about that now. If we don't get to Joseph and bring him back, he will die! Do you want that on your conscience?'

Milne shook his head, and took a great, ragged breath. 'Come on,' he said, taking hold of my hand. 'Don't let go. We mustn't get separated. Understand?'

'I understand.'

'And tread carefully, Alec. Tread carefully!'

Together, we stepped out into the fog. Now, all three of us were outside the lighthouse. We had broken the cardinal rule, but for the best of reasons: to save a fellow Lightkeeper. Perhaps, I thought, this was how Ducat, Marshall and MacArthur had met their ends. This was how easily we could all be lost.

We moved further into the blinding white miasma, calling out Joseph's name as we took careful, tentative steps, for even the ground beneath our feet was invisible to us. We were no strangers to such phenomena, but I had never seen fog this thick and all-encompassing – not even the *haar*, the great sea-mist that sweeps in from the east, obscuring everything beyond a few feet. As we moved, I realised that something else was deeply, confusingly wrong with our environment, but such was my state of mind that it took me some moments to realise precisely what it was.

All around, there was total silence. Even the constant low whisper of the sea was gone.

I noted this aloud to Milne.

'Yes, I know,' he replied and called out Joseph's name again.

Our hands were still clasped together, and I felt his tremble in mine.

'What did you see, John? From the balcony.'

'Not now.'

'If this doesn't lift, how will we find our way back to the lighthouse?'

'Look behind you, Alec.'

I did as he asked, and high up in the whiteness, I saw a faint but unmistakable pulse of pale illumination.

'The light itself will guide us back,' he said.

And so on we went, shouting Joseph's name into the fog, holding hands tightly, moving our feet slowly and carefully, constantly mindful of any change in the land beneath us that might warn of our proximity to the edge of the island. Apart from our desperate calls, the only sound to disturb the awful silence was that of our own breath, rasping and tremulous.

And all the while I glanced here and there, in this direction and that, behind me and to the sides, ever watchful not only for Joseph, but also for the three figures we had seen out here. I wondered why Milne would not tell me what he had seen from the balcony. Was he sparing me the fear that had seized him? Did he think that I would have refused to come out here with him, had he described it to me? Could it be that he was literally *unable* to describe what he had seen? That last question was the most difficult for me to entertain, and it made me yet more afraid.

I already held Milne in high regard, but now my opinion of him grew further, for he had obviously seen something that had shaken him to the core of his being, and yet, he had put his terror aside and had come outside to look for young Joseph. I knew then that I would follow him to whatever fate awaited us.

The slope of the ground told me that we were still moving away from the lighthouse, probably directly south. I halted and said to Milne, 'He couldn't have come this far, not in so little time. We've missed him. We should head back, and go from side to side, to cover as much ground as possible.'

'Good idea, Alec,' he replied.

I was about to ask why Joseph hadn't responded to our calls. Could he have stumbled and knocked himself unconscious? That was unlikely: there was nothing but grass on this part of the island. I did not want to think about the alternative: that Joseph was being prevented from answering for some unimaginable reason.

Was he now gone from the island?

Were Milne and I, even now, walking slowly and carefully towards the same inconceivable destiny?

Again I glanced about me in all directions, wondering if this is what a wild animal feels when it knows it is being hunted. But there was nothing but whiteness all around, silent and unending.

As we went on, I began to see things in the whiteness: strange, flitting shapes that seemed to fly chaotically away whenever I looked directly at them. More than once, I cried out, pointing with my free hand, only to lower it again, bewildered and consumed with an unbearable unease.

From time to time, Milne did the same, making a quiet, whimpering sound, a sound of abject fear and despair that no man should ever make, and I wondered what fearful pictures his imagination was drawing upon the featureless canvas that surrounded us.

'Can you see them, Alec?' Milne whispered.

'Yes. I don't know what they are…'

'Nor I. They seem to be all around us.'

We called Joseph's name again, although it chilled my blood to do so. By shouting so loudly, we were revealing ourselves to be out here in the open, betraying our exact location. But shout we did, again and again, for the sake of our friend, as the shapeless things darted all around us.

Presently, however, I began to form a suspicion of what they were, and I almost cried out in relief when I realised that the shapes I was seeing were the tiny things that float within one's eyes, and which can be seen drifting across the field of vision on occasion. Such was the utter featurelessness of our environment that these unfocussed particles had impinged totally upon my concentration, so that they seemed as external objects floating in the air before me.

I explained this to Milne.

'I think you're right, Alec,' he replied, his voice suffused with relief. 'Yes, I see… that's what they are… thank God that's all they are.'

And then my shuffling foot connected with something soft, and I cried out to Milne to stop. I looked down, but could see nothing, and so I stooped and felt with my left hand, my right still clasping Milne's hand.

'It's him,' I said. 'It's Joseph. Dear God, we've found him!'

Milne bent down also. 'Is he conscious? Joseph!'

There was no reply, but poor Joseph's body shuddered so much that it was quite clear he was awake.

'Get him on his feet,' Milne ordered. 'Back to the light, now!'

We hauled Joseph's shivering body up between us and went as quickly as we could up the slope towards the faint pulse of light hanging blessedly above us. I think I was most fearful during those minutes, as we stumbled through the fog with our friend alive between us, with the light growing steadily nearer, with the relative safety of the lighthouse within reach. Just a few more moments, and we would reach the low stone wall surrounding the yard; a few more moments and we would be across the yard and inside, with the door firmly bolted against whatever might still walk here.

'We're nearly there,' said Milne through clenched teeth. 'Keep going.'

We reached the wall and did not bother to feel our way to the gate. Milne clambered over, and I heaved Joseph to him and then climbed over the wall, and together we dashed across the yard to the house's front door.

Once inside, I slammed the door and bolted it fast and turned to look at my companions.

Joseph was curled up on the floor, still shivering, his eyes wide and glassy. Milne was crouched beside him, and I realised that the immense courage and resolve he had shown in leaving the house to look for Joseph had deserted him, now that we were back inside.

And I watched with a beating, painful heart as John Milne began to sob.

17
Joseph Moore's Fever

For the next two days, we took turns watching over Joseph. We had put him to bed, and at first had tried to get him to speak to us, but he wouldn't, or perhaps couldn't. He simply lay there, staring up at the ceiling, his eyes empty, his body still, apart from the occasional shiver that rippled horribly through him. His breathing, at least, appeared normal. He did not respond to our repeated questions, nor would he take any food. Milne said that Joseph could do without food for a short while, but not water, and so periodically we tried to get him to drink. When we did so, sitting him up in bed and placing a mug to his lips, most of the liquid dribbled uselessly down his chin, but some went into his mouth and down his throat. We hoped it would be enough.

The day after we saw the three shapes in the fog – the 25th of January it was – I went up to the lightroom, where Milne was doing duty. The fog had since lifted, revealing the island and the sea beyond, and we saw that they were as they had been before, with no clue that anything untoward had happened.

Milne was checking the mercury at the base of the light, on which the lens assembly rotated. On a table nearby, a mug of tea stood cold and untouched.

'I need to talk to you, John,' I said.

'Aye.'

'I want you to describe what you saw from the balcony, when I went after Joseph.'

'No, Alec, you don't,' he replied, still with his back to me.

I moved closer to him. 'Please, John, I need to know.'

'Why?'

'Because we three are alone here; because we are doing this duty together, and what one sees, the others should know about. You said yourself: anything that might have a bearing on our safety, on our ability to do our job, should be shared with the others.'

'Not this.'

'*Especially* this.'

He turned to face me. 'Joseph must have seen what I saw. That's why he's in his present condition.'

'Then why aren't you in the same condition? Joseph is a sensitive lad, but he's not *that* sensitive, John. He must have seen or experienced something else. I don't know, and in a way it doesn't matter – or at least it has no bearing on what I'm asking you now. I'm only an Occasional, but right now I'm a member of your crew. You *owe* it to me to keep me informed of everything that happens.'

Milne was silent for some moments. Then he sighed and sat down in the chair, and ran a hand through his hair, and looked up at me with bleak and haunted eyes.

'When you went after Joseph, they came close to the house. The fog was so thick, I shouldn't have been able to see them clearly: as you said yourself, visibility was practically zero. And yet I *did* see them clearly, for the fog seemed to move away from them as they walked. And they were not Ducat and the others.' He shook his head slowly. 'No... they were not Ducat and the others.'

'Who were they?'

'Not "who", Alec... *what*.'

'Was I right, then? Were they not men?'

'No, they were not men. I don't know what they were.' He gave a fitful, miserable sigh, a sigh of confusion and fear and helplessness. 'Their shape was that of men, in a manner of speaking... but there was something terribly wrong with that shape... as though they were something's *idea* of what a man should look like.'

I didn't understand what Milne was saying. Perhaps he didn't understand it himself. His brow was deeply furrowed, as if he were trying hard to recall something that drifted on the edge of his memory.

'And their colour was like no colour I've ever seen, as if a new colour had been created just for them.'

'Were they wearing clothing?'

'No, I don't think so... or they might have been – I don't know.'

'And their faces... did you see their faces?'

'Ah... their faces.' Milne laughed a soft, sad, humourless laugh and stared at the floor, and I could see tears welling in his eyes. 'They had no faces... nor did they have heads... but something else.'

'What else,' I asked, feeling a nausea rising steadily within me, a sickness and dizziness more of the mind than the body. 'What else, instead of faces and heads?'

'Their heads went into stars.'

'What... what do you mean?'

Milne tried to swallow, but I could tell that his mouth was too dry. 'From their shoulders... great fountains of space... holes in the world, and inside... *stars*.'

I could think of no response to this. I merely stood there and looked at him.

'Fountains of black space rising from their shoulders... rising up, up, up... never ending, into the white sky. I felt the coldness of it, more bitter than any cold imaginable... the coldness of the deep heavens, the void between worlds. Were they angels?' he asked then, and I realised that he was asking himself the question, rather than me.

'I don't know,' I whispered.

'It's strange, Alec,' he said. 'I never thought that Heaven might be so very cold. So hard and cold and dark... the stars so bright and pitiless. Nothing for us there... nothing we could stand.'

'What did they do to Joseph?' I wondered. 'He went outside... what if he met them, stood beside them?'

'Whatever happened was too much for him. Too much for his mind… I wonder if he'll recover.'

'I hope so.'

It was all I could think of to say.

*

That night, while I was taking my turn in the lightroom, I heard Joseph cry out, his voice loud and desperate, like the voice of some pitiful, frightened ghost drifting through a house that should never have been built. I went to the top of the stairwell and listened. He cried out again, and I heard Milne's footsteps leaving his bedroom and going into Joseph's.

The night beyond the lighthouse was mercifully quiet; there was practically no wind, and the sea had regained its voice and continued to mutter softly in the near distance. For some moments, I stood at the head of the stairs and listened.

Presently, Milne's voice drifted up to me, telling me to come down. This filled me with yet greater trepidation, for he was telling me to leave the lightroom unmanned in the dead of night. I hesitated and then made certain that the lens mechanism was fully wound, and I went down to Joseph's room.

Milne was sitting in a chair beside the bed, holding Joseph's hand while the lad writhed this way and that, his face a blank mask, his eyes vacant, his brow wreathed in sweat.

'He has a fever,' Milne said, turning to me. 'Go and fetch a cloth and some water.'

I did as he asked, and when I returned, Milne dipped the cloth in the saucepan of water and dabbed gently at Joseph's face.

'He's raving,' he said.

'What's he saying?' I asked, coming closer to the bed.

'I don't know. It makes no sense… no sense at all.'

'Joseph,' I said. 'Can you hear me?' I took his other hand and held it tightly. 'It's all right. You're safe – John and I are here.'

Joseph gave a low moan and said, 'The bodies... the bodies that intersect.'

'Dear God,' I said. 'John, what are we going to do?'

Milne shook his head and again wiped Joseph's brow.

'The solid bodies that intersect... I see them... the magnetic ring and the windowless solids... dimensionless... look at the moon! The bridge... how can that be? The moon bridge... the living crystals... the axial translator...'

He thrashed and shrieked so horribly that I wanted to run from the room. I couldn't begin to imagine what his fevered mind was seeing. Were we anywhere in the world but here, I would have pitied a poor wretch seized with some mental malady, confident in the knowledge that his mind had turned on him and was tormenting him with hallucinations of its own fevered devising. But there was no such surety here, far from the world of rational thought and logical explanation, and I found myself entertaining the awful suspicion that Joseph was *not* hallucinating, that whatever had happened to him while he was outside the house had afforded him a glimpse of a reality utterly unlike our own.

Suddenly, Joseph stopped writhing and lay still, his eyes fixed upon the ceiling. 'Oh God,' he said. 'Please stop the sound...'

'What sound?' said Milne. 'Joseph! Listen to me. What sound?'

'The sound, John,' he said.

'He's responding to you,' I whispered. 'Keep talking to him.'

Milne nodded. 'Joseph, tell me about the sound.'

'The sound of the stars moving. The noise of the axial translator. They're coming closer... make it stop!

The nameless cylinder that transforms the sky... the rim is carved... the eyes are open... eyes in the darkness... wings in the undying night...'

'It's all right, Joseph,' I said, feeling wretched and helpless.

'No... no, it's not all right,' Joseph whispered. 'It can never be all right... never again... with them, walking... the walkers among the eternal lights... serene and primal... no one sees them, but they are here... they are everywhere, from inside our minds, out, out to the farthest ramparts... the uttermost limits of space and time... and beyond that, beyond into the black spaces where no man will ever dwell.'

'Who are "they"?' I asked.

'Who are they? What is their nature? Not material things... not spirit... something between and beyond... from places where things are not as they are here. A great sound, like metal and mist and dust and stars... the sound of night... the sound of many voices. We are coming. We are coming close now. Do you see us? Will you speak to us?'

Milne looked at me for a long moment and then said, 'Is something speaking through Joseph?'

'Will you speak to us?' Joseph repeated, and his voice was light and gentle as a child's.

'What do you want?' I asked.

'We are close.'

Suddenly, Joseph shut his eyes tight and let out a long, mournful cry, a cry so full of despair that I wanted to run from the room and the house and to plunge into the sea and put an end to myself.

And so it went on. Joseph continued to whimper and shout abnormal things, while Milne kept talking to him, trying to bring him back from the dreadful darkness of his inner mind and from the things that moved there. Several times I returned to the lightroom to make certain that all was in order, but each time I quickly returned to Joseph's bedside, hoping that somehow Milne might have brought him a little further back to us.

With agonising slowness, Joseph became more and more aware of his surroundings and of Milne and me, and by the following morning his fever seemed to have left him, and he slept. Exhausted, Milne and I left him to his sleep and to dreams upon which we preferred not to speculate.

I did not expect Joseph to remember anything of his fever or the things he said while he had lain in its grip. In truth, I did not want to think of them myself, for while they had seemed to be no more than the ravings of a sick and overheated mind, there was something in them... a strange coherence that I found deeply disturbing, as if he were describing things that really existed.

As if he were seeing things that no man had ever seen.

John Milne had a similar reaction. While we talked quietly in the kitchen of the previous night's events, he said to me that it was as if Joseph were not mad, but was a sane man *looking* at madness. I asked him to elaborate, but he couldn't; he merely said that that was the feeling he had.

'What about the things he said?' I asked him.

Milne sighed and shook his head. 'I don't know, Alec. I've never heard the like of it. If we were anywhere but here, having seen all that we've seen, I would have put it all down to sickness and delusion. But we saw those things with our own eyes: they were *out there*, as real as you and I... perhaps *more* real.'

I closed my eyes and slowly rubbed my temples with both hands. 'Where did they come from? Lord, what is the origin of all this?'

'Joseph said that they come from places where things are not as they are here.'

'Aye, I remember. But what does that mean?'

'Perhaps there are men in the world who might know... or at least might know enough to make a good guess. But not us.'

'Is this what drove Ducat and the others to their deaths? Did they eventually become so afraid that they could no longer tolerate their own existence in this place, even though they knew that relief would come soon? Or were they taken away by something?'

Milne looked away. 'We have five more days before the *Hesperus* arrives. Then we'll be off the island.'

Five more days.

I wondered if the others had told each other the same thing. Not long now… soon… a few more hours of duty, and then we'll be away from Eilean Mòr – if we can just stay alive and sane until the lighthouse tender arrives. Whatever catastrophe overtook those unfortunate men happened very close to the date of their relief, just a few days before the *Hesperus* was due to arrive.

'And what then?' I asked. 'What about the keepers who will come after us? What do we tell the Lighthouse Board, John?'

'I've been thinking about that a great deal, and the truth of it is I don't know. If I report events as they really happened, even if you and Joseph corroborate everything, we'll be seen as weak-minded fools who were driven half mad by solitude.'

'Are you so sure? Doesn't your record as a Lightkeeper speak to the contrary?'

'It may well do, Alec. But I don't think it will make any difference.'

'But what about the Flannans?' I persisted. 'Their reputation is well known…'

Milne laughed softly. 'The Phantom of the Seven Hunters? Aye, we all know about that – especially the other Keepers. But that's only a legend, and the Board cannot afford to take account of legends – however true they may be.'

'Would Superintendent Muirhead support us?'

'Privately, perhaps; he's a good man. But officially?' Milne shook his head. 'The only thing we can do is warn the other Keepers in private about what to expect when they do duty here. Keep it amongst ourselves.'

'Assuming we survive.'

'Aye... assuming that.'

We heard footsteps on the stairs and turned to see Joseph come into the kitchen. He looked tired and dishevelled; his face was drawn and deathly pale, but his eyes were clear, and I immediately had the impression that he was himself again.

'How are you feeling, Joseph?' asked Milne, rising to his feet.

'I feel well enough,' he replied.

'Do you remember anything of yesterday... of last night?' I asked.

Joseph nodded slowly.

'You do?' Milne and I looked at each other.

'You sound surprised,' he said, regarding us each in turn.

'You had a fever,' said Milne. 'A fever... or at least some malady of the mind and body. I didn't expect you to remember anything.'

The lad frowned. 'I don't think it was a fever or anything like that.'

'Do you remember going outside?' I asked.

'Yes... and I owe you an apology, Alec.'

I waved it aside, although my face was still throbbing dully from his blow.

Joseph came and sat at the table. 'They are here,' he said.

'Who?' Milne asked.

'I don't know. They have come from a long way away... and yet they have always been here, because where they come from is both far away and very close. What I'm about to tell you won't make any sense to you – I'd wager all I have on that. Nor does it make any sense to me… I can only describe to you the things I saw while I was outside – the things they showed me.'

As I listened to Joseph, I noted something strange in his voice and bearing. He spoke very quietly, and his eyes seemed to have become unfocused, as though he were reciting some body of information from memory. I wondered at the reason for this: was he still suffering the effects of the terrible shock he had experienced? It seemed a logical enough assumption, but there was both fear and wonder in his voice: a dark and mysterious wonder that might rend the mind and soul with its intensity.

'Tell us what happened to you, Joseph,' said Milne.

'I was a fool to go outside, I realise that now, of course. But I was at the end of my tether, with everything that's happened. I had to confront whatever it was that… well, I went outside into the fog. And I saw them.'

'John saw them, too,' I said.

Joseph glanced at him. 'Then you know that they were not Ducat and the others, as we had hoped. They were not men at all, but something else. They hold infinite space within them, for that is where they are from. I saw this within them as they stood around me; they showed me things and places that exist on the other side of the sky, the other side of the blue of daytime and the black of night.'

'What are those things and places?' asked Milne.

'Different… they are different from this world.' Joseph frowned, and again I had the impression that he was trying to remember something, or to understand something that he *did* remember all too clearly. 'There is another order of being, outside the realm of God and men, that existed before both.'

'*Before* God?' said Milne. 'How is that possible?'

'Our understanding of God is incomplete, John. We can't begin to contemplate the true way of the universe, for there are places and things that will not fit into the human mind. Regions beyond... and minds that are not parallel to us or to anything we know or have dreamed. Through some accident, some random movement-that-is-not-movement, this world has strayed too close to theirs, or theirs to ours, and they have crossed over – or at least some *part* of them has crossed over... the part that is capable of doing so. And they are here, now, and they are curious.'

'What do they want?' I asked, trying to make some sense of what Joseph was saying.

'They want to know us... to speak with us... perhaps, you might say, to *commune* with us. But they are too different; there is no common ground.'

'There must be a way,' said Milne.

Joseph shook his head. 'There is no way. I can't describe how different – how very *different* – they are. Everything that has happened since we arrived on the island, everything we have seen and heard, has been an attempt by them to speak to us. That strange, metallic sound... the light we saw on our first night... the white fox... whatever prevented you from going into the store room outside... what happened to the sky... what came out of the sea and distorted our memories... the discoloured grass and rock on the north side of the island... all of it was their attempts to speak with us!'

'But those events,' said Milne, 'have nothing to do with *speaking*, with communication.'

'I use the word "speak" only as it applies to us. *They* do not "speak", not in any way we would understand.'

'Perhaps,' I said, 'it is a form of sign language, as we would use signs to one of our own race who did not speak our language... or the way we use flags and flares to communicate when the voice will not reach.'

'Yes,' said Joseph, 'I believe you may be right. But their minds are so different from ours that their signs are incomprehensible: they are emblems for things we have no hope of understanding.'

'How do you know all this?' asked Milne.

'I *don't* know, John! It's what I suspect, what I *feel*... it's no more than the impression I got while I was with them. And I had other impressions as well... vague intimations of what it is like where they come from. I felt my mind... or perhaps my soul... leave my body, and in leaving I was able to see something of their places, through the thin veil that now separates our world from theirs. There was light and movement, and the things that moved there were unlike anything the mind of man could conceive. Spheres and planes and cubes... vast towers made of space, that changed shape... the inside and the outside seen at once, as though what we think of as dimension has no meaning there – or at least a meaning so at odds with our world that it no longer has any useful significance. Great bridges linking stars – or things that seemed like stars, but which thought and spoke to each other through a bright, bright void. And shapes, faceted like jewels, that changed the angles of the intersecting planes through which they moved.'

Joseph paused and regarded his folded hands, which rested upon the table in front of him. 'Is that really what it was like?' he said, more to himself than to us. 'Or is it only what my mind was capable of seeing? Is *our* world really the way we see it, or is there more to it than our minds can understand?'

'Tell us, Joseph,' said Milne, leaning forward. 'Are they responsible for what happened to Ducat and the others?'

'I don't know, John. I'm sorry.'

'Are you sure?'

Joseph nodded. 'I had no... intimation... of what's happened to them. I don't know where they are.'

We all sat in silence for some moments, and then something occurred to me. 'What about the stone?' I said.

Joseph glanced at me. 'The stone?'

'The carved stone I found. Do you know what it was, what it meant?'

'I'm not sure... perhaps another attempt to speak with us... or perhaps something from their place.'

'Something from their place,' I echoed, recalling the shape of the stone, at once incomprehensible and deeply unsettling.

'Very well, Joseph,' said Milne. 'Let me ask you this: do you have any idea – any notion, however vague – of what they are *going* to do?'

Joseph shook his head. 'All I can say is this, John: whatever they are going to do next, we will not understand it.'

19
THE LAST DAY

Joseph's words did not sit well with us, although we knew that he spoke the truth. Until then, we had tried to determine some rational explanation for the things we had seen and heard, to apply the reason of intelligent, experienced men to the mystery into which we had come. But according to Joseph, there *was* no sound and logical explanation for the forces at work here: at least, nothing that could be understood by the narrow, earth-bound human mind.

Again I wondered if we were experiencing what Ducat, Marshall and MacArthur had endured before they vanished from the world. I wondered if whatever had come to Eilean Mòr had tried to speak with them as well. I speculated that those forces might have grown frustrated, even enraged, when the impossibility of 'communion' (as Joseph had strangely put it) became apparent. Might they grow similarly frustrated with us? Might they tire of trying to communicate with our limited minds and cast us into oblivion, perhaps without even realising that they were doing so? Perhaps in their incomprehensible realm there was no such thing as death; perhaps they hardly understood the torment they were inflicting upon us, or the annihilation they might rain upon us without even intending it.

I felt like a man suffocating in the darkness just before dawn. Escape from the island was only a couple of days away... but what might happen in those two days? I wondered if we, too, would be lost – and if not, whether there would be anything left of our minds when the *Hesperus* finally arrived.

As we continued with our duties, there was a great tension between the three of us. John Milne, Joseph Moore and I were bound together in our isolation, but the possibility that that isolation might result in our destruction made our bonds all but unendurable. We maintained the light unthinkingly, automatically, like the mechanism we were tending… and all the while waiting, waiting for the next encounter, the next unfathomable experience.

*

Our last full day on Eilean Mòr was the 30th of January. It began with a moaning wind out of the north east, emerging from the darkness of the night carrying with it a torrent of stinging, icy rain. The sea was all grey fury, roiling and heaving like a great beast in pain, and the sky was a solid mass of cloud the colour of gunmetal.

It was with great relief that I concluded my watch in the lightroom, and rang the house-bell to summon Milne to take over from me. He came up the stairs without delay, and stood beside me for a short while, and together we looked out through the diamond-paned windows at the furious grey world beyond.

'Wind's still rising,' said Milne presently.

'Aye.'

'No one goes outside today, not for any reason, understood?'

'Understood, John.'

'Kitchen slate's clean. All transferred to the log.'

'I'll put down my observations.'

'And help Joseph to make everything ready for the next crew.'

'I will.'

Milne fell silent, which I took as a dismissal, and so I walked back towards the stairs leading down through the tower into the house.

'Alec,' said Milne.

I stopped and turned to him. 'Yes, John?'

'Thank you.'

I hesitated, for there was a look on his face that implied he wanted to say more.

'You're welcome.'

'I'm going to recommend to the Lighthouse Board that you be offered the position of Assistant Keeper. You've acted with responsibility and diligence... it's been good to work with you. I wanted to tell you that now.'

'I appreciate your confidence in me, John,' I replied. 'But why now?'

He turned away from me, and returned his attention to the windows and the great seethe and gyre outside.

'Because this isn't over yet,' he said quietly. 'And I wanted you to know.'

*

I found Joseph in the kitchen. He was busy writing the Monthly Return, carefully noting which provisions we had consumed, how much fuel and water we had used during our duty and so on, and checking the Inventory Book containing details of the lighthouse's apparatus, furniture, tools and utensils.

He didn't look up as I entered, and so I continued on into the sitting room and began the cleaning and dusting which was required of us in preparation for the arrival of the next lighthouse crew. As I worked, I thought of what Milne had said to me. I was, of course, glad that I had acquitted myself well – at least in the Principal's eyes – although such was the terror and confusion I had felt over the last month that there seemed to my mind a strange hollowness to his words. I felt that I had managed to avoid being a burden to my professional colleagues, but that was all. If I had achieved anything beyond that, it was merely to have survived, as they had, with my reason intact.

I also recalled Milne's statement that this wasn't over yet. He had wanted to make me aware of his satisfaction with my performance, now, a full day before we were due to leave the island, and I wondered why. Was it because he was afraid of what the next twenty-four hours might bring?

The moan of the wind grew louder and more intense as I left the sitting room and walked along the corridor to the bedrooms, and I heard the spattering hiss of the rain on the windows, like steam from a straining engine. The faint sound of creaking issued from unseen quarters of the house as the weather pressed insistently upon it, as though trying to push it from the island into the waiting sea.

And then I heard a whispered voice nearby. The voice said, 'This is the last day.'

I gasped and stopped and stood perfectly still, my breath held fast in my lungs.

'Who's there?' I said. 'John? Joseph?'

There was no answer. I glanced back along the corridor. It was deserted. Muted sounds from the kitchen told me that Joseph was still there, and Milne would not have left the lightroom.

'Who is there?' I repeated, but the only response came from the wind that howled all around. I forced myself to breathe normally. That must be it: my mind must have transformed the sound of the wind into human words.

I continued into my bedroom, with the intention of changing the linen, thinking again of Milne's words.

This isn't over yet...

I stripped the bed, folded the used linen and put it in a corner, then turned to the tall wardrobe next to the door with the intention of taking some fresh linen for the bed.

I froze, my heart suddenly racing, and I moaned aloud when I saw what was on the wardrobe door.

Etched in the wood, taking its form, it seemed, from a warping and twisting of the grain, was a human-like figure. It extended for the entire seven-foot height of the wardrobe, and although its lower extremities were indistinct in the grain, its chest, shoulders and head were easily discernible.

How can I describe what it looked like? I am haunted by it still, and I know that my memory will never be free of it. In the dance of flames in a hearth, I see its elongated form; in the scattered clouds of a bright day, I see its stretched, mitred head; in the shifting waters of rivers and lakes, I see its eyes staring at me, wide and alive and ancient beyond words, beyond thought.

Instinctively I recoiled from it and stumbled backwards onto the bed, and it seemed that those eyes turned and looked down at me, and I thought that I would die beneath that alien gaze. I don't know how long I lay there, paralysed with dread, panting with confusion and inexpressible terror. Time itself seemed to flee from the room in the face of this utter abnormality. My unblinking eyes remained fixed upon it, unable to look away, and I saw the grain in the wood of the wardrobe, the dark striations from which this thing had composed itself, begin to shift in slow, subtle waves, as if it were attempting to free itself, to emerge fully into the world.

Somehow, I knew that if I stayed in that room, it would be the end of me, and so I threw all my effort and resolve, every last fragment of my instinct for survival, into forcing my muscles to move, to get up off the bed and make a stumbling dash for the door.

This I managed to do – though it was like running across the bottom of the ocean, with the weight of all the world's water pressing down upon me. And then, when I reached the door and threw myself into the corridor outside, I found myself plunged into darkness. Turning in spite of myself – for I did not want to look into the bedroom again – I saw through the window that it was now night: the sky was black and thick with stars. The writhing storm clouds had gone, and with them the wind that had howled so plaintively just a few moments ago.

'Impossible,' I whispered, repeating the word to myself over and over again as I moved along the corridor. 'Impossible! Impossible!'

In that sudden darkness and horrible, unnatural silence, I went in search of Joseph, but when I looked into the sitting room, I found Milne there, indistinct in the darkness, sitting hunched forward in a chair, rocking back and forth like a terrified child trying to comfort himself. He was weeping, the tears rolling freely upon his face, his eyes tightly shut. He was whispering something, and as I drew nearer, I realised that he was praying:

'Almighty and ever-blessed God... our souls do magnify the Lord, our spirits rejoice in God the Saviour; for he that is mighty hath done great things for his people, and his mercy is on them that fear him. We pray to our Father in behalf of all mankind. May the day-spring from on high arise on those who now sit in darkness... and may grace and mercy and peace from the Father, the Son and the Holy Ghost be with us forever.'

'John,' I said. 'John... it's night. How can it be night? The light...'

The room was in near-total darkness, and I waited for the pulse of illumination outside that would tell me that the light was still in operation. I counted fifteen seconds, but the darkness outside remained unbroken.

'Oh God, the light,' I said, as I fumbled upon the mantelpiece for the matches. I struck one and put its tiny flame to the wick of a storm lantern. But although the lantern burned brightly, the room remained in darkness. I held the lantern aloft, but still it failed to illuminate the room: it merely hung above my head like a great star burning alone in an empty universe, while John Milne continued to pray.

'Bless us, O our Father! Give us thy grace in every season of trial. Give us thy protection in every hour of danger. Prepare us for the dispensation of thy Providence; prepare us for the discharge of duty; prepare us for the inheritance of the just.'

I called out Joseph's name, but there was no answer. 'Joseph!' I cried. 'Where are you? Get up to the lightroom, now! Get the lamps lit, for God's sake!'

Still there was no response, and so, taking the all-but-useless lantern, I stumbled blindly from the sitting room and made my fumbling way up the spiral staircase leading to the lightroom. Several times I tripped on the stairs, for still the bright lantern offered no illumination. How that could be, I had no idea: it was as if the very air itself were made of darkness that refused to admit the passage of light.

When I reached the lightroom, I found the lamps extinguished and the lens assembly stopped. I also saw both Joseph Moore *and* John Milne standing at the windows, looking out to the west.

'John!' I cried in disbelief. 'You're... how can you...?'

Joseph turned his head slightly, without taking his eyes from what they were both looking at, and said, 'Alec, come and see.'

'John, I don't understand,' I said, still standing at the head of the stairs. 'I've just left you in the sitting room... weeping and praying... what in God's name is happening?'

'Come and see, Alec,' said Milne quietly.

'The two of you be damned!' I shouted, and instead of joining them, I set about checking the lens mechanism, the oil fountains and the wicks, with the intention of re-lighting the lamps.

'We don't need the light, Alec,' said Milne. 'Not now... not here.'

Something in his voice made me stop and turn to look at them. They were still standing at the windows, still gazing off into the distance. Their arms hung limp at their sides, and their eyes were wide, their faces expressionless. It was then that I became aware of a strange quality to the atmosphere outside, which seemed to be the opposite of the impenetrable darkness inside the house. It was still pitch dark, but the sliver of ocean I could see from my vantage point seemed to be luminous, as if lit from underneath. I could not prevent myself from leaving the light and joining Milne and Moore at the windows. In spite of the darkness, I could see everything outside with absolute crystal clarity. And what I saw was not the world I knew to exist in the region of the Flannan Isles.

The islands were gone, and all around there was a perfectly flat plain of shimmering quicksilver light. Whether it was water or something beyond the knowledge of man, I couldn't say, but it extended from horizon to horizon, just as the ocean once had. Overhead, the stars ranged in an overwhelming, unbelievable profusion, and I realised that this must be the reason for the strange quality of the atmosphere, which was steeped in night and yet bright as daylight. And as I looked, I saw that one star amongst all that multitude was moving, falling slowly towards the earth.

'The world is gone,' said Joseph.

'And in its place... what?' I replied.

Milne pointed through the window. 'Look there... what is that?'

We looked out over the western part of the island, where the body of Eilean Mòr sloped down towards the sea, or what once had been the sea. Where the island ended, something else began – something that had not been there before.

'It looks like a causeway,' I said.

'I think you're right, Alec,' said Milne. 'It looks artificial.' His voice was flat and quiet, and I realised that Milne must be experiencing the same numbness of mind that I felt. Numbness... yes, that's what I felt. This new phenomenon was too much to accept, and it seemed to me that my mind was like a muscle that has been tested beyond endurance, so that all its strength leaves it, and it becomes limp and useless.

'The world is not gone, Joseph,' I said. 'We are gone from the world.'

The causeway – if that is what it was – extended out in a straight line from the edge of the island for perhaps half a mile, before curving away towards the northwest horizon. It was about fifty yards wide, and was pale grey in colour, its surface quite flat. The horizon upon which it seemed to terminate, however, was not flat, but was curiously irregular, with minute serrations and irregularities. I picked up the telescope from the table and put it to my eye.

'What do you see?' asked Milne.

'I'm not certain... it looks to me like a *city*,' I replied, and handed him the instrument. 'See for yourself.'

He scanned the horizon for a long time. 'I can see buildings... towers, bridges... great grey cubes and pyramids... all at different angles...'

'Let me see,' said Joseph, and Milne handed him the telescope.

'Is that where they come from?' I wondered.

'It looks like a horrible place,' said Milne.

'What's that?' said Joseph suddenly, handing the telescope back to Milne. 'Look!'

Milne raised the instrument again.

'What is it?' I asked.

'Something is coming along the causeway.'

I seized the telescope from him and looked through it towards the 'city' on the horizon, and I saw tiny objects moving out from it, along the ribbon of grey that connected it to the island upon which we stood.

'They are coming,' Joseph whispered. 'What can we do?'

'Nothing,' Milne replied. 'There is nothing we can do.'

'I don't want to go with them,' Joseph said. 'I don't want to go to that place.'

I looked again through the telescope and saw the shapes approaching, slowly and steadily along the causeway, while Joseph's panting breath sounded in my ears.

'I don't want to go,' he repeated. 'I don't want to go.'

The shapes were now more than halfway along the causeway, in spite of their slow movement. I didn't understand how that could be, until I realised that 'movement' itself must have obeyed different laws in this unknown region. They were now close enough that we could see them clearly without the aid of the telescope.

And Joseph started to weep, and whispered, 'No, no, no...' over and over again.

I glanced at Milne and saw that his eyes were shut and he was praying, his lips moving soundlessly.

'I'll throw myself into the sea before I go with them,' said Joseph through his tears.

'But there is no more sea, Joseph,' I replied.

And then I decided to join Milne in prayer and looked up to the sky, to the infinite, motionless stars... and the single star that continued to descend towards the earth. As I watched, I realised that there was something familiar about that star's appearance. Again I took the telescope and this time I trained it upwards.

And then I realised that it wasn't a star.

It was a flare.

'The *Hesperus*,' I said. 'The *Hesperus* is here!'

Milne and Moore looked at me, and I pointed up into the sky. 'Do you see that? They've fired a rocket. The tender has arrived!'

'Then let us be gone,' said Milne. 'Perhaps we can get away from here... and if not, then we will meet our fate alongside our fellow men.'

Joseph pointed through the window. 'They've reached the island. They're coming onto the island!'

'Then hurry!' Milne shouted as he ran to the stairs.

We followed him down into the house, and together we dashed from the building, out into the strange, bright air. We left out oilskins on their pegs and took nothing with us but the clothes on our backs.

'Which landing?' asked Joseph. 'East or west? There's no time to check both!'

Milne looked up at the flare which was still continuing its sparkling descent. 'East,' he said, and began to run in that direction. From the corner of my eye, I saw the shapes emerging onto the western side of the island, and I silently thanked God that the lighthouse tender had come to the East Landing, for if it had been at the West Landing, we would not have been able to reach it before the shapes were upon us.

We fled across the uppermost shoulder of the island, towards the cliffs that looked out upon that strange, silent, unmoving sea. We should have been able to see the neighbouring island of Eiean Tighe from there: it should have loomed large in the foreground – but it did not. There was no sign of it, or any of the Flannan Isles.

We threw ourselves down the steps cut raggedly into the rock, towards the East Landing, where the *Hesperus* waited for us, held fast upon the silent sea. I did not dare to think of the possibility that the tender was as trapped and helpless as we were; did not dare to suppose that it would never be able to pull away from Eilean Mòr through the ocean that seemed as solid as a sheet of glass. In that moment, I refused to see it as anything other than our means of escape, of salvation.

When we reached the East Landing, I stopped and looked again at the ship. It was perfectly still, its lights were burning, but I couldn't see anyone on board. Milne and Moore stopped also and looked at me.

'What are you waiting for, Alec?' Milne cried. 'Come on!'

Everything was silent, strangely, horribly silent. The island, the air, the unmoving sea, the ship. I turned and looked back up the stairway and caught movement at its head…

'They'll be upon us in a moment!' shouted Milne.

'The tender's deserted,' I said. 'We're already lost… we were lost the moment we set foot here.'

Milne grabbed me by the shoulders and shook me. 'We'll make our stand on the *Hesperus* if we have to. But we won't stay here. Understood?'

I realised that Milne was right: I would rather meet my fate on this tiny fragment of the world of men, than on that strange and terrible island that had been invaded by the unknown and incomprehensible. I nodded and turned back to the edge of the Landing. The lighthouse tender's larboard gunwale was just three feet or so away.

'Jump,' said Milne. 'Jump now!'

We leaped as one from the island to the ship, and at the very moment when my feet made contact with the deck of the *Hesperus*, I was consumed by noise and movement. The deck suddenly heaved up, slamming into me and knocking me onto my back, while sea spray drenched me, and the cacophonous noise of wind and rain assaulted my ears.

I felt hands upon me, pulling me to my feet and dragging me towards the hatch leading belowdecks, and I heard shouted voices, including Milne's. He was screaming, *'Get us away from here! Get us away!'*

The deck heaved again, and I fell and felt a tremendous blow upon my head, and the world of sudden noise and movement went away from me into darkness.

*

This, then, is how we left Eilean Mòr, how we escaped, how we were carried back to the world from that other place which had enfolded the island in its unfathomable embrace.

I can write no more, for I have no more to tell, save that

I still wonder at the alteration that occurred at the instant our feet struck the deck of the *Hesperus*, transforming it from perfect stillness and desertion upon an unmoving plain, to a fully manned ship in the grip of a violently roiling ocean.

I will never be able to answer that question, nor the question of what happened to James Ducat, Thomas Marshall and Donald MacArthur.

And yet... and yet I wonder still whether they live on in that other world, of which we caught a glimpse that final night, and from which, by the grace of God and the presence of our fellow men, we managed to escape.

This, then, is my story. My testament from the edge of the Universe from a place that forced us to question our sanity; that showed us things that passed our understanding and even imagination. And now that I have completed my story, in the hope that in so doing I may effect my own escape from the strange dreams and nightmares that afflict me still, I must address the question of what to do now. I do not mean professionally, for I have already refused the offer of a permanent post with the Northern Lighthouse Board, nor will I ever act as an Occasional Keeper again. John Milne and Joseph Moore have likewise expressed their intention to seek other employment.

The question I now ask myself is this: what should I do with this testament? Should I accept it for what it truly is – a warning to all the Light Keepers who will do duty on Eilean Mòr in all the years to come? And if so, how should I transmit that warning to hardened men of the sea, who may well feel themselves justified in scorning its bizarre contents? I hesitate to set down the answer here, for it chills my blood to think of it, and yet, it is the only possible answer, the only feasible course of action open to me.

I must return to Eilean Mòr, be it ever so briefly, and place this manuscript in the lighthouse, where it may be found and read. Let those who read it make of it what they will and do with it as they please, for it is a poor thing, a warning of danger against which there is no defence. But perhaps it may be better than no warning at all.

HERE ENDS THE TESTAMENT OF ALEC DALEMORE

TWELVE

WEDNESDAY 22 JULY
10.50 AM

Rebecca finished reading aloud Dalemore's manuscript, closed it and placed it beside her on the cold stone floor of the sitting room. She looked at the others; only Nick returned her gaze. Jennifer and Max were staring at the floor.

'That's it?' said Max without looking up. 'That's all he wrote?'

'That's it,' Rebecca replied.

'Christ, then we really *are* on our own.'

'Did you ever really think otherwise?' asked Jennifer.

Max shrugged. 'I was hoping for...' His voice trailed off.

Jennifer looked at him. 'For what?'

'For a clue... for something we could have interpreted in a different way from Dalemore... something that might have let us figure out what's happening here.'

Jennifer shook her head. 'It was beyond them, and it's beyond us.'

'What do we do now?' asked Rebecca. No one answered. She searched their faces but saw nothing but blank expressions, nothing but resignation.

Nick stood up suddenly and walked to the window. 'Look,' he said, 'we're getting picked up on Friday morning.

Just two more full days. All we have to do is sit tight and wait. We'll stay inside the house and… and wait it out.'

Max sighed. 'I don't see what else we can do. Nick's right; we'll be okay. All we have to do is keep our heads together and wait for the boat.'

'Two more days,' said Jennifer quietly. 'It's going to be hard to get through them… even if nothing else happens.'

Max stood up and went to check on Donald. He was apparently in REM sleep, his eyelids twitching rapidly, his breathing deep and regular.

'What the hell happened to him?' Max muttered. 'What did he see in that room that could… that could fuck him up like that?' He glanced over his shoulder at the others. 'What if *we* see it?'

'How can we defend ourselves against something that can unhinge the mind at a single glance?' said Jennifer.

'Yeah…' Max looked at Donald again. 'Do you think he's gonna make it?'

'He'll make it,' said Nick. 'We'll all make it. We just have to keep him hydrated until we can get him to a hospital.'

They were all silent for a couple of minutes.

And then the daylight that had been streaming in through the window vanished.

Max was the first to jump to his feet. 'Son of a *bitch!*' He went to the window and looked out. 'It's night,' he said, shaking his head in disbelief. 'It's goddamned *night!*'

Rebecca buried her head in her hands as the room gradually became illuminated by a pale silver light.

'It's happened again,' said Jennifer, her voice weak, tremulous. 'Another… distortion of time.'

'Only this time we're awake,' said Nick. His face was bathed in the pale light, which gave it a strange, metallic pallor.

'The moon,' said Max, joining him at the window. 'It shouldn't be full. It should be a new moon... but it's full.'

'And it's too big,' said Nick.

Max pointed through the window. 'What's that in the courtyard?'

'Where?' said Nick.

'There. Is that... is that a shadow?'

'It can't be. There's nothing there.'

'But it *is* a shadow,' insisted Max. 'Cast by the moonlight.'

Rebecca sat and listened to them. She didn't want to; she wanted to put her hands against her ears and smother the sounds of their voices. But instead, she listened, her eyes tightly shut.

'How can something that isn't there cast a shadow?' asked Jennifer. 'How *can* it?' Her voice cracked, and Rebecca opened her eyes and looked at her.

'Keep it together, Jennifer,' said Max, without taking his eyes from the window.

Rebecca wanted to go to Jennifer, to put her arms around her and comfort her. She wanted to do that much more than to look into the courtyard. But she stood up and went to the window and looked out. The cobblestones glowed ochre in the moonlight, except for a large irregular patch of darkness about halfway between the house and the courtyard's enclosing wall. *It does look like a shadow*, she thought. *But there's nothing there to cast it.*

She thought of the entries in the logbook, which Joseph Moore had read to Alec Dalemore, the ones which described how Donald MacArthur had cried. Dalemore had wondered why, and Moore had spoken of him as a hard man who could look after himself in a fight. Moore had wondered what could have made such a man weep...

Max spoke up. 'Should we… should we go outside? See if we can find out what it is?'

Nick glanced at his friend. 'I don't think I want to know what it is, Max.' He looked up at the bloated moon, too large and too full, which hung in the black sky. 'I'm no expert,' he added, 'but from the length of the shadow, and the moon's position and elevation… I'd say that whatever's casting it must be about three metres tall.'

Rebecca continued to gaze at the shadow. There was something about its outline – all convex and concave arcs and deep, zigzagging furrows – that reminded her of something. 'The stone,' she said.

Nick and Max looked at her.

'It's like the stone… the same shape or something similar.'

'Christ,' Max breathed. 'You're right.'

Nick gave a single, slow nod. 'So, whoever carved the stone must have seen… *this*.'

'Or its shadow,' said Rebecca.

'I want to go and see what it is,' said Max, but he didn't move from the window, and Rebecca had the strong impression that he was waiting for someone to dissuade him.

Nick obliged. 'I think that would be a mistake. It's invisible, and yet it's casting a shadow. Whatever it is, it's defying the laws of physics. I don't think you want to go anywhere near it.'

Max shook his head in a horrible wonderment. 'What the fuck *is* it?'

'Maybe something's trying to communicate with us,' replied Rebecca.

'Communicate?' said Max.

'That's what Joseph Moore said. He said that everything that happened while he and Dalemore and Milne were on the island was an attempt at communication.'

'There's a strange kind of logic to that, I suppose,' said Nick. 'If there's an intelligence here, something utterly nonhuman, something perhaps from another dimension of existence, then nothing it did would make sense to us. It would be like us saying "hello" to an insect. It would be aware of us, and of the sound we had made, but the action would be totally without meaning to it. I think Moore was right: no human would have any hope of understanding what's happening here.'

Jennifer joined them at the window. She seemed to have brought herself under control, for which Rebecca was glad. She hated herself just a little for not having gone to her. 'Your insect analogy doesn't quite hold up, Nick,' she said.

Nick turned to look at her. 'Why not?'

'First, why would you bother saying "hello" to an insect? And second, even if you did, you'd know that it couldn't understand you, that there'd be no point in trying to communicate with it, and you'd leave it alone. A question therefore presents itself.'

'Which is?'

'Why continue the attempt? Whatever's here, why didn't it leave the lighthouse keepers alone? Why doesn't it leave *us* alone?'

Nick regarded her in silence for a few moments and then turned back to the window. 'Because it hasn't stopped trying. It isn't finished yet.'

Rebecca didn't want to look outside anymore. She turned away from the window and gasped. 'Donald!'

The others spun around as one.

'Christ!' said Max.

Donald's sleeping bag was empty.

A few moments later, they heard the front door opening and closing.

Nick and Max ran from the sitting room, into the corridor and out through the front door, while Rebecca and

Jennifer watched from the window. Donald had appeared in the courtyard; he was walking slowly, as if still asleep, although his eyes were wide open and glassy in the pale light of the unnaturally full moon. He appeared to be speaking: his mouth was moving, but neither Rebecca nor Jennifer could hear what he was saying.

'Donald!' Jennifer cried. 'Donald, come back! Come back inside!'

From his position in relation to the misshapen shadow that stretched across the courtyard, Rebecca could tell that he was standing right next to the invisible object. She heard muffled shouts from Nick and Max as they appeared and sprinted towards him.

Jennifer cried out as Donald reached forward...

THIRTEEN

...and then the air is filled with a raging metallic sound; a bronze cacophony that assaults their minds as much as their ears. Rebecca can taste it, can feel the flavour of blood flowering in her mouth and spreading through her nasal cavity and up into her brain. She screams, though she can't hear herself. She claps her hands uselessly to her ears and looks into the courtyard.

She looks at Donald, at what he has become, his head flowing into stars, a fountain of interstellar space erupting from his shoulders.

And she looks at what is standing beside him, the thing that has now been made visible by his touch.

And Rebecca screams so loudly and for so long that her vocal chords snap, while Jennifer runs from the window in such unheeding panic that she slams into the opposite wall, splitting her skull against the shelves of maintenance equipment.

Rebecca's mouth is wide open; she fills her lungs with air and expels it, again and again, no longer able to scream, to make any sound.

In the courtyard, Nick and Max fall to their knees, their faces distorted, no longer human, their teeth bared in mouths that are too wide, their heads extending into long mitres that burst upon the night and shower livid, glowing stars towards the heavens.

The horizon convulses and leaps towards the island like a monstrous tsunami, carrying with it not the ocean, but the twisted geometries of an absolute elsewhere. Rebecca can see vast cubes and ovoids, truncated cones and twisted cyclopean spires, inverted pyramids and revolving helixes. And rising from the island's flank towards the great mass of heaving, writhing shapes, the causeway which Dalemore described stretches like a piece of grey elastic, connecting Eilean Mòr with the alien horizon which now closes in upon it.

Rebecca looks at the shapes that have begun to appear on the causeway, shapes that are moving slowly and inexorably down towards the island, and somewhere in the depths of her screaming mind, Joseph Moore's words echo over and over again:

...the walkers among the eternal lights... serene and primal... no one sees them, but they are here... they are everywhere, from inside our minds, out, out to the farthest ramparts... the uttermost limits of space and time... and beyond that, beyond into the black spaces where no man will ever dwell.

We are coming. We are coming close now. Do you see us? Will you speak to us?

She flees from the window, past Jennifer's lifeless body, out of the sitting room and along the corridor leading to the kitchen. She presses herself into a corner, curling up into a foetal position and weeping uncontrollably. She shuts her eyes tight because she doesn't want to look at the white, five-eyed fox sitting on the table across from her, watching her impassively.

Dalemore, Milne and Moore were lucky, and Rebecca knows that soon she will discover the true extent of their luck. She remembers what Max said. 'Maybe it goes in cycles...' There were no further incidents reported after the relief keepers left the island in 1901. Through all the decades that lighthouse keepers came to Eilean Mòr since then, no strange events were ever reported.

Until now.

Maybe it goes in cycles.

Rebecca's lips curl into a silent grimace of anguish.

The kitchen door opens.

AUTHOR'S NOTE

While this novel is of course a work of supernatural fiction, it is inspired by the genuine mystery of the disappearance of three lighthouse keepers from the Flannan Isles light in the winter of 1900-1901.

I have always been fascinated by mysterious disappearances, from the *Mary Celeste* to the loss of Flight 19 over the Bermuda Triangle, and so I suppose it was only natural that I should use such an event as the departure point for a tale of strange and unexplainable happenings – especially an event as eerie and spine-chilling as the 'Flannan Isles mystery'.

Having said this, I should like to point out that I have stayed as close as possible to the historical record in describing the initial stages of the mystery: that is, the circumstances surrounding the tragic discovery made by the crew of the lighthouse tender *Hesperus*, when the ship docked at Eilean Mòr on 26 December 1900.

In doing so, I have relied on Mike Dash's excellent paper on the subject, which was first published in *Fortean Studies 4* (1998). However, I should also add that certain elements of the story (such as the entries made in the logbook by James Ducat), which Dash has shown to be apocryphal, have been retained for their atmospheric effect.

The likeliest explanation for the tragic deaths of James Ducat, Thomas Marshall and Donald McArthur is that they were washed off the island by a freak wave (just as Superintendent Muirhead suggests in my story). Nevertheless, writers of mystery books have speculated for decades that something altogether stranger happened to them – something of a paranormal or supernatural nature – and it is this idea which I have utilised in writing *The Lighthouse Keeper*.

The character of Alec Dalemore is entirely my invention.

DISASTER AT A LEWIS LIGHTHOUSE
THREE MEN DROWNED

A telegram was received yesterday morning from Callernish, Isle of Lewis, by the Northern Lighthouse Commissioners, stating that disaster had overtaken the three lighthouse keepers on the Flannan Islands. This group of rocky islets lies off the mouth of Loch Roag. They are seven in number and are sometimes called 'The Seven Hunters'. On the largest of them – Eilean Mohr, as it is called – the Northern Lighthouse Commissioners erected a lighthouse, which was first lighted on the 7th December 1899. Designed by Messrs. D&C Stevenson, C.E., Edinburgh, the Commissioners' engineers, it took four seasons to build, partly on account of the stormy waters around it, and also from the difficulty there was landing stones and material.

This island, which is egg-shaped, has cliffs all round of not less than 150 feet in height. Above the cliff line there is a steep grassy bank facing south, which carries the land of the island to a height of over 200 feet. On the north side the cliffs have a straight descent to the sea. The lighthouse was erected on the highest land, and was a stone structure fitted to resist the gales that blow in wildly from the Atlantic. There is no land between the Flannan Islands and America. The tower of the lighthouse rises 75 feet above the island, and the light, which is of 140,000 candle power, could be seen for 24 nautical miles. The chief purpose it served was to give a lead and direction to vessels going from the Atlantic by the Butt of Lewis to the Pentland Firth, or coming from the Firth to the Great Western Ocean. The Commissioners made two landing places, one at the east side and the other at the west, to be used according to the way the wind was blowing. From these they had to cut a zig-zag stair up the face of the cliffs to the grassy slope already referred to. And they also constructed a trolley tramway, worked from the lighthouse by an engine and rope, for the purpose of taking stores from the landing stages to the lighthouse. At each of the landing stages, but higher up the cliff, is a crane for unloading stores from the Commissioners' steamers. There are, it may further be explained, four lighthouse men attached to this station. Three of them are always on the rock attending to the light. Each of the four in turn is six weeks on the island, and a fortnight on the mainland. During that fortnight they reside in the township of Breasclete, on the north side of Loch-Roag, where the Commissioners have built substantial cottages for their staff, their wives and families, or other relations. The Flannans are visited every fortnight by the Commissioners' steamer *Hesperus*, and it was on this vessel, which is under the command of Captain Harvey, making her usual call at the lighthouse with stores on Wednesday, that the unfortunate discovery was made that the whole of the lighthouse staff were missing. But for the lighthouse men these rocky and lonely islands are uninhabited.

The *Hesperus* left Oban on Monday and took on board the keeper, who after his fortnight on shore was returning to relieve one of his comrades. On the boat's crew landing at Eilean Mohr no one was to be seen. The tower and residences of the keepers was searched, but none of the men could be found. A rocket was fired, but there was no response, and the painful conviction was forced home that the lighthouse keepers had been swept off the island and drowned. All the clocks in the building were stopped, from which it is considered possible that the disaster occurred about ten days ago – presumably on Thursday last, the 20th – the day of the terrific gale which did so much damage all over Scotland and wrecked part of the Shetland fishing fleet. How the disaster occurred to the lighthouse men is only as yet a matter of conjecture. When the first intimation of it arrived in Edinburgh it could only be guessed that they had been blown over the cliffs, as nothing was said about any damage to the lighthouse itself. What they were doing outside in such a gale could not be conjectured. The names of the men missing are James Ducat, principal keeper, who is married and has a family of four; Thomas Marshall, unmarried, and an occasional keeper, Donald Macarthur, who is married, and who had temporarily taken the place of one of the regular keepers who is ill on shore. The relief keeper, whose name is Moore, and three of the crew of the *Hesperus* were left on the island to attend to the light, while the vessel returned to anchorage for the night to Loch-Roag. On Thursday the *Hesperus* again made for the Flannans, but the sea was too rough for a landing to be effected at either of the stages. Captain Harvey, however, got into signal communication with the men on the island, and learned that one of the cranes already referred to on the cliff had been destroyed, and it is now thought that the unfortunate men could have ventured out of the lighthouse in the gale in order to try and save the crane, and been washed away. It seems that at Breasclete, on the mainland, there is a look-out station, from which the Flannans Lighthouse can be seen. The signalman there, seeing no adverse signal from the lighthouse, apprehended nothing wrong, though he did not see the light for these last few nights past. That he attributed to the thickness of the atmosphere. This, it seems, is quite an unprecedented calamity in the history of the Northern Lighthouse Commission. The last disaster was nearly fifty years ago, when an attending boat, running between Kirkcudbright and the Little Ross Lighthouse, was lost with all hands.

Telegraphing last night, our Stornoway correspondent states that during the day information of the disaster was received there, though nothing definite beyond the fact that the three lighthouse keepers had lost their lives, was known. The people of that part of Lewis which is nearest the Flannan Islands, he adds, were alarmed when for two or three nights past they could see no trace of the Flannan light – a fact which was communicated by telegraph to the Lighthouse Commissioners.

The Flannan, or 'Flannel Isles', as they are called in the Statistical Account of Scotland, are rather interesting rocky islets, and are supposed to have been the residence of ecclesiastics in the time of the druids. They are called by Buchanan *Insulae Sacrae*. There is at least one ruin on Eilean Mohr of some small ecclesiastical chapel – known as the 'blessing chapel' – just below the spot on which the lighthouse is now erected. The islands, which are attached to the parish of Uig, are, as has already been stated, a rocky cluster, seven in number, with narrow water ways between them. The total area they cover would be about two miles by a quarter of a mile, the long way being east and west. The largest of the group, Eilean Mohr, is barely a quarter of a mile across. The cliffs are of gneiss. Nearly all the members of the group have this in common: that their sides are precipitous. Formerly, a few sheep belonging to people on the main land were grazed on the islands, but this has been given up for many years. McCulloch speaks of the islands as being a great resort for sea birds, but people who lately visited them say that in this respect there is nothing very remarkable about them. With connection with what has been said as to the association of the Druids with this lovely group of rocky islands, it may be recalled that at Callernish, near the head of Loch Roag, are the celebrated Druidical standing stones – forming one of the most complete remains of the kind in the kingdom, while at the neighbouring town of Carloway is one of the largest and most perfect Danish forts or dounes to be met with in Scotland. It was on the sand of the bay of Uig in 1831 that a number of small sculpted ivory figures, resembling chessmen, were found, and being of great antiquity, were transmitted to the Antiquarian Society of Edinburgh.

ALSO FROM ALAN K BAKER
AND SNOWBOOKS

The Martian Ambassador

A BLACKWOOD AND HARRINGTON MYSTERY

&

The Feaster from the Stars

A BLACKWOOD AND HARRINGTON MYSTERY

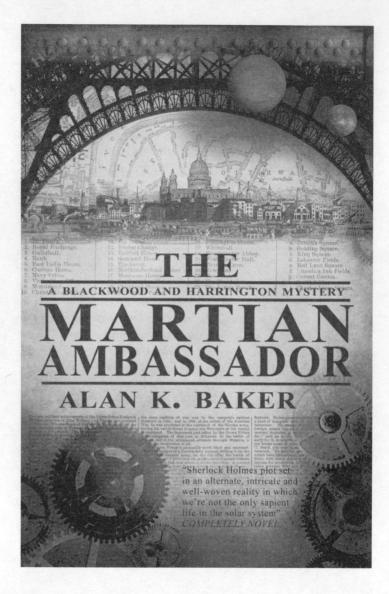

THE
A BLACKWOOD AND HARRINGTON MYSTERY
MARTIAN
AMBASSADOR

ALAN K. BAKER

"Sherlock Holmes plot set
in an alternate, intricate and
well-woven reality in which
we're not the only sapient
life in the solar system"
COMPLETELY NOVEL

WELCOME TO LONDON, 1899

It has been six years since the discovery of intelligent life on Mars, and relations between the two worlds are rapidly developing. Three-legged Martian omnibuses stride through the streets and across the landscape, while Queen Victoria has been returned to the vigour of youth by Martian rejuvenation drugs. Victorian computer technology is proceeding apace, thanks to the faeries who power the 'cogitators'; while the first 'ther zeppelins are nearing completion, with a British expedition to the Moon being planned for the following year.

Everything seems to be going swimmingly until Lunan R'ondd, Martian Ambassador to the Court of Saint James's, dies while attending a banquet at Buckingham Palace. The discovery of strange, microscopic larvae in his breathing apparatus leads Queen Victoria to suspect that he may have been the victim of a bizarre assassination. The Martian Parliament agrees, and they are not pleased. No Martian has ever died in such suspicious circumstances while on Earth.

An ultimatum is given: if Her Majesty's Government cannot solve the crime and bring the perpetrator to justice, the Martians will! Enter Thomas Blackwood, Special Investigator for Her Majesty's Bureau of Clandestine Affairs. Along with Lady Sophia Harrington, Secretary of the Society for Psychical Research, Blackwood is charged with the task of solving the mystery of Ambassador R'ondd's death, before the Martians take matters into their own hands, possibly igniting an interplanetary war in the process!

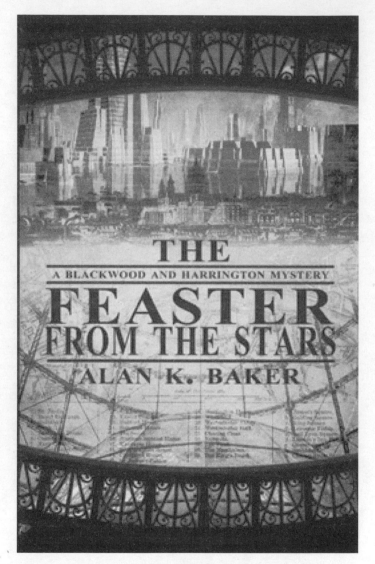

THE

A BLACKWOOD AND HARRINGTON MYSTERY

FEASTER
FROM THE STARS

ALAN K. BAKER

SOMETHING STRANGE IS HAPPENING ON THE LONDON UNDERGROUND.

The ghosts which haunt the platforms and tunnels are being seen much more frequently than usual, and it seems that they have become angry and frightened for some reason. There is something on the network of which even the dead are afraid, and the train drivers and other staff are becoming increasingly reluctant to work there.

When a train driver named Alfie Morgan is driven insane by something indescribable in the remote section of the network known as the Kennington Loop, Queen Victoria instructs her Bureau of Clandestine Affairs to investigate. Enter Thomas Blackwood, Special Investigator, and Lady Sophia Harrington, Secretary of the Society for Psychical Research.

Along with Detective Gerhard de Chardin of the Metropolitan Templar Police and the famous occultist Simon Castaigne, Blackwood and Sophia plunge into a terrifying adventure which takes them from the dank tunnels of the London Underground to the depths of interstellar space and a dying planet known as Carcosa, where a horrific being from beyond the ordered universe has set its sights on Earth. Unless Blackwood and Sophia can prevail, it will descend upon the Earth and consume every living thing upon it!